Abramo's Gift

Abramo's Gift

Donald Greco

Abramo's Gift
Published by Bridgeway Books
P.O. Box 80107
Austin, Texas 78758

For more information about our books, please write to us, call 512.478.2028, or visit our website at www.bridgewaybooks.net.

Library of Congress Control Number: 2008925262

ISBN-13: 978-1-934454-29-9
ISBN-10: 1-934454-29-X

This is a work of fiction. All of the characters and events portrayed in this book are fictional, and any resemblance to real people or incidents is purely coincidental.

Top cover image supplied by the Mahoning Valley Historical Society, Youngstown, Ohio

10 9 8 7 6 5 4 3 2 1

Angie,
Of moments too brief
and sweet beyond redeeming.
This is for you, with all my love
and homage and gratitude forever.
Till we meet again...

DG

Chapter 1

HE STARED AT THE waves, countless shallow whispers being called home toward the distant statue in the harbor. He took a deep breath, wiping furtive tears from his eyes, looking around to see if other people noticed him. No one did. All eyes were on the Statue of Liberty. More and more of the passengers were coming on deck as the ship made slow but steady progress toward their dreams. He shook his head to himself. How could they be so trusting of the future? You can't trust dreams. Had not his own been shattered in a few minutes, all of them gone because Angelina was gone?

He studied the couples standing nearby on deck and looked with envy at the fathers and mothers clutching children to their sides, full of expectation, full of trust in happiness. Why? Why had he and Angelina not been given that chance? They were so much in love, so full of promise. She would have been a beautiful mother—gentle, warm, and adoring.

He watched in silence as more people emerged from below deck. There was strange quiet as they communed with themselves about their places in the new world. He shook his head. What would his life be like? He would find work as a laborer, not an artisan, and he would live as a boarder in someone else's house, and he would be alone; that much he knew. Angelina's resting place was behind him, and the little girl she had given him lay by her side. And he had come to this new country perhaps never to see their graves again, left to harbor only frail memories of what might have been. And their graves would be an ocean apart: his in America, theirs in Italy.

Horns sounded as the ship drew nearer to Ellis Island. The deck was full now as the boat slowly entered the draft of the harbor. He could see the buildings on the island, and his anxiety increased. Would *Zio* Michele be there as he said? The ordeal at Ellis Island would be long and torturous, he knew.

After disembarking, he and the others were directed to sit on benches while they waited to be examined by doctors. The wait lasted through the night, and the entire time he was haunted by the thought of being marked with coded-colored chalk on his name tag that signified a contagious disease. Though he did not have any of the dreaded diseases, like trachoma or tuberculosis, that would mean immediate expulsion back to Italy, he was dispirited enough to entertain those demons and agonize silently through the night. But by morning, when his turn came, he was judged fit enough. And after another three-hour wait in a line, he finally arrived at the registration desk: his last hurdle. If he made it over this one, he would be sworn in to citizenship.

"Name?" the clerk said without looking up. He hesitated, fumbling through his pocket for a small packet of papers he had brought from Italy. "Name?" the man repeated testily.

Finally, he thrust a scrap of paper, a baptismal record that contained his name in perfect script, on the table. "Abramo Cardone," he said aloud, and the man looked up at him. He gazed back at the clerk steadily but uneasily. The clerk hesitated a minute then repeated it. Abramo smiled slightly at the pronunciation and nodded. The man brightened a little and wrote Abramo's name carefully, pointed at another doorway, and handed him a document to carry with him. On the document was his name, written exactly as it was on the crumpled paper he had brought from his homeland.

He breathed deeply, as if for the first time since his encounter with the clerk. He had heard stories of some people coming to this island with historic family names, such as Lagomarsino and Boscheratto, and entering the new country as March and Bosh forever after. No one dared to correct the surly men who sat at desks interviewing thousands of people per month.

His clerk was businesslike and curt, but at least civil. Some were sadistic and cold, seeming to enjoy returning some families to the hell they had left in Italy, to war and factions and gang rule. The reasons for rejection were sometimes hasty judgments by harried physicians who had minutes to decide if a patient was feeble-minded or diseased. But a mistake by the doctor would often be enough to break the hearts of the mothers and fathers who were forced to turn their children from the gates of paradise back to the uncertain and tumultuous purgatory they might never leave again. He shook his head to banish the thoughts. He thought of Angelina and her beauty and devotion to him, her gentleness and femininity, and he shuddered to think of what she might have endured if they were rejected by one of the less competent doctors. For the first time in four years, he was glad he was alone.

Finally, he entered one last line where he was examined for his devotion to this new country and made to vow allegiance to no other country but the United States. He said a small prayer and walked into the sunlight to the barge that would take all the new Americans to Battery Park to meet their relatives.

As the ferry approached the dock at Battery Park, he set down his bags and moved to a rail to look over the crowd. But he could see no one he knew. Maybe he couldn't find his uncle because there were so many people. But what would he do if Zi'Michele were not there? It had been many years since they had seen each other. What if he didn't recognize him?

He walked along the rail and looked again into the bedlam of voices and strange languages, of people moving around, of people sitting and waiting. Still no Zi'Michele. When he realized how long he had been looking, he panicked, thinking someone might have taken his carpenter's tools. He retraced his steps and found the bags with the tools still in them, guarded by an old Polish man who knew they belonged to a skilled worker. He shook the old man's hand and bowed slightly, muttering thanks in Italian as the man offered acceptance in Polish. He returned to the rail and paused for a moment, nervously scanning the crowd. Then a booming voice call his name.

"Abramo!" He turned toward the sound and peered into the mass of people. At first he didn't recognize anyone. Could there be someone else with that name?

"Abramo!" He heard it again. Finally he saw a massive, square man in a derby waving his hands in his direction. "Abramo!" he said, smiling with glistening teeth and a thick white mustache. Finally their eyes met.

"Zi'Michele," he shouted in return. Abramo pointed to the gangway at the edge of the holding area. Michele nodded. In a few minutes, Abramo walked to the head of the gangway and stared out into the crowd. Again he saw his uncle, eyes shining and mustache white and formidable.

At first, Michele stayed still as Abramo came toward him and stopped. The two men stared at each other for a short time. Abramo tried to fathom what the old man was thinking.

Then suddenly Michele advanced toward the young man and kissed him. "You look so much like your mother, God rest her soul," he said in Italian as he hugged him.

"It's good to see you, *Zio*," Abramo answered, also in Italian. "Thank you for coming for me…for bringing me here."

The older man snorted in response and put his arm around Abramo's shoulder, urging him forward through the crowd. They were going to take a trolley ride through the city. Michele grabbed one of Abramo's satchels with one hand and ushered his nephew into and out of trolleys and through streets massed with people, farther and farther into New York.

When they left the last trolley, they walked several blocks through streets and sidewalks roiling with life: street vendors, policemen, children playing tag, women carrying sacks of groceries, men telling stories, horse-drawn wagons full of trash. Everywhere people called out to friends, priests, Mafia bosses, and God for filling their lives with evil landlords, corrupt politicians, unmindful children, thieving grocers, and accursed wives and husbands.

Abramo had seen Rome, but he had never seen anything like this. Rome was noisy, sweaty, and hectic, but the scale was much smaller than this city. And Rome bore the restraint of a thousand ages that seemed to make it more placid than New York. This new city seemed ready to explode.

As they walked, Michele talked constantly, occasionally stopping to catch his breath, saying hello to passersby, buying an apple for him and his nephew. He gestured proudly at the tall buildings, as though presenting the city to Abramo. He would catch himself talking from time to time and suddenly stop to look into the eyes of his nephew, his face now reddened much more than it was when they first met. "Are you okay, Uncle?" Abramo would say.

"*Sì*," his uncle would answer. A few minutes later he would stop again.

"Are you comfortable, Abramo? Hungry? Tired?"

"No, Uncle, I am fine," was always his response in Italian.

"We are almost there," he said. "A few more streets."

Finally, Michele stopped in front of a set of stairs that led to double doors in brown chipped paint, leaded glass fronts, and huge brass doorknobs. Michele put down Abramo's satchel and hesitated. Then he turned his thick body directly in front of his nephew and put his hands on both of Abramo's shoulders.

The young man looked uneasily into his uncle's eyes. "Abramo." He hesitated. "My son…I'm so sorry about Angelina and the child. I'm sorry you were not there to see them buried." He stopped for a second, watching his nephew's eyes fill up with tears. "You know, Abramo, I have always believed that looking on the face of the dead—especially that of the beloved woman who held you in her arms by night—never does a man any good. Now your memories will only be of life and warmth and beauty. You will remember

Angelina for the first time you saw her, for the first time you held her naked in your arms, for the joy she had on her face when she married you. And you will not remember, as I do, the face of the dead, of cold skin and hard touch. Keep your memories in the sunshine...of the child you never knew; remember that she came from the love you shared with Angelina."

He stopped to catch his breath and to look questioningly into his nephew's eyes to see if he understood. Abramo nodded once in understanding, then again in agreement. "The child is an angel, Abramo." He hesitated, then resumed. "As you grow older, the story of the child will be revealed to you, and you will remember these words of mine. Just as I have carried the story of my sister, your beloved mother, in my heart for all these years. You are its fulfillment."

Abramo hugged his uncle. The older man cupped his head and bent to kiss the boy on the forehead. After a few moments he said, "Come with me, son. This hotel is where we will stay the night."

When they were in the room, unpacked and refreshed, Michele sat on the side of the bed and pointed to an old, stuffed chair about five feet away. Abramo, who seemed puzzled by the things they were doing, about their presence in this old hotel, sat in the chair staring quizzically at his uncle. "Where do you live, Zi'Michele?" he said finally.

"You are asking why we are in this hotel?" he said in response. Abramo shrugged in agreement. "I have not lived in New York for many years, Abramo. I live in a small town in Ohio, near the border of Pennsylvania, called Youngstown."

Abramo was troubled. "But will I have work in such a place? I thought New York—"

"It's okay, Abramo. You will have work…and a place to live… and my friends will be your friends. Youngstown will be your home…if you let it. Do you want to do this? If you want to stay in New York or in Pittsburgh, I have some friends who—"

"No, signore, I will go where you go."

Michele smiled in relief. "Then tomorrow we will ride to the station and take the train to Youngstown. It will stop in Pittsburgh first. By night, we will be at my apartment, and your Aunt Renata will greet us. Come—wash yourself of the dust of Italy. We will go out to a restaurant to eat."

Finally, the train began to slow down as it approached the center of Youngstown at dusk. The B&O Station was large and well lit. As the train slowed to a stop, Abramo and Michele grabbed their satchels and stood waiting for the car to empty out. Michele stepped down first from the car, pausing at the bottom, looking around as though expecting someone. Abramo took two steps down and waited silently for the older man to move. Suddenly, he heard a voice calling from a small crowd of onlookers. Michele reacted quickly to the call of his name and, without turning toward Abramo, walked in the direction of the voice.

He encountered a man about his own age and shook his hand. Then he gestured back over his shoulder in Abramo's direction. Abramo stood, waiting, as his uncle turned toward him and urged the stranger over.

"Abramo, this is my dearest friend, Marco Bevilaqua. Marco, this is my nephew, Abramo, son of my beloved sister, God rest her soul."

"Welcome to Youngstown, my boy," Marco said.

Isabella Chianese was a widow with three young children. She boarded men in her house to make enough money to supplement the income she earned from washing and ironing clothes for the prosperous people in the neighborhood.

Abramo marveled at the woman. Michele had told him on the train ride that she had a very hard life, and yet she was pleasant and talkative, and yes, quite beautiful. He wondered what she would be like as an old woman. She was forty-one years old, Michele said. How long could she live with this life's burden? Perhaps some day a man in the neighborhood would see her goodness and spirit and would marry her. Perhaps he too would marvel at her untiring optimism and singular lack of self-pity. But she avoided men—maybe for the sake of her children. And though men yearned for her and dreamed of her in their beds, none of them wanted the past that came with her, and the future with someone else's three children.

"This is Abramo Cardone, the son of my beloved sister, God rest her soul," Michele said. "Abramo, meet your landlady, Isabella Chianese."

"I am honored to be in your house, Signora Chianese," said Abramo.

"You are welcome, Signor Cardone," she said softly.

Isabella showed them to the room where Abramo would stay.

"This will do you fine," Michele said, lowering the satchel as the woman left them.

In a few minutes she was at the door again, this time holding towels and soap for their use in the newly installed bathroom that had running hot water. Before leaving, she asked Michele if they were ready for supper. The men looked at each other quickly, and she smiled before they answered. "The meal will be ready at eight o'clock," she said.

The food the widow Chianese cooked was simple but delicious. Abramo was quiet, more so than usual, as he kept his eyes on the hostess. He studied her as she moved around the table in the dining room, bringing food from the kitchen, talking brightly of the glories of the new land.

Angelina would have been just like her, he thought. She would have worked hard, would have smiled through her adversity, would have had hope…and would not have been defeated. He was struck by the goodness of Isabella, by her faith and spirit and wisdom beyond her years. And he made a wish for her. He wished her the love of a good man and happiness in her old age and, always, healthy children. He wished her all the things he, himself, despaired of having.

"You are quiet, Abramo," Michele said later.

Abramo shrugged. "I do not talk much lately, Uncle."

Michele gazed at his nephew for several seconds. He was nothing he had not expected. He was not as tall as his father, but more slender and muscular…and disheartened. He was his mother's son: black hair full of waves and curls, quiet and thoughtful as she was. How Michele missed his sister now! This son of hers would have to become known to him, just as his mother became known to him as they grew up. He would tell Abramo of his illness on another day.

"Abramo, you will not have a job as a carpenter or cabinet maker. You know that."

"I know, Zi'Michele. As long as I earn a living, I don't care what I do."

"You must make your way in this country, my boy. You must save your money for the family you will have." Michele regretted saying it as soon as he did. "I'm sorry, Abramo, I was only thinking about your future. I should not have brought forth memories."

"It's okay, Zi'Michele, I have to do many things now…without Angelina. I know that."

The Ancient Order of Hibernians, the AOH, was housed in an old building that was part residence for the owner's family and part tavern, the most important part being the tavern. It had been remodeled two years earlier and was a showcase club for the Irish on the East Side.

Two great wooden pillars of beautiful blond oak anchored each side of the bar. A series of glass mirrors ran thirty feet between them, in five-foot sections. The joy of the club was a Saturday night crowd aligned along the bar and at crowded tables, all hounding the harried bartenders for food and beer and shots of bootleg whiskey from bottles arranged on step-like shelves. The shelves led up to the base of the mirrors, which were tilted slightly so that bar patrons could easily see themselves drinking, laughing, and telling truths that had to be told.

A taciturn, middle-aged man with a large mustache worked behind the bar. Occasionally he would utter a word or two to ancient patrons, but he was perfunctory and short with customers he either disliked or did not know.

A tall man with a rumpled shirt and stiff collar came out of a door in the rear of the tavern and walked up to the bar. He, too, was morose and quiet, as though preoccupied by troubles not of his making.

"Where's Conor, Eddie?" he said to the bartender.

"He said he had to go out," Eddie answered. "Had something to do."

"Did he bring up that beer from downstairs?"

"No."

"Why the hell not? Did you tell him?"

"I told him three times, and he got mad at me. So, I said the hell with him."

"You told him I wanted that beer upstairs?"

"Yeah. He said he'd get it later…that you don't need it up here now."

"Goddammit, I decide what we need up here, not him." He slammed the heel of his hand onto the bar. "This is the last time that kid is gonna do this. Next time he can go down to the mills and get his own job. Damn it!"

"I'll bring it up little by little, boss…Maybe I—"

"If we get a crowd in here tonight after that ball game, we won't have time to haul up that beer. We'll have all we can do just with food orders." The man stopped and pondered what to do. "All right, Eddie, I'll bring the barrels up to the landing here, and you can roll 'em and stack 'em."

"But, boss, that'll be hard work for you…maybe I—"

"You think I can't do hard work, goddammit? Do as I tell you. Stack the barrels as I bring them up."

Kieran Harty had been boss of the AOH for sixteen years. He started as a boy cleaning spittoons and worked his way up to ownership of a set of properties that constituted the club and several adjoining buildings, almost an entire block fronting Sloan Street. He was prosperous and respected. He was also known for his quick temper and, in his youth, his ability to drink large quantities of whiskey. He had a dark sense of humor that surfaced from time to time. He was also known, to those closest to him, for a strange softness of heart for people he felt were unfortunate in life. His charity almost seemed like a contradiction of his tough, cranky outward demeanor. Yet, quietly, he would send food to grieving widows and poor people who had suddenly become laid off or sick. He would see to it that the old man whose back had been broken at the Valley Mill had a wheelchair and whiskey, and regular visits from Irish neighbor ladies who would clean his house and bring fresh soda bread and meat. No one was told that the kindness was all at Kieran Harty's expense.

Kieran also had three sons and one daughter. Conor, the eldest, was irresponsible, spoiled, and unintelligent. The youngest, Paul, was brighter and a better worker. Ross, the middle boy, was an intelligent and kind man. Harty's daughter, Máille, almost from the day she was born, was known as Molly.

As children, the boys were never quite sure their father cared for them. His anger at one of their transgressions was usually disbursed to all three boys, and all of them provoked their dad's wrath in one way or another. Yet the boys respected him enough, or perhaps feared him enough, to be on the good side of the law around the old man. Gradually, the quiet kindnesses of their father became known to them as they grew up, and because of that, the boys honored their father, despite their resentment at his seemingly irrational demands upon their lifestyles and behavior.

But if ever the boys had doubts about their father's affections toward them, they had no doubts about his love for Molly. She was said to be the image of Cara, their departed, sainted mother. Though there was only one unclear and fuzzy photograph of their mother in the family's possession, Molly, they were told by aunts and friends and relatives, was Cara's incarnation.

She had large, sparkling hazel eyes, a small upturned nose, pale, freckled skin, and light auburn hair, with highlights that glistened in the sun and made her striking and beautiful. She was also a complete contrast to her combative, rough-hewn brothers. She was gentle and feminine, but tough-minded and intelligent. She was her mother, the woman that Kieran loved and lost a dozen years ago. He had never been able to cope with her loss until Molly began to grow into the picture he held in his memories.

Molly was small and, like her mother, almost frail, though she was hardy and worked tirelessly in the kitchen and the bar of the

AOH. Occasionally Kieran would admonish her for working so hard that she looked tired and sickly. She would quietly ignore his directives and prepare the evening meal for him and her brothers. She knew instinctively the hold she had on her father, but she never abused the leverage the bond between them gave her.

Her favorite brother was Ross, the middle son. He was a year older than she, and he was the closest to her in temperament. He had a less volatile temper than his father, but he alone among the boys had his father's hatred of injustice and compassion for God's unfortunates.

"Hi," he said to his sister as he entered the dining room.

"You were up late last night," she answered.

"I was reading," he said.

"Reading what?"

"A book...about radio. We should have one, Moll. You hear people talk from New York and Cincinnati and Pittsburgh. It's amazing."

"You know Daddy won't have one. Who has time to listen to it, anyway?"

"We should make time. We can learn more about this country."

"You mean more about the people who hate the Irish, don't you?"

"They don't all hate the Irish, Moll. Just like there are good and bad Irish at the club, there are good and bad Americans... even Italians."

"You really believe that?" said Molly.

He shrugged. "I don't know. They work cheaper than others and undercut good men who are trying to feed families. So many are in gangs...You think there are any good ones?"

"There must be good in some of them," Molly said thoughtfully. "They're Catholics, right? I guess they just want to feed their own families…like we do."

Ross shook his head again. "I don't know, girl. Some Catholics tortured people in the Vatican. Remember how Uncle Eamon used to tell us how the dagos brutalized people in God's name?"

She huffed. "Whenever Daddy wasn't around, you mean?"

Conor and Paul entered the dining room and sat down, without a word, and helped themselves to the bread and butter on the table.

"Paul and Conor Harty, you get back out there and wash you hands and faces," Molly said. "This isn't a boarding house. You come to this table clean."

"What about him?" said Paul, nodding resentfully at Ross.

"He has enough manners to come to the Harty table with clean hands and face."

Ross grinned smugly at his younger brother.

"Now, you get out of this dining room, Paul Harty," Molly said.

Paul looked at Conor, who snorted disgustedly and then stood up and walked out of the room. Paul followed shortly behind.

Ross was beaming after Molly's outburst. She slapped the back of his head as she walked by. Then, their father entered the room. "Where are Conor and Paul?" he said as he sat down in his place at the head of the table.

"They've gone out. They'll be back directly," said Molly.

Ross was grinning as he sat down across from his father. "What's so funny?" Kieran asked his son.

He shrugged. "It's fun to watch Molly beat up on my brothers."

"Hush, Ross," hissed Molly.

Kieran's expression brightened a little just as the two other men returned to the room. "What did ye do, Molly, to put the fear of God into your brothers?" he asked.

"I'll not serve pigs at my table," Molly said defiantly, gazing at Conor and Paul.

"Your table?" Conor said. "Isn't it Pa's table? You make too much of yourself, girl."

"It's my table as long as the food you eat is prepared by me," she said. "When you make your own food, it's not my table, Conor."

"All right, now. That's enough. You boys know your sister's right. You come clean to this table"—he paused for a moment, a slight smile playing on his lips—"your sister's table...like civilized men, not like some goddamned Black Hand cutthroats. That's the way your mother would have wanted it."

"But she's not our mother," Paul said.

"But in this room and in that kitchen, she speaks with her authority...and with mine. You are not savages, so you clean yourselves of the dirt of the day in your own house."

"You mean her house, Pa. Don't you?" Conor muttered.

"I mean my house, and don't you forget it," his father answered.

Later that night, Kieran was back at the bar, and some of the regulars were long in their cups and lamenting all that God had done to them. "Christ's sake, every time you turn around another trainload of them dagos is coming into town."

"Yeah. And next thing you know, they'll be taking our jobs because the goddamned bosses make them underbid us. Only mill that doesn't do it is Reid-Carnegie."

"It's getting just like with them Pennsylvania mines. They come off the boat and right away you got family men looking for jobs because some polak or dago underbids them."

Kieran had heard the arguments before—long enough to be sympathetic to the men who feared losing their jobs. Yet, he was uncomfortable siding with some of the men who he had no respect for. Hell, he mused, as boss of the AOH, he didn't have time to worry about some new dagos or polaks just getting off a boat. They weren't the ones putting up the "No Irish Need Apply" signs, anyway. The Irish had enough problems of their own.

"Hey, barkeep, how about a glass of good red wine?"

Kieran was facing away from the bar, but he knew well the voice that was taunting him. He didn't turn right away, playing his role in the game that had developed over the years between the two men. "There's a dago bar about a half mile down the street, Luigi."

"But I have a special dispensation from the Pope, another dago."

Kieran finally let out a laugh and turned toward his tormentor. "Damn you, Hugh. Have you forgotten so much about hard work that you have to come down here to harass honest men as they do it?"

"All I see is a boss who gives orders to underlings...and works a few hours a week behind the bar just to keep up appearances."

Kieran reached out his hand. "Hugh Connolly, I hear that you make so much money now that you've forgotten the friends of your youth."

"Those that are my elders I still look in on. We young folks still have to show respect."

"You bastard, I'm only two months older than you."

"So how old are you today, Harty? Tell the truth before God and everybody." Kieran smirked. "Before God and everybody," said Hugh again, grinning broadly.

"Fifty-two," Kieran said, grinning back.

"And how old am I then?" Hugh said.

"How the hell do I know? You think I have nothing better to do than remember birthdays of rich men who show up once in a while in the AOH?"

"How old now?" Hugh persisted.

"Fifty-one and be damned," said Kieran, still holding the hand that he had clasped when it was extended across the bar.

"And don't you forget it, boyo," said Hugh.

Kieran was silent for a few seconds, looking at the face of the man he had just greeted. "Damn, it's good to see you, Hugh. How come you and I go weeks without seeing each other? You're one of the few Irish politicians I can stand."

"We've been friends for fifty years, Kier. How'd we manage that without breaking each other's noses?"

"Ah, we came close a few times, remember? But I used to spare your life because of your sister," said Kieran.

"The hell you say. Are you sure it wasn't my left hook?" Kieran huffed, shaking his head as they both laughed. Then Hugh grew more serious. "How long dead, Kier?"

"Twelve years in February."

Hugh shook his head. "How are you doing, son?"

"Can't complain, Hugh. Like you, I'm making a little money, and I'm trying to get the boys to grow up enough to take over the AOH."

"How are they doing?"

"One thing about them: Except for Conor, they're hard workers if not hard thinkers."

"And Molly?"

"She'll be back here in a little while…and glad to see you."

"And I her. She was always the gift Cara left us, especially you."

Kieran raised his eyebrows in agreement. "I don't know what I'd do without her, Hugh. Every time I look at her, I see Cara. She's the joy of my life."

"You'll have to let her go some time, boyo. Some strappin' Irish lad will come up here and take her away."

"He might have her, but he'll not take her away. I'll see to it that they stay in Youngstown."

The two old friends chatted more, and then in a lull in their conversation, Kieran said, "So what's the trouble, Hugh?"

"What makes you think I'm here about trouble?"

"Because I've known you for fifty years, that's why," Kieran answered. "What's up?"

"The Hannons have formed their own AOH," Hugh said. "They just got chartered."

Kieran was quiet for several seconds. "So, that's why my old friend came up here to see me, huh?"

"You know it's more than that, Kieran. I just thought you might want to hear it from me."

Kieran looked at his friend. "Yeah," he sighed, "rather from you than from someone else." He paused. "How far along are they?"

"They just converted that old beer garden they've had for a few years. The sign went up today."

"You think they'll make a go of it?"

"I wouldn't bet money on it. They're the worst sons o'bitches in the Valley. Jack Hannon would pimp his own mother if he could get money for her."

"I still think it was the Hannons that beat up Ross a while back."

"Yeah…but they're making a run at *you* now. Be careful, Kieran. Bide your time around here. You have a good quality place and you're honest. Jack Hannon wouldn't know quality if it bit him on the ass."

"I don't know, Hugh. It'll be tough going if he takes a quarter of my business away. Christ, there are already five AOHs in the Valley."

"Stay the course, boyo. Remember, you're quality and he's not. I'll help you any way I can. You know that."

Kieran smiled and poured a drink of whiskey for his old friend. When Hugh reached for his wallet, Kieran stayed his arm and shook his head. Hugh protested. "I don't need a drink for telling you the truth, Kier."

"It has nothing to do with that. This is for you making superintendent."

"How'd you know? It just happened last week."

"I have spies everywhere, Connolly."

"So, let's go out to dinner some night at one of the best places downtown…like we used to do when Cara and Aileen were alive. My treat."

"You miss her as much as I miss Cara?"

Hugh nodded. "Yeah…only I wish I could have had that little girl, as you have Molly, that makes me think of Aileen every time I see her."

"I'm sorry, Hugh. I wish it would have been different. She was beautiful even through all the sickness. The two of you would have had wonderful children."

"Thanks, boyo." He tipped back the rest of his drink and set the glass on the counter. "Listen, it's time for me to go. Say hello to the boys…and to Molly. Let's have that dinner, okay?"

Hugh Connolly was not only one of three superintendents at Reid-Carnegie but also a precinct committeeman for the Democratic Party, long a minority party in the Mahoning Valley, but one that had a strong Irish contingent. He sat in his new office overlooking the rollers in the plant, set high in the second story behind a large wall of windows that gave a perspective of the mill.

He was having coffee, eating a sandwich, and reading the latest Ku Klux Klan handbill that had circulated through the plant. The Klan was tightening its grip on Mahoning County, especially upon Youngstown. The dagos were catching more hell than the Irish, Hugh thought to himself. The KKK hated the Italians more than any group except Negroes, and they were making inroads into every neighborhood in town. Any horse's ass could put on a dunce cap and be a grand wizard or grand buzzard or something. All they had to do was hate the right people.

The door to his office opened, and the assistant plant manager, George Carter, walked in. Hugh stood up and greeted him. "Coffee, George?"

"No, I'm okay…Everything all right?"

"Yeah. The steel is rolling."

"How are those new hires working out?"

"Mostly okay. I had to let one go for stealing a couple of wrenches."

"One of the dagos?"

"Nah, an Irish kid. I know his father, so now I have a sworn enemy in the precinct."

The assistant manager snorted then walked over to the window wall and studied the men working on the floor. "How's that Italian kid we hired last year doing…the one who just got off the boat?"

"You mean Abramo?"

"What's his last name?"

"Cardone."

"How's he doing?"

"Hell, I wish I had a hundred like him. He's quiet, minds his own business, catches on to everything quick…and he works hard. Tom's real happy with him."

"You know his uncle got him the job? Michele della Malva, that dago who's a precinct man in the First Ward. Do you know him?"

"No, but I've heard well of him. I hope the guy has a few more nephews," Hugh said.

Carter turned from the window. "Let's keep an eye on Cardone. If he's that good, we might be able to put him on as a foreman after he learns some things. It'll be good to have a dago foreman who can deal with some of those Italians who'll cut your throat soon as look at you." He headed for the door and clapped a hand on Hugh's shoulder as he passed. "That's what got you your first leg up. You were the last one who could handle them."

Michele della Malva sat in his easy chair puffing on his pipe. Renata Paccioli, his sister, sat opposite him, crocheting beautiful lace edgings for the altar cloths at St. Rocco's Church. They were both silent and content. They had eaten one of Renata's delicious meals and the house smelled of fresh-baked bread and coffee. Michele was busy with his thoughts, and his sister noted his silence, so unusual for her brother. He would sip some wine from time to time but then would settle back into his large, faded and worn easy chair.

"How do you think Abramo is doing?" Renata asked her brother in Italian.

Michele shrugged. "He's like our sister. You never know what he's thinking. He learns quickly." He looked over to her. "Have you heard him speak English? He's been in Ohio eighteen months and already he talks to the men he meets at work or on the street in English, easily and well."

"There are books in his room on English, his landlady says."

"Wasn't his mother just like that? Always reading, always asking the priests and nuns for books. Remember?"

"Has he made anything for you yet?"

"No. Where is he going to find room at my place?"

"But he can come here."

"I've told him. But he says he wants to do other things first… repairs for Isabella, learn English. He goes to English classes at St. Rocco's every Friday."

"Do you have anything for him to do?"

"No." He shook his head. "He's a finish carpenter, an artisan. It's a shame to make him do only repairs."

"He will never be happy at the mill. Those damned Irish and Germans will torment him, and the bosses will not protect him."

Michele shrugged. "It is said that he works under a new superintendent named Hugh Connolly. I have heard he is a good and decent man."

"That's fine," said Renata, "but he needs something more than that."

Michele sighed. "I don't know. I have tried to introduce him to young girls. He is polite…but distant."

"He must still dream of Angelina."

"I know he does. Have you noticed that he still talks of her daily? Even after five years? Angelina did this, Angelina did that?"

Renata was quiet for a few seconds, thinking about what her brother had said. "He still hurts, Michele."

Michele put the newspaper aside and stared back at his sister, then looked away. He shook his head. "He can never heal that wound himself, Renata. Someone else must do it…if he can find her, if he will let her."

Chapter 2

ABRAMO HAD BEEN IN America more than eighteen months before he knew he was accepted by the men in the mill. At lunch, the old hands sat at the few crude tables where they set out their lunch buckets and their food. Those places were earned by time served or job classification or gang affiliation or length of time in this country. Abramo knew that he was short by all measures, so he stayed on the periphery of the tables, sitting, along with other lesser mortals, on the crates and boxes that bordered the room.

On that day, Joe Hannon was holding forth as usual at his table. He was a big, loud man, one of the bullying kind that needed constant reinforcement from his coworkers to know he was the toughest, the shrewdest, the strongest, the greatest stud and ladies' man. As usual, he was surrounded by toadies whose own status derived from their closeness to the main man in the shop.

Joe Hannon's boorish attitude and crude manners were learned over years of tolerance and encouragement. In his family, his behavior was smiled upon. His father would beam at the stories of Joe beating up "niggers" he encountered in their neighborhood. Joe was his father's son, with fewer brains, but what he lacked in the old man's cunning he made up for in cruelty and viciousness.

Being the oldest brother, he would one day wear the Hannon mantle as head of the gang. His father was pleased with his son's reputation as a tough guy and encouraged tough behavior whenever he could.

"My brother Sean and me, we saw these two niggers come walking on our part of the North Side, carrying some flour sacks and oil to one of the dago stores. So Sean says to one of them, 'Hey, nigger, what are you doin' here on the North Side?'

"'Just passin' by,' this one nigger says. 'We workin' men—delivery men.'

"'You ain't men at all. You're just a couple of niggers.'

"'We don't mean no trouble,' says one of the niggers.

"'But you are trouble, boy,' says Sean. Just then my other two brothers come along. Then the one nigger says, 'We don't want no fight. I got a family, and I'm just trying to work for some food.'

"'We got too many niggers in this world already. If you got all them mouths to feed, it ain't our fault. You fucked them black whores, and now you have to feed the kids. Too bad for you.'"

Abramo sat next to a young Polish Jew, named Mateusz Wroblewski, who had become his friend and work partner. They glanced at each other and shared a look of mutual disgust. They were sickened by the crude lout whose bellowing voice daily darkened the lunch break with vulgarities and banalities that sometimes made them not want to eat.

Mateusz was a glass blower in Poland who came to America with his wife and two children when soldiers took over his small factory and the half acre of land that went with it.

The bond between the two men began with their love for America and their passion for the English language. Abramo and Mateusz, who worked side by side as rollers, deliberately found reason to talk to each other in English. They corrected each other, asked the meanings of new words, and taught each other new phrases and pronunciations and usage.

The more they learned, the more they realized that men such as Joe Hannon spoke poor English, crude and vulgar at that. Mateusz whispered something in English to Abramo after one of Hannon's diatribes. Both men smiled knowingly and continued silently to eat their lunches.

Hannon saw the exchange. "Hey, you—Wroblewski. If you don't like my stories, maybe you shouldn't come to this lunch-room, huh? Maybe not even the yard, or even the plant. You don't like working with Americans? Then get the fuck out."

Mateusz didn't answer. He knew Hannon was only looking for a pretext to fight. He was meant to be the next sacrificial victim to show the others that Hannon was still the top man in the yard. Mateusz was short and slender—no match for Joe Hannon. He also had a slightly crooked right arm; Abramo had noticed it before. He did everything he could to compensate for the deformity, but there were times Abramo knew Mateusz's arm ached enough to bring water to his eyes when they rolled the steel on cold and cloudy and humid days. Once when they were resting after a long and grueling job, during what Reid-Carnegie called a water break in the summer time, Mateusz held his arm and was unusually silent. Abramo asked, "How did you injure your arm?"

Mateusz shrugged. Then he looked at his friend, who seemed to really care about his pain, and decided to talk. "I was a young boy...soldiers were riding through our village, and my little sister was in their way. I ran to get her out of the way, and this sergeant's horse jump up. The man almost fell...one of his feet came out of the...What is that word, Abramo?"

Abramo pondered for a moment, but couldn't think of the word either. Mateusz gestured with his foot and then when on with his story. "But when the horse was calm, the sergeant come off his horse and was angry with me. He take his...mace...from his saddle and hit me two times in the arm. The first time near the shoulder knock me down. The second time in the, um..." Mateusz pointed to his elbow.

"Elbow."

"Thank you, Abramo. Jews had no doctor in our village...but the old man who helped such things said my...this..." He pointed to his elbow again. "He said it was broke, and my shoulder bad, too. He said I never use it anymore. Every day I try to use, and I get better. But some days now—days like today, damp and dark? I have a hard time. Hurts like hell."

Joe Hannon too had noticed that on certain days Mateusz favored his right arm during some of the jobs. That was why he had picked Mateusz over Abramo as his scapegoat. "Well, how about it, kike? Are you gonna stick around here even when you can't do your job right? Like a goddamned cripple?"

"I do my job. I only don't want fight. No fight," Mateusz answered.

"If you were a man, you'd step to it, Jew-boy," Joe said.

Joe looked around at his cohorts and saw that they were enjoying the spectacle. As usual, he couldn't resist giving them more. "But you're not a man, are you? See, I'm gonna just have to stop fucking your wife, boy. I ain't doing you no favors anymore. Now if you want someone to service your wife, you'll have to pay me."

Abramo had heard much in the lunchroom in the months he had worked at Reid-Carnegie, but he had never heard the squalid personal insults that Joe Hannon had leveled at Mateusz.

"You are a pig," Mateusz hissed at Joe, and then stood up to leave the lunchroom. Just as he did, one of Joe's henchmen, a vicious little man named Dilworth, found a cue in Joe's voice to confront Mateusz. He stepped in front of him and pushed Mateusz backward. Mateusz, far lighter than the other man, fell over his chair, losing his footing and falling sideways on the right, landing sprawled upon the floor. He had used his bad arm to break his fall and grasped it in pain.

Abramo stood up and helped pull Mateusz erect. Then Abramo turned toward Dilworth and said, "His arm hurts from an old injury. Leave him alone."

"You his keeper, dago?" Joe Hannon bellowed over Dilworth's back. Abramo didn't answer but still stood his ground between Dilworth and Mateusz. "So, are you gonna arm wrestle for him, then?" Hannon said.

"No," said Abramo, still looking directly at Dilworth.

"Then it looks like I might have to start fucking your wife, too—just like I have to do for that kike over there."

Abramo glared at Hannon now as Dilworth withdrew back to the table. Then he turned to Mateusz and moved toward him, concerned about his friend's arm.

Joe hated being ignored, and like a child who couldn't handle frustration, he grew angry. He called to Abramo's back as the Italian talked to his Jewish friend. "Hey, boy, what's your wife's name? If I'm gonna start fucking her, I'll have to know it—just to keep it straight from the Jew's over there."

Abramo's face was a mask of rage; Mateusz held one of his forearms with his left hand. "Abramo, I'm sorry for this."

"Hey, dago, what's the name of your wife? I always like to get cozy with these women before I—"

Finally Abramo broke. He turned and faced his tormentor. The whole room was silent. "Her name in your mouth would rot your tongue, animal!"

Joe Hannon was shocked at the vehemence of Abramo's response, as was everyone else in the room. Joe suddenly became uneasy, not because he feared Abramo, but because he felt he was losing the favor of the crowd. This time, Joe realized he may have gone too far. All the men recognized Abramo and Mateusz as good workers: always willing to help another with a heavy job, always calm, always polite and friendly. And those who knew that Abramo had lost his wife were sickened by Hannon's vulgarity.

"Animal, am I? You fucking dago. What are you gonna do about it?"

"You want to wrestle? Then we wrestle, and then you shut up forever."

"No, Abramo," Mateusz whispered.

But Abramo was angry and outraged. He really wanted to arm wrestle Joe Hannon. Suddenly, through all the resentment and bitterness and anger over Angelina's death, through all the confusion and loneliness and bewilderment, he saw one thing clearly: He saw Joe Hannon as the personification of all the hurt that had tormented him in the years since Angelina died. He wanted to beat this fool and bully who felt that he was better than all other men.

Abramo walked toward the table where the ritual arm duels were always done. For a half second, he hesitated as he approached the table, doubting himself again, almost believing that the years of labor in Italy had left him undeveloped and weak. But from childhood, Abramo had performed the steady, consistent exercise that built strength and endurance and power, if not great size, into a man's arms. From the age of five, he had worked with his father, a rough-stone cutter, hauling stone. Soon Abramo, even as a young boy, was able to carry heavy stones in both arms, all day long, in jobs that would have exhausted most grown men.

Then, when he showed more interest in wood than the stones that he had grown up with, he cleared woods and carried felled trees back to the artisan's shop where he learned to treat wood as something living and beautiful, something that came from God through the hands of artisans to the people.

His apprenticeship was one of pleasure and learning. His master was a man who loved the smell and feel of wood. He honored wood when he worked with it. He blessed, anointed, and cherished it. And he taught Abramo to feel the same way. The young man was a willing pupil, as natural to the trade as his master.

And now, in this strange place, Abramo's past had to do him justice in an ordeal that might injure and humiliate him, might cast him out of Reid-Carnegie, might drive Joe Hannon's lewd insults into his heart. The one way Hannon had given Abramo a chance against him was to challenge him in a duel of arm strength.

But Hannon had no doubts about the slender Italian. Abramo was too small to cause him fear. How could this crowd be so dumb? To think that this little guy could do what so many bigger, better men had failed to do? Hannon had the size, weight, and height advantage. He was well over six feet in height, with a heavy, thick body. Abramo was well under six feet, with a muscular but slender body. As in all his past physical contests, he would prevail against the Italian. In this one, it was arm strength and leverage that mattered.

Hannon glared at the young Italian. His withering gaze had always helped intimidate his adversaries in the past. He knew that besides sheer strength, there was a psychological component to these bouts. Sometimes belief that he might fail rendered an opponent incapable of dealing with the sudden thrusts or bursts of energy or periods of strain that Hannon used so well. It gave him a split-second advantage that could not be undone. And once he had the advantage, he never gave it up.

The same man who was the unofficial referee in all Hannon's bouts stood beside them. He had adopted the air of a ring announcer and advertised the contestants as though they were boxers at a prizefight. After his introductions and a respectful time to allow cheers from the partisans, the ref was ready. "Clasp hands, gentlemen," he said officiously.

Abramo opened his right hand, and Joe Hannon grabbed it roughly. Joe leered at him, but Abramo avoided his gaze while quickly catching a glance at Mateusz's frightened face as the contest was about to begin. "Ready? Go!" said the ref.

Joe quickly bore down on Abramo's arm, and he saw the surprise on his face. He began to crush Abramo's hand, drawing himself closer to the table with his face directly opposite their hands. This time Abramo met his gaze. Strange, thought Hannon: this Italian's eyes lacked the fear that he could so easily detect in other men.

Abramo felt neither fear nor confidence. He had been through too much in his life to be so sure of himself. He knew that chance was involved, that this was no time for panic and no time for fear to overwhelm him.

Joe pushed a little to his left, and Abramo's hand moved with it. But as he pushed, just as slowly, Abramo's hand resisted. Joe smirked. How many of these moves could the Italian stop? In a moment he tried moving his hand left again. But as he moved, Abramo stiffened, and Joe's arm stopped.

The noise around them was deafening. Joe's partisans shouted to him to stop toying with the man and end it quickly. Abramo's supporters, at first prepared for an inevitable, if not sudden, defeat, were amazed that the contest, after two minutes, had not ended. And reluctant as they were, they gave in to their hopes and let themselves believe that this slender Italian just might have a chance. So many other men at this point had been reduced to sweating and trembling, with eyes hollowed by fear and humiliation. The noise surged from behind Abramo and filled the room to overflowing.

The six foremen of the day shift who ate lunch in the small but well-kept anterior room adjoining the men's lunchroom stirred at the sudden increase in noise coming through the walls. "What the hell's going on?" said the general foreman.

"I'll go see," said another foreman, instinctively aroused by the strange tone of the noise. In a few seconds, he was back at the door of the small room. "Hey, Tom," he called to Abramo's foreman, "come over here and look at this."

Tom glanced in puzzlement at his colleagues and then started for the door. The whole contingent followed him. They entered the lunchroom from the rear and could see only the face of Joe Hannon and the back of the Italian. The noise was deafening as they advanced to the edge of Abramo's crowd, just enough to give them a view of the fight.

Shocked, the foremen looked at each other. Not many of them liked Hannon, and Tom detested the loud and arrogant Irishman. He had run-ins before with the politically connected Hannon and would have fired him long ago if it were not for the restraint applied by the old general foreman.

Tom was elated by what he saw. By now, Hannon's legend had grown to the point that anyone who gave him a good fight was serving him humiliation. By not delivering a crushing, quick defeat, Joe Hannon had allowed Abramo a moral victory.

Every move was countered, every tactic thwarted, and even more terrifying still, Joe's muscles were beginning to tire. He tried staring at the dago, only to be met with steely resolve. These goddamned dagos were all devils, he thought.

Abramo was expressionless, showing neither fear nor confidence. He held on, and he could see a change in Joe Hannon's eyes, a change in his spirit brought about by fatigue. Abramo knew that the fatigue was new to Joe Hannon, and the four or five minutes they were grappling and straining had unexpectedly taken their toll on the arm of the big man.

And then, just once as time was passing, Abramo saw fear. Joe Hannon was frightened by the specter of possibilities to come. How could he come to work if he lost to this little dago? What would the men who were now cheering him think of him if he lost? How do you command respect if everyone has seen you lose? And how do you face your conqueror when you have insulted him by degrading his wife? And what do you tell your brothers who always looked up to you as the best and the toughest? And finally, how do you face Jack Hannon, a man and father to be feared, if you have lost to an Italian? An Italian that you provoked and insulted? That you forced into a fight?

Joe Hannon was sweating, and Abramo was waiting; he didn't know for what. He thought of Angelina; he thought of his life as a soldier; he thought of his old father who had died not long ago in Italy. And he thought of his baby daughter: a dream of love now lost. He could hear Mateusz shouting behind him—hold on, hold on.

And if there were any emotion visible on Abramo's face, it wasn't smugness or pride of victory. It was relief and hatred together. Relief because he had finally found a release for the pent up bitterness within him that had turned his lonely, aching life toward Youngstown. And hatred because now he had a chance to avenge himself upon all the evil that had visited his life in the person of this cruel and bigoted and callous lout. The anger he felt over Hannon's defilement of Angelina's memory had brought him to this table and sustained him through six minutes of arm wrestling that were now being called out by the referee as each minute passed.

And just when Abramo was feeling that he was now a match for Hannon, another thing occurred. Joe Hannon's eyes showed it first. It was bewilderment and wonder. The changes were noticeable only to Abramo, whose face was as close as six inches to Hannon's. There was the look of pain.

Joe Hannon looked almost betrayed. Suddenly the great arm that he had used so many times to destroy opponents was faltering. Suddenly the arm was more than tired; it was breaking down. At second glance, Abramo knew it for sure. Something was happening to Hannon. And there was no doubt now that his arm was hurt.

Abramo looked questioningly at him. Did he want to quit? But the conciliatory look that would have ended the match at a draw was ignored by Hannon. When Abramo lessened the strain against him, instead of relaxing, Hannon brought his arm sideways, attempting to pin Abramo's arm to the table. He hated Abramo, and Abramo's conciliatory gesture was returned with a grunt and more effort against him. Then he sneered and muttered, "Your wife, you bastard dago."

When Abramo heard the words, and when he felt Joe's pressure against his right hand, he knew that he had felt the best that Joe could use against him. Joe was summoning every bit of his strength and resolve to beat him. Abramo was finally free of any feelings of fairness or compassion. Now he wanted to beat Hannon, to humiliate and hurt him.

Each time the surge of Hannon's hand was weaker. And this time Abramo was thinking not about not losing but about winning. Where in the past six minutes he had only been holding on, now he was aggressive.

For the first time, Hannon could feel the strength on the other side, movement against him, and he could see a sure knowledge in the eyes of the Italian that he could win. Slowly and steadily, as the ref called seven minutes, Abramo grew defiant. Then Joe's nightmare began against the backdrop of all the shouting voices and the foremen standing by. Suddenly his hand began to move, and a slight smile played on the mouth of Abramo. The dago was actually pushing his hand away against his best efforts. Hannon was terrified. He gave a grunt and watched his hand being held still. Then moved slowly, inexorably backward—again.

This couldn't be happening. It had to be a bad dream. But the terrible pain in his arm was not a dream. Joe frantically punched his hand against Abramo's steady and controlled pressure. And almost in an instant, his partisans were quiet. From Joe's back, they could see his hand moving, and at Abramo's back there was bedlam.

But Hannon had one last gesture he could make. From deep in his chest he made a low growl that shot through his mouth as a loud bellow, almost a scream. And once more Abramo gave, but once more Hannon's arm moved to a stop. And within a few seconds of his shout, Joe's arm was again going backward toward the tabletop. The look of disbelief on Hannon's face was only erased by a look of horror. Hannon felt it first, and Abramo knew it second. The snapping sound, the collapse of Hannon's arm, and then the scream of the vanquished champion at the terrible, sudden pain. Something had broken, and his arm was useless.

Hannon shivered and tried to stand up, pushing himself away from the table with his other arm. He fell backward as he stood up, as though his legs were broken. And when he pushed everybody's hands away from their offers of help, he stood finally and looked around at his silent supporters and back to Abramo's host. He was in a daze, not recognizing who he saw or where he was. Then to the horror of friend and foe alike, a dark wet spot began to appear at his groin on his pants, getting larger and larger before the eyes of all men in the room. He turned to run but fell down, screaming in pain.

Abramo, standing now with tears in his eyes for what he'd seen and done, looked exhausted and disoriented. Mateusz came to him and slipped a hand under his shoulder. Soon another hand helped, and then another. Abramo walked back to his lunch pail and stood looking at it, not even hearing the congratulatory wishes of his friends, old and new, or the clapping noise as the whole crowd gave him an ovation—all of his partisans and most of Hannon's.

"Better let Connolly know, Tom," said the general foreman. "I think Hannon's finished."

Kieran Harty felt the drop in his trade. The Hannon district AOH was cutting into his business, and the general slowdown in business in the Valley was hurting all bars, especially the AOHs. Besides, he had just recently bought the last building on the block and now owed several hundred dollars more a month to the banks. And he would soon have to buy a truck, because it would be quicker and cheaper to go get his supplies rather than wait to have them delivered. And he could put the new truck to good use by renting it out to other businesses for deliveries.

But what he needed now was time. Just a few months of good business and the last part of the block would be his. But, of course, what he needed, he never got, he thought morosely.

He sat in the kitchen of the bar, watching two dozen eggs boil. Hard-boiled eggs were always a staple at the bar, and Kieran seemed to know how to make them to everyone's liking.

At the moment of his darkest thoughts, Molly entered the kitchen. Kieran brightened when he saw her. Of all people in the world, she best could change his moods. She was carrying a cup of coffee for him. "What're you doing, Da? Brooding about money?"

Kieran shrugged. "Nah, just wondering where the hell my coffee was and when you'd get around to thinking of your old man to bring him a cup."

"Well," she said smiling, "I'd about decided that you're too cranky to deserve one, but then my soft heart got the better of me."

"Sit down here and talk to me," Kieran said, cradling her elbow as she set the cup before him. He liked touching her. She was his link to his memories of Cara. All those years when he busied himself with acquiring things, owning things, becoming respectable, he counted on her to remember the past. Cara was the treasurer of dates and times and memories of the children, the family, and their marriage. But in an instant she was gone, along with all the memories and most of the dreams. Kieran was lost. Only Molly reminded him of the life that was and might have been. And as she grew into a woman, the lost memories didn't hurt so much, because she was the fulfillment of them all.

"Pa?" Molly said finally.

Kieran's heart sank. Whenever she used that soft tone, he was defenseless. It was almost impossible to withstand her, even when he was angry about something, but when he was sitting alone and dreaming of once and future happiness, when Molly used that tone, he was doomed. "Yes, daughter," he sighed.

"I was talking to Mary Catherine—"

"Good that you didn't talk to someone silly," he muttered.

"Pa! Will you listen, please? Mary Catherine works as a domestic to some family on the North Side. Well, she says she can get me a job—"

"Oh, no," Kieran said, "there'll be no domestic jobs for you. Kieran Harty's daughter will not do such servile work."

"Why not?"

"Because I'll not have my daughter do such work for rich people," he said.

"No, but you'll have me do it here for you, will ye not?"

"That's different."

"It is not."

"Don't argue with me, girl. You'll not have such a job."

"Pa, here I clean the house and the club, clean the men's toilet, I mop floors and clean spittoons. I wash towels—sometimes filled with blood and vomit—and I say nothing. Why does getting paid to clean a house with much less filth and mess than this place bother you so? It should bother me, not you."

Kieran stared at his daughter. Like her mother, she never stopped surprising him. Every day he discovered new facets of her character. Every day he realized how intelligent and special she was.

He walked away from her a few paces. "It bothers me that it bothers you," he said softly. "It bothers me that I still haven't given you the life I wanted for you."

"My life is fine, Pa. I know you love me. And in their own ways, I know the boys do, too. And we're just starting to see daylight...only now the business is falling off just when we've bought new things. And it's not a long-term job. It'll be just for a few months while the wife recovers and the new baby is well."

"Temporary, is it? But why do you set your head on such things, Moll?"

"Because all of us—each of us—should do whatever we can for this family. And I know I can help."

"But, my dear, we'll get by. You don't have to do this."

"But I want to, Dad." She hesitated for a few seconds. Again Kieran couldn't imagine what she would say next. "You know, Daddy, that Ross wants to go to school?"

"What? He's done with school."

"He wants to go to college."

"To do what?" Kieran said incredulously.

"To be an electrical engineer."

"Engineer? How come he never told me about this—never mentioned a word?"

"I'm the only one who knows. He told me one day when we were having a long talk. He wouldn't tell you because he knows you're short of money and have a lot of bills."

"I would have found a way to send him if he wanted to go," muttered Kieran.

"Sometimes boys have a hard time talking about things to their fathers…especially boys like Ross," Molly said hesitantly.

"You mean Ross is not close enough to me to talk, don't you?"

"He thinks you're closer to Conor and Paul because they spend more time at the club. He thinks you're…disappointed in him."

"I never said anything to him about being disappointed." Molly just stared at him without saying a word. Kieran stared back sheepishly. "But somehow I let him believe it, right?" he said finally.

"If I can work this job, I can help Ross—"

"It'll take a lot more than you'd make," Kieran huffed.

"But I'll help…and Ross will know…I mean, he won't have to give up his dream, will he? Please, Da?"

Kieran took a deep breath. He glanced at her again. She had done it once more. By virtue of her mind, her beauty, and her charm, she had beaten him and gotten just what she wanted. And he was an old fool to fight. He was lost. He nodded imperceptibly. She threw her arms around him and kissed him. "Get away, Máille! Damn you, girl, you've bewitched me," he said, with a slight smile playing on his lips and his arms around her.

Hugh Connolly watched Abramo working beside Mateusz Wroblewski. Damn, that had to be the strangest pair he'd ever seen in the plant. Of all the hundreds of Italians in the place that Cardone could have paled up with, he chose a Polish Jew. As Hugh watched them, it was like watching a matched team of horses.

Every move they made was in concert, every move designed to make the job easier, every move fluid and economical. They had a kind of subliminal communication that animals have when they are in a group with a common purpose.

The lunchroom was a lot quieter now than it was before—and much less tense. Productivity after the lunch break had increased measurably. The men were coming out of the lunchroom relaxed and refreshed. There was no more of the strain imposed by one man with a need to dominate others physically and spiritually. There was more table talk and easy laughter, and newcomers sat at tables now. There was no longer a pecking order; whoever arrived first took a place.

George Carter, the assistant plant manager, came into Connolly's office. Seeing him looking out over the plant, he said, "So, how are things?"

"Okay," said Hugh. "You see the latest figures? Better to be lucky than smart, huh?"

Carter nodded as he drew up beside Hugh and began to look over the plant. "Take credit for it, son. It happened on your watch. But it's amazing how things are, isn't it? If we would have seen this while it was going on, we could have sacked Hannon a long time ago. Who would have thought that his going would have such a benefit?"

"He was a bully," said Hugh. "I guess none of us could believe he had such tight control of the crew."

"Whatever it was, he sacrificed productivity for his own good—and no one, until you came along, was sharp enough to find out."

"Oh, come on, George…"

"It happened on your watch, son," Carter said again, waving his objection off. "If they blame you for other things you can't control, then take credit for this one. I've already told the old man you're responsible."

"Jesus, George, he'll want me to work miracles from now on."

"Just keep doing what you're doing. The men like it when you go around on the floor. They know you're one of them. And they like to think that there's a way for some of them to move upstairs off that floor. We didn't know about the bad effect Joe Hannon was having, but we might have found out sooner if we'd have done more of your kind of visits to the floor and the lunchroom."

"That Italian kid down there knew."

"Have you talked to him since the fight?"

"Nah, I stayed out of it. Tom handled it well. Funny thing— he said that Abramo came to work the next day and, to look at him, you'd never know he knocked off the meanest son of a bitch in the plant."

"But every guy out there knows it, right?"

"They sure as hell do."

"And yet he's not throwing his weight around, huh?"

"No," said Hugh, thoughtfully. "George, is that job still open for a courier?"

"Yeah, it is," said Carter, "but it's only part-time."

"How would it be if we let that kid do the job? He'd be able to use the extra money."

"You mean work in the plant three days and be a courier two?"

"It would give him a chance to learn more of our operations. And the raise will let him know that he has some future with us if he keeps his nose clean."

"Well, offer it to him. See what he says," said Carter.

Later that day, Abramo was ushered by a secretary into Hugh's office. Abramo looked pale and fearful. He was sure he'd be fired for hurting a long-time employee like Hannon.

"Sit down, Abramo," Hugh said, pointing to a chair opposite his desk. Hugh was standing, and Abramo, seated, wished he didn't have to look up at the boss as they talked.

Abramo couldn't control his anxiety. "Am I fired?" he asked.

"Why? What have you done?" Hugh said with a slight smile.

"I fought with Joe Hannon."

"That wasn't a fight, as I heard it. It was a contest, right? And didn't he challenge you first?"

"Well…" Abramo hesitated, looking at Hugh, trying to figure out why he was so non-threatening, even though he had called him up to his office.

"Enough about the lunchroom. I have a proposition for you." Abramo didn't understand, so Hugh paraphrased himself in Italian.

Abramo looked amazed. "How do you know Italian?"

"When I was a young foreman, my first crew was an Italian gang that nobody wanted. I asked the men to help me learn Italian. Then I went two nights a week to the Italian church to study more. I was their foreman for seven years. When my wife died, they were very good to me. We're still good friends, all of us. And I get invitations to weddings and such. So I learned to speak, and now the lady who cleans my house—I still talk to her in Italian."

Abramo nodded. "I am trying to learn English," he said in Italian.

Hugh stared at him for a few seconds. He could have had a son the age of this boy. And he liked this young man. It was more than his being a good worker, or that he beat that asshole, Hannon; it was that he was honest and quiet and genuine.

Finally Hugh said, "We have been watching your work, Abramo…and we like what we see."

Abramo said, "*Grazie*—thanks."

"There is a job that is available now. It is part-time, two days a week."

"But I—"

"This does not mean that you will lose your place here," said Hugh. "If you take it, you will come to this office every Tuesday and Friday, and be a courier—messenger—for the mill."

Abramo still seemed amazed. "But my English is not good. You would want me for such a job?"

"It will pay you half again what you are making now for those two days."

"Half again?" Abramo had obviously not heard that expression. "What is half again?"

"You make three dollars a day now. On the new job, you will increase by half…to four-fifty."

"Just for delivery and messages?"

"You will be making important deliveries. We will be trusting you with information and correspondence that is 'sensitive.'" Hugh said the word in Italian.

"You think I can do this, signore?" Abramo said.

"I know you can, son," Hugh answered. Abramo stared into the room, away from Hugh. "You would be driving a truck for us, and your hours would be the same as they are now. And on other days, you will report to Tom, and he'll probably still let you work with Wroblewski."

"I would like that," Abramo said. Then the quality of the offer dawned on him. "But now I would be paid for six days when I only work five?" he said.

Hugh nodded, surprised at his quick arithmetic. "What do you say, Abramo? You will work here on Tuesdays and Fridays. And you will learn more about the company…and it will help you be a foreman sooner."

Abramo seemed dazed but thrilled with his good fortune. He stood up finally and said in Italian, "My fight with Hannon had nothing to do with this?"

"No," said Hugh. "It's your work, your attitude, and your willingness to learn."

Abramo gazed at Hugh for a few seconds. This Irishman was as nice as anyone in America, outside his family, had ever been to him. He was told by neighbors on the street and other Italian workers that the Irish were to be feared and not trusted. But this was an honorable man.

"I will be honored, signore," Abramo said.

"Good. Do you know how to drive a car?"

"No," Abramo answered anxiously.

"All right. When you start next Tuesday, Tom will get someone to teach you how to drive."

Chapter 3

HUGH WALKED INTO THE AOH and noted how sparse the crowd was, unusual for this time of the year. He nodded to Eddie, the bartender, who pointed to the back room where Kieran was poring over ledger books on the money spent and received. Hugh knocked on the door frame and walked in. Kieran brightened when he saw him.

"How are you, Kieran?"

"Getting by. What are you doing here on a Thursday night? Didn't you have a precinct meeting?"

"It ended early. I just thought I'd stop by to invite you out to dinner Saturday night." Kieran hesitated to answer for a moment. "Now I'm not going to let you think up a lot of reasons why you can't do it. I'll pick you up at seven."

"I don't know. Molly may not be home yet."

"Where will she be?"

"She's working a short-term job as a domestic with her girl-friend. It's for a family on the North Side."

"The North Side? How does she get over there?"

"She takes the trolley over, but if she's late she has to walk home. I always send one of the boys to meet her."

"You say this is temporary?" said Hugh, not wanting to ask the reason why Kieran would allow his daughter to work late as a domestic—and on the North Side.

"Yeah," Kieran said. Finally he tried to answer the question that Hugh had on his mind. "She wants to help out, Hugh. I tried to talk her out of it, but she'll not be told."

"Could you ever talk my sister out of anything she set her heart to?" Hugh responded. "Would you expect her daughter to be a pushover?"

Kieran huffed in agreement. He was grateful to Hugh for having deftly avoided asking the obvious but discomforting question about his financial state. But he felt close enough to his brother-in-law to share a confidence with him. "I'm okay, Hugh. It's just that I bought one of those corner buildings at the east end of the block, and—"

"That real old one?" Hugh interrupted.

"Yeah," said Kieran. "Only I didn't think it would happen at the same time as Hannon's AOH. I'm down about twenty percent."

"I told you the Hannons will piss all over that business in a few months. It's bound to happen. Just hold on, boyo...Kier, I can loan you money for—"

"There's no fucking way I'm gonna take money from you. You've worked too hard to get it."

"Remember I offered. And it'd be a short-term loan, anyway. Just don't let yourself get too deep in a hole without asking me for help."

"Yeah," said Kieran. There was a long stretch of silence before he looked up again. "So, what have you been up to?"

"Not much. Just learning my new job." Hugh leaned back against the door frame. "Speaking of Hannons, we had to let Jack Hannon's oldest kid go."

"What'd he do, steal something, the son of a bitch?"

"No, nothing like that. See, we hired this Italian kid a couple years ago who's bright as hell, minds his own business, and does excellent work. Anyway, Joe Hannon—he's a big guy, even bigger than his old man, and a bully besides—well, this Hannon runs the lunchroom like a goddamned Viking overlord. He beat up a bunch of people and then shoved a foreman, a good one, and got the old general foreman to hire him back after his old man put some political muscle on him.

"Anyway, for years he's been arm wrestling guys. And of course he'd pick the guys, insult them, challenge them, then shame them into a match, which he always won.

"Well, last week he started on this Italian kid. Hannon tried every trick he knew, making faces, getting the jump on the kid, but the kid outlasted him. Every time Hannon pushed, the kid stopped him. It went on for about seven or eight minutes and finally Hannon couldn't do it anymore. He gave one last heave and his goddamned arm broke...and Abramo pinned his hand.

"Then, when Hannon stood up, he started screaming, and suddenly—I swear to God—he pissed his pants. Then you know what the Italian kid did? He went back to his table and started crying." Hugh shook his head. "How about that? He beats the biggest blowhard and prick in the Valley and then feels sorry for him."

Kieran listened to the story with fascination and disgust. The thought of seeing a Hannon, especially Joe, so publicly humiliated was pleasing to him. But he had a belief in the dignity of men that made the image of a grown man urinating in his pants after being beaten in a contest horrible to him. The hair on his forearms and back of his neck stood up with the chill he felt at Hugh's story. "Jesus Christ," he muttered.

Isabella Chianese was busy washing clothes and hanging them outside to dry, going into and out of the cellar with load after load of newly washed clean clothes. It was hard labor, not just to wash the clothes, but to put them through the ringer after rinsing them twice and carrying the heavy baskets of wet clothes outside. She glanced out the window and saw the man whose backyard abutted hers from the street behind light a fire in a big steel drum full of trash. It was Monday, and only a fool would burn trash on washday. Pontello was always a fool.

Her face reddened, and she ran to the backyard and screamed at him. Soon she was joined by a chorus of other women who likewise cursed and damned Pontello. Reluctantly, he stopped up the fire and tried to put enough water on it to stop the smoking and sooting up of the white towels and sheets and underwear hanging on the lines across the neighborhood. He growled at the women and muttered curses at them as he went back into his house to face the embarrassed screams of his own wife, who was mortified at his breach of neighborhood protocol. Pontello often settled arguments between him and his wife by brutalizing her. Today he decided not to do it.

Isabella was still angry at him for his stupidity, and because he was a wife-beater besides. She mopped her brow with her apron and then quickly took the exposed clothes off the line. She worked hard every day and was known as the "lady of the three orphaned children." But by now her children were nearly teenagers. Gianina was thirteen and Roberto was ten and Guido was nine, born after his father's death.

Isabella was lovely to begin with, but the dark crown of black hair and large beautiful dark eyes set against creamy northern-Italian skin, flawless and clean, made her stunning.

She was almost forty-two years old and had lived as a widow for the last nine years. Her husband had been killed in an accident at the Valley Steel Mill. She was given a small settlement, and with it she made a down payment on her house. Along with boarders and taking in laundry and baking and selling bread, she managed to scratch out a living and to almost pay for the house that she lived in with her children.

She had also heard the rumors about her and the young boarder in her house, a mere fourteen years her junior. She had learned as she lived through the harsh times that befell her that some people envy others' successes. If she survived in the dark days after her husband's death, if her children, though poor, were clean, intelligent, and respectful, some people resented her for her steadfastness. But she didn't care, as long as her children prospered. The two old men, boarders for years, were like uncles to her. They would see to it that she and Abramo would do no harm to the name of Isabella's husband and children.

Her brow furrowed as she worked, washing clothes and wringing them through the clean water. These people had no hearts, she decided. Who suffered her pain, her loneliness? So when a respectful young man, the nephew of Don Michele della Malva, became her boarder, was she to be ashamed? She knew she had done nothing wrong. Why should she care about their idle talk?

That day, after supper, as the old men smoked cigars and drank wine in the living room, Isabella asked her daughter, Gianina, if she had seen Abramo go to his room. Her daughter said she hadn't. Isabella and Gianina cleared the table and washed the dishes. Once or twice she thought she heard something strange, a noise in the house. But when she stopped to listen, she heard nothing.

Later that night she decided to take some clothes she had mended down into the cellar to wash. As she went down the steps, she was suddenly frightened. She heard a noise in the basement, coming from one of the rooms in the cellar. She approached the room slowly, waiting to see who was in this place that only she and her children had ever seen. "Abramo?" she said in Italian as she entered the room. "What are you doing?"

He just looked at her in response and then pointed to a table he had made. She came further into the room, looking at the table in wide-eyed amazement. "You did this?" she said. He nodded. "This is beautiful. How…?"

"I brought my tools from Italy," he said. "I was a carpenter."

"You never told me, Abramo. How lovely!" He shrugged, and she understood. He was not a person to talk about himself. She had not even heard of his exploits at the mill until a neighbor lady told her at the market that Abramo had vanquished one of the evil

Irish in a fair fight, defending the honor of a Polish Jew who was his friend. "Where did you find the wood?"

"There is an old junk room at the mill, and I brought a piece home each night. The foreman said I could take it."

"Are you going to put it in your room?" she said.

"No." He hesitated. "It is for you…for your kindness to me."

"No, I can't accept this. It is too valuable. I don't—"

"Signora, this is my gift to you for all your help. You must take it."

"I…" She had tears in her eyes. He reached out with his hand and touched her arm gently.

"I didn't mean to embarrass you," he said.

She took a deep breath, gathering her composure, and then spoke. "I know, Abramo. You have been wonderful to me and the children."

"You have made this a home for me, Isabella. Your children, the old men…they are like my family."

"God bless you, Signor Cardone. My prayers are that you will do well in America." Then she came to him and hugged him. Abramo, who was not used to having young, attractive women in his arms was at first hesitant, but then he embraced her in return.

In a few moments, she stepped away and wiped her eyes. "I have to put oil onto it," Abramo said. "Then it will be ready."

"Can I show the children?" she asked, now animated and happy about her table.

"Now?"

"Yes, now," she said, smiling.

"Okay."

She ran upstairs, leaving her basket of clothes in the room. In a few minutes, she was downstairs again. With her were her three children. Gianina was the image of her mother—gentle, affectionate, and sensitive. The boys were noisy and talkative, but playful and kind, the same as their father, the old men told him. Gianina walked toward Abramo in amazement and held his hand.

The table was made in the style Abramo had developed: different colored pieces, red and dark and light woods oiled and stained. The table was simple, yet beautiful.

"This is lovely," Gianina said to Abramo. He squeezed her hand in response.

"It's for your mother," he said.

"Mama, it's ours," she said in English. Isabella nodded.

Later, as Abramo was cleaning up the room after he had oiled down the table, Isabella returned to the basement. "Abramo," she said, and he looked up. "I never use this room, and I don't need it now, so if you ever want to use it—not for me—you can do your work here…always."

He nodded in acceptance. "Thank you," he said.

Hugh Connolly asked one of his assistants, "How's Abramo doing with the truck?"

"Okay," said the assistant. "He catches on quick, and Tom told me he's just about ready to go out alone."

"Good," said Hugh. "Before you send him out alone for the first time, tell him to come up here and talk to me."

Renata brought Michele a cup of hot coffee. "Have you seen Abramo this week?" she asked her brother.

"It's only Wednesday," Michele answered, not looking up at her as he read the newspaper.

"But I thought maybe he would come here to show you the truck he was driving."

"If they send him this way," said Michele.

"Imagine. He gets into a fight with an Irish and he gets a better job besides," she said.

"It's because he's a good worker, Renata," said Michele, not really wanting to talk.

Suddenly they heard the front door open. It was Abramo. "So the truck driver is here," Michele said, finally seeming to rouse from his lethargy.

"Not-until-Friday truck driver," said Abramo.

"Will you stay for supper, Abramo?" said his aunt.

"*Sì*, thank you," said Abramo. Renata immediately left for the kitchen.

"Sit here, son," said Michele. "How are you doing?"

"I'm fine, Zi'Michele. The job is good, and they teach me new things." He grinned. "And I will make more money—one whole day's wage more each week."

"I know, Abramo. I'm proud of you," the old man said. To Abramo he looked as though he had something on his mind, but that he was having trouble saying it.

"Zi'Michele?" Abramo said softly.

"Abramo, you have become a son to me—the son I never had. I want you to be happy here in Youngstown…and in my old age, I wish I could hold your children in my lap." Abramo raised his open right hand upward a few inches and then placed it back on his knee. In Italian it meant acceptance and gratitude, and Michele understood. "But I must warn you also, Abramo. You will be driving a truck and making deliveries in parts of Youngstown where you will not be welcome. The Germans, the Poles, the Irish will all mistrust you and be your enemies."

"But Zi'Michele, I am friends with those very people at work."

"I know, Abramo. Your Jewish friend, your Irish bosses—but those are special people. You must know that there are many of them who would hurt you if they could. Hell, there are bad ones in every group. Do you think all Italians are good?"

Abramo shook his head, remembering that Angelina was killed by Italians. "But I must go where they send me, right?"

"Yes, but you must be careful in those places—in every place. Mind your own business, trust no one, and do your job. Then come home safely, understand?"

"I understand. But you know that I keep my mind on my business."

"I know, I know. But I'm reminding you because I want you to be safe." Abramo nodded again. "Now tell me, have you met a girl that you like yet?"

Abramo chuckled. He knew his uncle and aunt were anxious for him to meet someone. But he wondered, when they importuned him to meet some young woman so often, how it was that they themselves were widowed and still alone.

Abramo kept himself busy even during his free time. He visited Mateusz and his aunt and uncle several times a week. He studied English and read books from the free library. He spent evenings talking to Isabella and the children, and also with the two old boarders. His life was full, yet it was empty.

He did miss the companionship of a woman. But he missed more the touch, the tender whispered words that entered his soul and cleansed and soothed it. He missed the soft words they would speak when they held each other in bed, warm and safe, full of dreams for the future, full of the promise of life that came from their love, their hard work, their honesty, their openheartedness. He missed the reflection of his love that she would provide.

And despite the worries of his aunt and uncle, he did notice women. He looked furtively, and looked again. Yet, of all he noticed, there were few who had the look that was the key to his heart. Some who did, like Isabella's daughter, Gianina, were too young. Most were married and could not be looked at a second time.

He knew that they had to be in some way striking, if not beautiful. Beyond that, he had to see something in their eyes, the same thing he saw when he looked at Angelina. He couldn't describe what he felt, but what he wanted was the look that made his heart sing. It was the look of sincerity, of innocence, of playfulness, of brightness.

But who was he to be so demanding when there were other, more worthy men who should be as particular as he? Yet he still dreamed of finding her. Maybe she was looking for someone, too. Maybe for that special look in the eyes of a man who made her heart sing?

Yet what could he say to Michele and Renata? That he was waiting for lightning to strike twice in his life? That after Angelina, there would be yet another one for him who was beautiful and tender and loving and wise? Abramo shook his head to himself. But where was she? Was she waiting for lightning to strike, too? Could she ever be his if she didn't even know he was alive? "I have not met this girl, Uncle. Where is she? Do you know her?"

Michele smirked. His nephew was taunting him, and it was a new experience. The comfort of closeness and belonging had given Abramo the ease of playing with his aunt and uncle. "You know, Abramo, if you sit and wait, you will not find her. But if you live your life, and if you always look, someday she will be behind you or in front of you or will somehow touch you. And then you will know you have found the girl who has been waiting for you."

"Does the God who took my lovely wife and the child I could have had in my old age now concern himself with my happiness, Zi'Michele?"

Michele was surprised at Abramo's bitter tone. This was a side his nephew had never shown. He was more human than he had believed, Michele thought with some satisfaction. Abramo was angry with God. Maybe when his life changed, he would know that the pain had made him wise.

Kieran had just finished stacking barrels beneath the bar of the AOH. He was still fuming at the delivery of bad meat that had been sent that afternoon. Damn that bastard Creagen! He was sick of having to fight him all the time and then eat the costs himself. Creagen thought his customers were stupid and would accept crap without a word of protest. But that's what he got for dealing only with Irish, Kieran thought. One more bad shipment and Creagen was out as a supplier. Next time, he was going to the Jews or the dagos.

Conor came into the AOH and grabbed a hard-boiled egg. Kieran eyed him coolly. "You have to go get Molly," he said.

"Damn it, Daddy, I go more than both the others combined."

"Your sister needs you, boyo," Kieran said wearily.

"She doesn't have to do this. She can get a job here on the East Side. Why the hell do we have to walk an hour just to get her back…and on the North Side yet?"

"Conor, go get your sister and shut up."

"But why can't you send one of the other boys?"

"Because the other boys are busy working, something you don't have a habit of doing."

"I work. You just don't pay attention to what I do."

"You don't put in half the work in a year that your brothers do…or a third of what Molly does. I'm through arguing with you. Now go get your sister, and you damn well better be there on time because I don't want those two girls walking through Walnut Way alone. And, Son, if anything happens to your sister on your watch, I'll flay you alive."

Conor glared at his father for a few seconds, grumbled something, then turned to leave the tavern.

Abramo walked up the stairs to the superintendent's office, wondering what Connolly wanted to talk to him about. He thought he was doing well as a driver. Tom told him he'd soon be driving on his own. He approached the secretary, and she showed him through the maze of small offices to the superintendent's door. She knocked and admitted Abramo.

Hugh Connolly turned in his desk chair to greet him. "Hello, Abramo. Come over here and have a seat." Hugh pointed to a chair opposite his desk. Abramo walked over and sat down uneasily. "Tom tells me you're ready to go out on your own," said the superintendent.

"Yes, sir. Next Tuesday."

"Do you like the work?" Hugh smiled.

"Yes, sir. It's interesting, and I see the outside…get to know Youngstown."

"But you have to be careful, son. Remember that there are men out there who will assault you just because you're Italian or Catholic or curly-haired and dark-skinned."

"Yes," Abramo said thoughtfully, shaking his head. "It's strange that this happens in America."

Hugh was surprised by the comment, but he nodded in appreciation of the point. "Abramo, we often make deliveries on the North Side. But when you go there you have to stay away from the Irish bars, understand? Do you know Joe Hannon's father owns an Irish club on the North Side? Called an AOH?"

"Yes, Mateusz told me. But I thought it was on the East Side?"

"There are five in the Valley. The newest one is on the North Side. You see what I mean? Just be careful, and remember to avoid a fight whenever you can. I'd rather that you miss a delivery than get brutalized by one of those thug bastards."

Abramo smiled at Hugh's language. He had heard the fore-men use profane language, but never one of the big bosses. But this Connolly was a real man, not a phony. He started as a worker, a natural, likeable man with a connection to ordinary people. He had a good heart.

"Abramo?" Connolly said in a changed tone of voice. "What are you doing this Saturday?"

"I help out at my uncle's warehouse most times..."

"Oh."

"Do you want me to work here?"

"No...Well, yes. I want you to come with me to pick up some things—to drive the truck. You'll be paid, of course."

Abramo nodded. "I can do it."

"I don't want to interfere with your work at your uncle's."

"But I'm not a regular worker...I can do it."

"All right. We'll be going over to Mrs. Reid's house to pick up some things...and to do whatever else she wants." Abramo let his puzzlement show. "Mrs. Reid? Do you not know of her?" Hugh asked. Abramo shook his head. "She's the widow of Anthony B. Reid—you know, the Reid in Reid-Carnegie? She still owns controlling interest in this company…and is the most important Irish person in the Valley, probably in the state. You don't mind working for Irish, do you?" Hugh smirked.

Abramo smiled, more at ease now with the superintendent, and ready to respond to his humor. He also sensed that Hugh liked him—at least enough to curse freely and to taunt him. Yes, a man this good would not disguise his feelings. Abramo liked him.

"All right. Let's meet here at seven o'clock—she goes to Mass daily, so we can't go too early—in this office. We may have a thing or two to bring to her house. Uh, wear some better work clothes, okay? One false move on our parts and she'll eat us alive—superintendent or not, truck driver or not."

"Okay," Abramo said. "I will be here early. Thank you, sir."

"You say he is going with you? The superintendent?" said Michele, amazed at the turns Abramo's life was taking. For Irishmen to be so kind to Italians? For an Irish mill superintendent to be so close to an ordinary worker, newly come to this country?

"Will you mind if I go?" said Abramo.

"Of course not. That is your job." Both men had developed a pattern of speaking that was maddening to others who knew either English or Italian alone. They would begin in English and then lapse into Italian and back and forth into the two languages. Renata, who had learned little English, was often irritated by their crazy speech patterns.

In the nearly two years that Abramo had been in America, he had become as knowledgeable in English as his uncle, who had been in America more than twenty years. The young man had a passion, not only to learn his new language, but to learn the patterns and intonations of speakers native to the country. Every night he would spend a short time reading the grammar and language texts he had bought from a downtown bookstore. And he would read the great literature that was available from the Reuben Macmillan Free Library, a treasure house of wisdom, knowledge, and adventure.

"You don't know what you have to do?" Michele said, referring to Abramo's meeting with Mrs. Reid.

"No. The way the superintendent talks, she is rich and does not like fools."

"Well, you are surely not a fool, but be careful. That's all you can do."

Chapter 4

MOLLY AND MARY CATHERINE Meade walked wearily home from the Parsons family estate. They had scrubbed and cleaned and polished almost the entire house. Their hands were raw and their knees ached. And they were hungry. Tomorrow they would return to clean up the debris from tonight's party.

The Parsons family was wealthy and unworthy, both girls thought. They were lazy, arrogant and stupid. For every attempt the father made to help his children show some dignity and class, he was rebuffed by manifold outrages and shames. His wife was vapid and dumb, his children prodigal and ignorant. He alone had a sense of dignity, and some belief that wealth comes not by birthright but by work and frugality.

The girls crossed Blair Avenue and walked through the park near Warfield Auditorium. Then they walked down through the notorious Walnut Way, moving almost at a run to get through the seedy quarter, averting their eyes from anyone on the sidewalk for fear of being stopped. Luckily, they were walking through the supper hour, and the cold October wind and early darkness were enough to keep most people off the Way at night. It was only after they crossed the Sloan Street Bridge that they could see Conor running toward them in the distance.

When he drew near, he was red-faced and distressed. "You won't tell Pa about my being late, will you, Moll?"

"Where have you been Conor? We've walked the whole way without you. Damn you! I should tell Pa just to see you thrashed."

"Don't tell, Moll. Please. I promise I'll be there on time from now on."

"You'd better be, Conor. Mary Catherine depends on you too, you know."

"Hi, Mary Catherine," Conor said, appealing to her with a smile. "You don't mind if I'm late, do you?" Mary Catherine shrugged.

"Of course she does, Conor. You moron," said Molly.

"Please, Moll. Don't say."

"All right. But no more. I don't want to cross Walnut Way or the mill yard alone, or get home in the dark with all those drunks and bums around."

"I swear to God, Molly Girl. I won't do it."

"You won't have your card game at the Crab Inn you mean," she said disgustedly.

Abramo entered Hugh Connolly's office at seven o'clock Saturday morning. "Good morning, Abramo. We have to bring some pipes to Mrs. Reid's house today. Let's go down to the truck, and I'll help you put them on. There are not many."

The two men walked down to the truck, Abramo walking quietly beside the superintendent. The few pipes that they had to take were loaded onto the truck, and then Hugh handed Abramo the key. "You drive," he said as he entered on the passenger side. Abramo, surprised, did as he was told and started the truck. As they drove, according to Hugh's directions, they passed a small neighborhood restaurant. "Stop here," said Hugh. Then he looked at Abramo. "Well, come on, man. It's too early to deliver these pipes to Mrs. Reid. We'll have some breakfast."

Abramo hesitated, not sure if he had enough money for a full restaurant meal, but Hugh could read the look on his face. "Don't worry about the money," he said. "The company pays for this because we're on a special assignment."

Inside, the two men sat down. Both ordered eggs and ham and potatoes, and both wanted coffee, Abramo black and Hugh with cream. After they ordered, Hugh began speaking.

"Remember, now, you mustn't take personally what this old lady says. You never know what might offend her. She's a good soul, but I've seen her drive men out of her house because she thought their clothes smelled strongly of cigarette smoke."

"And her husband owned the mill?"

"Yes. He was a genius at making steel and started it as a young man. It grew into that giant place. But then he got sick and gradually let Carnegie buy in. When Anetta Reid dies, Carnegie—well, now U.S. Steel—will buy her out of the rest of the mill."

Abramo nodded, not understanding about ownership of giant corporations. Finally he spoke. "But why does a superintendent of the mill make pipe deliveries to her house?"

"Because I know her. You see, I'm a Second Ward precinct committeeman, just like your uncle. You know what that means?"

Abramo shook his head. "I'm in Democratic politics in my neighborhood, and sometimes I have dealings with the city council or the mayor. It's one of the few ways the Italians and the Irish work together without killing each other," he said sardonically. "And once…I did her husband a favor when he was alive. We were at a Second Ward party and he was guest speaker. He had a little too much booze and got drunk. So I took him home and would not take any money from her. Nor did I tell anyone of it at the mill. Hell, I'd done it for my dad and my uncles many times. Anyway, she's liked me ever since…the way a lion likes a water carrier. But I'm sure I'm superintendent because of her influence."

They ate their breakfast unhurriedly, the conversation between them easy and natural. Abramo spoke with a combination of respect and friendliness, and Hugh responded to Abramo's careful conduct with naturalness and warmth.

Hugh genuinely liked the young man, and the Italian was charmed and respectful of the kind and garrulous Irishman with easy manners. Somehow Abramo told Hugh about his last few months' service in the Italian provincial army. Hugh mentioned Abramo's wife's death out of respectful curiosity, just trying to know better this young man he was growing to like more each time they met.

Finally Abramo told him that he volunteered to be in a firing squad. After the rape and murder of his wife, he was so bitter that he did his job out of blind hatred. But after five executions, the work began to take a toll on his spirit. And the bitterness was replaced by horror at what he had become; Angelina's death was being dishonored and defiled by his hatred of the soldiers who were on the same side as the killers of his wife. So finally he left the service.

As he spoke, always in Italian during their meal and through their intimate conversation, Hugh saw one quick gesture by Abramo: he quickly wiped a tear from the corner of one eye with his fingers, in a movement carefully discreet, as he spoke of Angelina's death. He liked the boy now as much as he had liked any young man, as much as Ross, and certainly more than Conor and Paul, his nephews.

It was nine thirty in the morning, and Anetta Reid had just come home from Mass and had a modest breakfast alone. She was in a depressed and cranky mood, fostered by the young priest that she didn't like, who botched the offertory prayer and whose voice cracked twice during the Paternoster. The organist was a substitute who was mediocre and uncaring. The altar boys were slovenly and uninvolved with the Mass.

But there were more than those trivialities that darkened her spirits and promised her a day of gloom and depression. As always, she missed her husband, Anthony; she had never recovered from seeing him die a slow and debilitating death. But for some reason, today she felt the loss of her only child more acutely than she had in recent days. The wagging tongues of neighbors and parishioners had sharpened the memories of his tragic death into a sword that pierced her proud heart every day she went abroad in her car. Her driver often bore her wrath if he drove so slowly that bystanders could gawk through the windows at the stoic, solitary figure in the passenger seat in the rear of the large car. And they would cluck obviously to each other, expressing theatrical, but insincere, sympathy for her. For her! Wretches who knew nothing of her son were willing to believe the rumor that he was executed for cowardice or desertion. The official reason for his death was only that he was caught behind enemy lines in France. The true reason that she knew, and could not tell, was that he was a spy who had been found in hostile territory by German soldiers and was summarily executed as he led a small squad on a rescue mission for captured French prisoners.

He was a gentle child, brilliant and sensitive, more like a poet than a soldier. But after years of enduring the barbs and taunts of those who envied his social position, or who envied his slender, graceful body or his beautiful blond hair or his handsome face, he felt he had something to prove. So he joined the army and volunteered for spy duty.

"Mr. Connolly is here, ma'am," her butler said as he entered the library quietly.

"Show him in then," she muttered, stiffening expectantly. She liked Connolly but labored not to show it by being too familiar or overly civil. He reminded her of the brother, long since dead, who was her favorite in the family she remembered not so fondly as years passed.

In a few moments, Hugh walked in to the room, followed by Abramo. Mrs. Reid brightened slightly upon seeing Hugh but darkened again upon seeing the ruddy companion who held a hat in his hand as he entered. "Good morning, Mrs. Reid. I hope you're feeling well today."

"Connolly," she acknowledged stiffly, still not taking her eyes off Abramo.

Hugh sensed her interest immediately. "Mrs. Reid, may I present Abramo Cardone, who works for me at your mill."

She glanced at him fiercely as Abramo bowed slightly from the waist. She made no other acknowledgment.

"So, Connolly," she said, "did you bring my pipes?"

"Yes, ma'am. The men will start Monday. By the end of next week, you'll have water in all parts of the wing. We will also relieve some of the burden on the drainage system. I know you'll be pleased with the results."

"I will if your assessment is correct, Mr. Connolly," she said, seeming preoccupied with other ideas. Hugh knew there would be other duties he'd have to perform for this woman. He had seen the look before.

"I am going to give these books to St. Mary's School," she said, pointing to one corner shelf in the library. "But I must insist that the older children be made to read them and learn more of their Catholic heritage. The lack of reverence in these children is appalling. The nuns are permitting slovenly, unkempt altar boys to serve the early masses and allowing them to be inept and irreverent on the altar." She was huffing, becoming more agitated as she spoke.

"But, ma'am, oftentimes those are the children who live closest to the church in the poor neighborhoods within easy walking distance. Most of them haven't had breakfast and little to eat from the night before—"

"Don't lecture me on poverty, Mr. Connolly!" she said. "Poverty is no excuse for irreverence."

"I didn't mean to lecture, ma'am. I was just—"

"That's enough," she said. "The servants will have the books ready in boxes by Tuesday. Come to get them then…and tell Father Quinn that they must be put in that glass-enclosed bookcase outside Sister Regina's office. And they must especially be made available to those children who seem to have vocations for the priesthood or the sisterhood."

"I'll talk to Father Quinn tomorrow after nine o'clock Mass. I'm sure there will be no question about where the books will be placed or how they will be used."

"See that you do…and while you're at it, tell Father Quinn that I'm very displeased with his new assistant pastor. What are they teaching in the seminaries these days! The young man gives sermons at low Mass—during the week! The very idea! And they're interminable driveling homilies at that. Who ever heard of a low Mass taking an hour and five minutes? An hour and five minutes! And how are the few Christian souls who attend Mass during the week going to get to work on time or to get home to do their daily chores? With children playing in the schoolyard at eight o'clock and noise just outside interfering with the prayers of the Mass? And that young man acting as though he were a saint upon the altar, sent by God to drive us to distraction with his theatrical prayers and pompous sermons, a man barely twenty-five years old!"

God Almighty, Hugh thought to himself. This had the makings of a real bad morning. She was in rare form and only now getting started.

While Mrs. Reid and Connolly were talking, Abramo noticed the picture of a handsome young man above the fireplace in the room. Unconsciously, he gravitated toward it until he was standing directly in front of the picture, gazing up at it and studying everything about the huge, tinted photograph so intently that he had not even heard the colloquy between Mrs. Reid and Mr. Connolly.

"I want that young priest told that he does not yet wear a cardinal's hat, and...What is he doing there, Connolly?" she said, suddenly conscious of Abramo standing before the picture.

"What are you doing, Abramo?" Hugh said in Italian. Abramo didn't respond or change his gaze, intent upon the picture. "Abramo?" he repeated, more insistently.

Abramo turned to Hugh. "This is the son of the *donna*," he said in Italian, gesturing slightly toward Mrs. Reid.

"Yes," said Hugh.

"He is dead," said Abramo.

"Yes. How do you know?" said Hugh.

"His eyes," Abramo said, gesturing toward his own eyes. "He knew he was going to die."

Hugh's expression changed to one of wonder and disquiet, as though forgetting that Mrs. Reid was there. As he spoke, Abramo stepped forward and touched the somber black frame slightly, running his fingers over its surface. Then he turned back to Hugh. "He died as a hero," he said softly.

Hugh frowned in amazement, as though not believing what he was hearing from Abramo. Mrs. Reid was also listening and watching, not understanding the Italian but fascinated and perturbed by the body language of the two men, especially Connolly's reactions to some of Abramo's comments. She knew enough to understand that the "donna" in Abramo's speech was she and that the word "morte" meant death.

"He said that Brendan was dead, didn't he?" she said softly.

"Yes," Hugh said, not looking at her.

"How did he know?" she asked, her voice quavering. "Was he told of it?"

"No." Hugh turned to face her, staring for a few seconds. "He said he could see it in his eyes," he said in amazement.

"Did he ask you if he was my son?" she said.

"He told me he was," Hugh said.

Mrs. Reid gasped softly, struck dumb by the connection Abramo had made with the photograph…and what he had seen in it. "He said something else. What was it?" she asked Hugh who had been watching Abramo again.

Hugh turned back toward her again with the same expression of troubled wonder. He took a deep breath, grimacing before he spoke. "He said your son died a hero."

She stepped backward, as though being pushed by some unseen presence, and held on to the back of the chair for support. She looked at Hugh, speechless for a moment. "He had to have heard it somewhere," she said plaintively.

"He never even heard of you until I told him Thursday," said Hugh. "And I never mentioned a word about Brendan."

She shook her head and sat in the chair, seeming to be dizzy. She was silent. Hugh turned back to Abramo, who was again touching the frame of the picture. "What are you looking at, Abramo? What is there about the frame?" Hugh said, still in Italian.

"This frame is ugly and speaks only of death. The man here should have one that speaks of his honor."

Hugh took a deep breath. "What did he just say, Mr. Connolly?" Mrs. Reid said, suddenly shorn of her imperious manner by the thought of Abramo seeing her son as few did, and from a picture he had never seen. Hugh hesitated. "Please, Mr. Connolly," she whispered in a manner as soft and natural as Hugh had ever seen in her.

"He said the frame is ugly and speaks only of death. He said Brendan's frame should be one that bespeaks...honor."

Mrs. Reid took a deep breath. She brought a handkerchief to her eyes and wiped them, holding her face in her hands for a few seconds. Never had Hugh seen this human side of Anetta Reid. No one would believe that this formidable woman could be reduced to tears by only a few words from a stranger.

Finally, she composed herself. Then she looked up at Abramo. "What would this boy's name be in English, Hugh?"

"Abraham," said Hugh, startled at hearing the familiar form of address from Mrs. Reid.

"Come here, Mr. Cardone," she said to Abramo.

Hugh nodded, and Abramo came across the room and stood before Anetta Reid, about six feet away from her. "Tell him I—"

"He understands English," Hugh said.

"Mr. Cardone, you have honored my son, and me, as few people who have ever come into this house. Your insight and vision is as extraordinary as it is welcome. I am pleased to have met you."

"Thank you, madama," Abramo said in English.

"What kind of frame would you say belongs on the painting?"

"Something warm and light and beautiful," Abramo said in Italian turning toward Hugh.

Hugh repeated the answer to Mrs. Reid. "Where does one get such a frame?" she said back to Hugh. He, in turn, asked the question of Abramo.

"I will make it," said Abramo.

"You?" said Hugh.

"I was an artisan in Italy. I can do it."

Hugh turned back to Mrs. Reid in amazement. "He says he wants to make one…"

"Then tell him…" She hesitated. "Mr. Cardone," she then said, looking toward Abramo, "if you make a frame the way you wish, I'll pay you well for your work. How long would it take?"

"If I can get the wood, some weeks…maybe months."

"Do we still have wood at the mill, Hugh?" she asked.

"Yes, we do," said Hugh. "I can get him anything he wants."

"Well, see to it that he has what he needs."

Abramo turned to Hugh and spoke again in Italian. "I must measure this picture."

Hugh turned to Mrs. Reid. "Can we get a ladder and a tape to measure the picture now?"

"Pull the cord there," she said, pointing to a thin piece of tapestry that adorned the rope used to signal the staff.

In a moment the butler entered the room. "John," said Mrs. Reid, "tell Tim and Mary to bring a tape measure and a ladder. We're going to take down Brendan's picture." The butler seemed confused but turned to do her bidding. Then suddenly she called to him again. "And, John, bring some tea and scones—three cups, now. See to it yourself." This time Hugh and the butler were both amazed. Mrs. Reid had never had refreshments with anyone, especially someone who came in through the back door of the house to work.

Abramo began deliveries the next week. He also worked each night on the frame for Mrs. Reid. It was becoming a work of art, something simple and beautiful the likes of which he had not set his heart on since the happy years when Angelina was by his side and the war was not with them. He made the inlaid wood patterns at the corners, the medium dark and light wood interplay along each edge that he liked so much. Hugh Connolly had allowed him the choice of any wood that could be ordered. And allowed him to rip-cut the pieces of wood for the edges of the frame and the thin pieces of alternating light and dark woods. And he gave him the oils and stains and glue needed to do the job. In fact, Abramo assembled the frame in parts at the mill and did the close work and carving at Isabella's house in the room she provided for him.

Uncle Michele came to see him several nights as he was making the frame, and plied Abramo with questions about the famous Mrs. Reid, and about the strange new friend of his, Hugh Connolly.

One night, while Michele was in the basement with Abramo, the doorbell rang. When Mrs. Chianese opened the door, Hugh Connolly was standing on the front porch. "Yes, signore?" she said softly, knowing instantly that Hugh was someone special. Hugh was startled by her loveliness, by the depth of feeling visible on her face. She was the perfect embodiment of earthy Mediterranean femininity and gentle, dutiful resignation to her fate. In the background, Hugh could hear the children talking in Italian about the "elegantone" who was at the door.

"Signorina," said Hugh, using the title for an unmarried woman out of respect, even though she was surely the mother of the children he could see in the doorway of the small vestibule, "is this the home of Abramo Cardone?"

He had spoken in Italian, and Isabella was stunned at his presence and his demeanor. He was obviously not Italian, or even Mediterranean, and yet he knew the nuances of address as though he had come from the Old Country.

"*Sì*, signore," she answered. "Please come in."

"Is he working?" Hugh asked.

"Yes, he's in the cellar," she said. "Come, I'll take you."

Hugh looked at Isabella and was overwhelmed by her beauty. She looked at him in sideways glances, trying to absorb all the dignity, intellect, and warmth of his presence. Their eyes met a few times, and both had to remind themselves to look away.

What made this one man, of all the others Isabella encountered daily, someone who drew her soul into his own body? And what made Hugh, who had been an eligible widower for so many years, by happenstance decide to visit one of his workers, something he seldom did, only to find this enchanting woman with the beautiful eyes as the first person he encountered?

Since her husband's death, the cares and worries that burdened Isabella's life made it easy not to pay attention to other men, attractive and available men who would have been overjoyed to have her in their lives. Yet when she opened the door to this stranger, she felt something strike her heart.

Hugh shook his head as he followed her down the stairs. He knew as he watched her lead him to the room in the cellar where Abramo worked that he would see this woman again. He had to see her.

Inside the doorway, Isabella said, "Abramo, Don Michele, we have a visitor."

Hugh entered after that. Abramo was startled to see the superintendent standing in the room where he worked, in the house where he boarded. "Hello, Abramo," said Hugh.

"Signor Connolly," Abramo acknowledged. Then after a few seconds added, "Signor Connolly, this is my uncle, Michele della Malva. Zi'Michele, this is the superintendent, Hugh Connolly."

Hugh put forth his hand to Michele and said in Italian, "Don Michele, I am honored."

Michele, shocked as he had never been, responded with a handshake and a quick comment. "I, too, am honored, sir."

Isabella watched the greetings then quietly turned toward the door. Hugh caught her movement out of the corner of his eye and turned toward her. "Thank you, signora."

"You are most welcome, sir," Isabella responded.

Michele caught the glance between Hugh and Isabella. He didn't know what he had just seen, but it was not the usual formal greeting between a man of high station and a widowed woman who ran a boarding house. Nor was it a coy, flirting look between two people who had an understanding between them. No, this was respect, almost awe. There was a connection.

"I've come to see the frame," Hugh said finally.

"Here," said Abramo, standing aside to show the frame resting on the table behind him.

Hugh advanced toward the table and was silent as he looked at the frame. Then he turned toward Michele as though not believing what he saw. Michele noted the look of wonder and nodded imperceptibly. Then Hugh turned back toward the frame. "Abramo, this is the most beautiful picture frame I've ever seen…and it's not even done yet." He turned toward Abramo. "In fact, it's the most beautiful piece of carpentry I've ever seen."

"Thank you, Signor Connolly," said Abramo. "And you think she'll like it?"

Hugh snorted. "Abramo, she'll be thrilled. That picture will glow once it's in this frame." Then he turned toward Michele. "He has too much talent to be a mill worker."

Michele smiled. "You see, nephew, it is not only your family or Signora Isabella that thinks your work is beautiful."

The words caught Hugh's attention. "Is that the name of the lady of this house?"

Michele nodded, an imperceptible smile playing on his lips, his eyes brightening slightly. He had been right about Hugh Connolly. The eyes of that lovely woman had looked into his heart.

Michele read the newspaper at his desk in the warehouse. He shivered slightly as he read of the Ku Klux Klan in the Mahoning Valley. The Ohio Klan had planned a march in Youngstown that had to be canceled because of bad weather and some violence at prior marches. All the Klan marchers that had come from out of town were put up at houses of local Klan sympathizers. Now they were going to start having marches in small towns on the outskirts of larger cities.

The Klan hated Blacks, but next to Blacks they also hated Italians. They were not only Catholic, they spoke a foreign tongue and were dark-skinned. And even though the Irish were not spared because they, too, were Catholics, they at least spoke English and looked paler and more British than the Mediterraneans, and so the Klan gave them less trouble.

The Klan was beginning to take over Youngstown politics. They helped elect two councilmen last year, and now they were determined to also elect a mayor.

Marco Bevilaqua, second in command at the warehouse, carried two cups of coffee to the table and handed one to Michele as he sat down at right angles to his friend. "What news is there?" he said in Italian.

"Ah, the Ku Klux Klan is going to march again…through small towns this time."

"I have heard these men talk of the Klan. Some of them like it."

"Even Italians?"

"Some of the stupid ones. They hate niggers and so like the Klan."

"Send them home, goddammit. I will not have the Klan talked about with favor in this place. Jesus Christ, Marco, those bastards would kill us all if they could."

"We must deal with the Klan, Michele. They want the Second Ward now that they have the Forth and the Sixth."

"There are enough good people in the Second Ward to keep the Klan out."

"What about the Irish?"

"There are many good ones, Marco. They're Catholics, aren't they? Why should they support those creatures who hate Catholics?"

"It is said that the Irish on the North Side support the Klan."

"I have heard that, too, but I'm not sure the Irish in the Second Ward are like that…You know, Marco, I have met one of their precinct committeemen from up on Sloan Street."

"Where?"

"He came to visit Abramo at Isabella Chianese's house." Michele made a wry smile as he spoke.

"Or, did he come to visit Isabella where Abramo lived?" Marco said, catching Michele's meaning.

Both men chuckled. All men on the East Side were awed by her beauty. "I don't think he knew about her…No, this man is a good man, honorable and decent. He is a superintendent at the Reid-Carnegie."

"To visit Abramo? Why?"

"He is a man, I think, that knows other men. He sees the difference between good and bad. And he sees the good in Abramo, and likes him."

"Does he have a family?"

"No. Abramo said his wife died when she was young. He never remarried and has no children. But he has helped Abramo get a better job in the mill—for more money. Last month he and Abramo drove out to the North Side to see the owner of the mill, Mrs. Reid. She has a large portrait of her dead son, an only child. Abramo said that the frame was ugly, and he could make one more beautiful. So, he has been making it, and the big boss wanted to see it."

"He was a carpenter before he went into the army, right?"

"Yes. He was so good that he became a master at nineteen. But when they put him in the army, they had him making stalls and stables for horses."

"I would like to see it," said Marco.

"We'll stop there tonight after work. Maybe we'll see the superintendent. I think he will find reason to visit Signora Chianese's boarding house more often," Michele said with a slight smile.

Abramo had to make one more stop on the North Side to deliver a bill to Nelson Concrete Supply, the concrete company that bought large tonnage of slag from the mill. It was getting dark so much earlier these nights. On dreary days like this one, the darkness seemed to begin falling at four o'clock, and it was barely November. Abramo made this the last stop of his day because it usually took so long for the company office to process the billing. When he first started as a courier, he would make Nelson one of the first stops on the North Side. But the office took so long for their paperwork that he was behind the whole rest of the day. He soon learned to visit Nelson at the end of the day when their people were eager to leave the office.

Abramo handed the bill to the man behind the counter. The man silently turned and handed the paper to a woman who set it down on her desk and continued working. Abramo had brought his English novel and began to read. He knew he was in for a half-hour wait.

Molly Harty was cold, walking home from the Parsons house. Mary Catherine would have to get well soon; she dreaded these long chilly walks home after work, especially now that the sun was down early and it was dark by time she arrived home. Even though Mary Catherine was sick, Mrs. Parsons said she expected all the work still to be done, and Molly was exhausted at the end of each day. At home, she tried not to show it, but her father worried about her. The few weeks she was supposed to work had now become two months, and he could see the weariness in Molly's behavior.

The wind was starting up. Damn that Conor! she thought fearfully. Of all nights to be late. She knew he wouldn't be there to pick her up in this weather. It was too easy to stay inside and play poker at the Crab Inn.

She shuddered. At least she was about halfway home now. And it was not yet black night. But still, she had to pass Walnut Way, along the set of bars, flophouses, and whorehouses that lined both sides of the street.

The men there were often unruly and violent, many of them derelicts who had abandoned their families, some others drifters who had nowhere else to go, all of them leading lives of dissipation and drunkenness that hurried disease and death upon their futures.

Several times Molly and Mary Catherine had come to Walnut Way under protection of one of the Harty brothers, and even then were frightened by incidents that stopped just short of violence. Now, as she walked alone, she imagined shadows lurking at a distance in corners of her sight, following quietly and with sinister stealth. Conor was not to be found. God, what would she do if trouble came her way? Wind, clouds, and the threat of cold rain were all around her, and yet she could also hear the noise of brawling and gambling and women calling cheap sex to passersby.

Abramo had finished his day's work and was on his way back to Reid-Carnegie in the truck. He drove slowly as the wind and drizzle bore into the open cab and made sight difficult in the impending darkness. There were not many people out now, and the ride was quiet even with the road noise. Only a short time longer and his week's work would be done. He was hungry and tired, and it would feel good to drop off his courier pouch at the superintendent's office and go home to Isabella's table. He would take a bath tonight and read in the big easy chair with the floor lamp overhead. He'd be in the remote corner, and the boarders would not talk to him much if they saw him reading. Isabella would only come over to him to bring him coffee royal that he would sip as he read until he was no longer able to keep his eyes open and the words he read lost meaning. Only Gianina, his favorite of her children, could disturb his reveries.

The wind was growing colder as he turned onto Walnut Way. In gusts, it shook the trees and blew trash barrels into the street. He thought once he heard a human voice as he drove slowly past the flophouses and bars and pool halls. Then again—a female voice that seemed to say no words. Each place he passed he looked for the voice, seeing nothing. The alleys and driveways between the buildings were dark, except for the solitary lights overhead on the side doors of the buildings, where contraband booze and beer could be brought in at night.

In one of the last driveways toward the end of the block, Abramo slowed the truck. He sensed the presence of someone in the dark driveway; the voice was coming from there. He listened, straining to hear. Again he heard something, not a spoken word, but something. He turned off the motor, this time stepping down from the truck and securing the courier pouch in the locked strongbox hidden behind the driver's seat.

He parked the truck on the opposite side of the street and crossed toward the sound. A moan. As he moved farther up the driveway, he could hear men talking. The closer he came, the more the dim light provided an image of what he heard. One person standing, one person down on his knees hunched over another figure on the ground, the one on his knees making rhythmic motions against the other. He heard the voice again.

"No, please!"

Abramo heard a laugh and another comment from the person who was standing. "Hurry up! If you don't finish soon and someone comes, I won't get a chance."

Abramo shouted into the driveway. "Hey! What are you doing there?" The standing figure cursed, and suddenly the kneeling figure stood. Neither one could see Abramo's face, but they knew that anyone could cause them trouble. "Get the hell out of there!" Abramo shouted.

One of the men, the shorter one, ran toward the rear of the driveway into a back alley. The bigger man hesitated. "For Christ's sake, come on!" the short one said.

Joe Hannon was troubled. There was something strange about the voice that called into the driveway. "Let's go!" his companion screamed.

Abramo advanced into the alley to the figure that was down on the ground. Joe Hannon had run to the back of the building, but stopped again, perplexed, and turned back toward the intruder, watching his silhouette.

Abramo knelt down to the figure on the ground. She was alive and breathing erratically. She was also sobbing hysterically. He reached for her to pull her up, noting her swollen lips and cut forehead and dark and swollen eyes. As he pulled her up, their eyes met, just a few inches apart. "Please. No more," she whispered plaintively.

He studied her for a few seconds as she did him in return. "I am not one of them," he said to her softly. For some reason she believed him, maybe his voice, or perhaps the gentle way he held her in a sitting position. She collapsed forward into his arms. He held her in an embrace, and she cried convulsively, making soft, squeaking sounds as she did. Her forehead rested against his chin. "I will not hurt you," he said.

As he spoke, his left hand touched her dress as he was trying to hold her upright. When he tried to position her better, his hand felt strange. When he brought it up to the dim light, he could see blood. "Oh, Madonna!" he whispered. "What have they done?"

She was crying still and shook her head to his question. "Oh, God. Oh, God!" she kept saying.

"Signorina, is that the only place you are bleeding?" he asked. "Signorina?" He slowly peeled back the dress and found the pantaloons underneath. They were not very different from those that he wore, but the crotch had been torn out and the tatters that remained were soaked with blood. She knew that he was looking at her nakedness, but she stayed still, not feeling in the least defiled by this man. Then, gently, he folded the tatters to put them back in place, to cover her and to soak up more of the blood. She stayed in his arms, clutching him tightly, holding herself against him and shivering.

In the few seconds it took Abramo to pull the girl up into his arms, Joe Hannon watched in fascination. The shadow of the intruder was familiar. He strained to hear the voice but caught only a few words that he spoke. Suddenly all of the sensations came together into one nightmarish vision. The shadow was Cardone. It was Cardone!

Hannon was trembling. His heart raced, yet he seemed paralyzed. What could this devil be doing on the North Side? Was this God's punishment for him, sending this dark angel to haunt him, a dirty bastard dago? Joe Hannon's mind seemed to play tricks on him. The dark shadows grew larger, then smaller, then larger again.

Even the driveway seemed to be moving at angles with the light. But he steadied himself and he whispered, "It's Cardone, Dilworth. It's Cardone!" He said it again and again. The two men watched from the distance, hidden in the dark, obscure end of the drive.

Abramo asked the girl again, "Signorina, are you still bleeding? Can you feel it?"

"I don't know," she said, holding tightly to him. "Please don't leave me like this. Please?"

"I will not leave you, but if you are still bleeding, you must go to the hospital."

"How much blood is on my dress?" she said finally, lucid now that she trusted Abramo.

He looked down at her dress, and it was soaked with blood around her groin. "I still can't tell," he whispered, "but the blood is red and fresh. They have hurt you very bad."

She sobbed again, and he held her, comforting her as best he could. "We must go," said Abramo. "I have a truck here. I will take you to St. Rita Hospital. Can you stand if I help you up?"

Abramo tried to stand up, but her hold on him slipped. "Don't leave me. Please?" she said, her voice cracking and strange as she reached for him again, as though he were a totem of safety.

He went to his knees and made her hold on to him again. "Hold tight to my neck," he said. "I will help you up."

"Okay...slowly," she said.

He braced first one knee and then the other into a crouching position. Then, slowly, he began to stand. She came with him as he lifted her, her weak legs aiding him as he began to pull her with him. "If I can get you up, I can carry you," he said.

At the one moment when all their efforts seemed to be coordinated, when her legs were beneath her and Abramo's had begun to push them both upright, they heard a yell. She felt Abramo's legs give out as he fell on top of her. The first blow had struck him across the shoulders and the back of the head. She could see the second blow fall on his back as he collapsed on top of her. She screamed hysterically as she saw the assailant hit Abramo with a large wooden board from a packing case. Then she heard the same voice again.

"Jesus Christ, let's get the fuck out of here before the police come. That screaming'll wake the dead."

The assailant dropped the board and turned to him. "I got him a good one, that dago bastard."

"He's probably dead now," his friend said. "Let's go."

They ran back to the darkness of the alley. Molly kept calling for help, but she was weakening. Abramo was draped across her body and was unconscious. She felt the light moving toward her, then moving away, then toward her, then away. After several times she closed her eyes and lost consciousness.

Chapter 5

"My God, Conor," said Ross. "You were supposed to get Molly. You mean you haven't even gone out to look for her?"

"Hell, she's home. She'll be all right."

"She's not home," said Paul. "And Pa's ready to skin you alive."

Conor's face grew pale. He knew how late it was. And if his sister wasn't home, that could easily mean some harm had befallen her. "God Almighty," Conor said. "Let's go."

He threw his cards down on the table, gathered his poke, and hurried out the door of the Crab Inn with his two brothers. They ran across the Sloan Street Bridge and through the valley that approached Walnut Way, frantically retracing steps they had made countless times in the past few months. There was no one out; the drizzle, wind, and cold kept everyone off the streets. Even in the whorehouses the red lights had been taken out of windows. They called to Molly, to no avail.

"We have to go see if she's still at the Parsons house," said Ross. "We can't go on all night like this."

"Pray God that she's there," said Conor. "Ross, you go. You talk better than us. We'll be looking through the Hollow. When you come back round, we'll see you in Walnut Way."

"Okay. If you find her, one of you stay by the old German church and wait for me. The other can get her home."

As Ross turned to head toward the Parsons house, Conor, filled with remorse, said, "My Lord, I hope you find her there, Ross."

Ross was breathless and red-faced by the time he reached the Parsons house. He stopped for a minute to catch his breath at the lower landing of their front stairs. Finally, he was ready to talk. He approached the front door and rang the bell with a twist. The porch was illuminated by ornate, wrought-iron sconces that cast subdued light over the faces of all who entered the doorway by night.

A maid came to the door and opened it, saying nothing to complement the look of surprise the late-hour unannounced visit induced. "Excuse me, miss. I'm Ross Harty, the brother of—"

"Who is it, Sophie?" a female voice called to her from the inside.

"Just a minute," Sophie said to Ross, leaving the door ajar and returning to explain.

"Did you close the door, for God's sake? James! James! There's someone at the door!"

James Parsons came to the door, annoyed at the intrusion into his quiet library smoking time. "Yes, what is it?" he said to Ross.

"Sir, I'm Ross Harty, the brother of the girl, Molly, who has been working here. She...Is she still here?"

Parsons turned to Sophie. "Is she still here?"

"I don't know, sir. Hilda would know. I'll go get her."

Parsons studied the boy. He looked intelligent, much like his sister. And he was at least presentable and respectful. "Come in here, son," he said softly. "It's too cold to wait out there."

"I'm okay, sir. I can wait."

"Come on," he said, gesturing with his hand to hurry the boy inside.

In a moment Sophie returned with Hilda. "Hilda, this is Molly's brother. He wants to know if she is still here," said Parsons.

Hilda blanched, and her face contorted into a pained frown. "No, sir. Molly left here about three hour ago…while it were still light. She should be home long since."

Upon hearing her, Ross's head fell forward toward his chest. He raised his hand to his face and covered his eyes with the fingers of his right hand. Parsons knew immediately what he was thinking. "Where do you live, son?" said Parsons.

"On the East Side, near Sloan Street and Bookman."

"And she walks home each night? Through the Hollow? And Walnut Way?"

"Yes, sir. My brother was supposed to meet her to see her safely home…but he didn't make it tonight," Ross said, by way of explanation.

Parsons nodded, understanding. Ross turned toward the door, thanking them and apologizing for the late intrusion. As he did, the lady of the house came back into the hallway. "What's going on here? Who is this man, James? What does he want so late at night?"

"He's the brother of the new domestic we've hired—Molly."

"But what does he want?"

"His sister left here about three hours ago and has not gotten home yet. Her family fears trouble may have befallen her," said Parsons.

"Nonsense. These young girls are so fickle and undisciplined. She's probably with a boyfriend right now."

"She's not like that, ma'am," said Ross.

"Nonetheless, she's your problem and not ours. If she is the cause of such trouble, we'll find another girl."

Parsons took a deep breath, not trying very hard to hide the disgust he felt for his wife's callousness. "Marian," he said finally, "let me handle this." He turned to the maid. "Hilda, tell Kurt to get the car."

"The car, James? Have you gone crazy? Why would you get involved with the personal affair of a transient servant?"

"Because she works for us…and because it's the right thing to do."

"James, I'll not have you getting involved in—"

"Hilda! Do as I say," Parsons said, ignoring his wife. "Tell Kurt to bring the car around front and take this boy along the path he came. Now." He turned toward his wife. "The rest of you get inside."

When they were alone, Parsons waved off Ross's sincere thanks. "Let me know if you find her. I'm hoping for the best. When you find her, Kurt will take you all home in the car. Use it as you need it."

In a few minutes, Kurt was driving Ross along the path that Molly always took back to their house. They saw nothing, even though both men strained their eyes through the darkness. Soon they were in Walnut Way, and in the distance Ross could see his brothers in the light of the bar signs and dim streetlights. When the car stopped, Ross called to them. The other boys, shocked to see the car, got in instantly. "What are we gonna do?" Conor said, anguished.

Kurt turned to the three boys. "I can't take the car through these driveways because there's so much trash in them. I may not be able to get back out. You boys go down each driveway and across the alleys behind the buildings. Maybe you'll find her."

"My God, you think she might be there?" Paul cried, silent so far through the turmoil.

"If she's okay, she could be anywhere along the way back to the East Side," said Kurt. "But if she's not okay, I'm guessing she'll be right here in one of these alleys.

"I'll go wherever I can on this side," he said, pointing to the opposite side of the street. Then I'll park the car across the street halfway down. If you find her, call me. I'll take you all home then."

"Okay," said the boys as they left the car. "If you see anyone, ask them, huh, Kurt?" said Ross.

"Yeah, kid. I'll do whatever I can. Good luck."

Each boy took a driveway along one side of Walnut Way. They were tired, cold, and hungry, and the fine drizzle chilled their spirits.

The driveways were filled with trash and garbage. In some cases there was barely enough clear space for a truck to get through to the back loading doors. It was dark, but the light from the open hearths of nearby mills brighten the sky and created a gold cast to the darkness that enabled dim sight. They trudged through the alleys, stumbling and bumping into the trash that lined the driveways, each afraid of what he'd find in the darkness.

After each trip through the driveways, they'd go into the bars and flophouses and whorehouses to ask if anyone had seen Molly. No one knew. Information was not offered easily on Walnut Way. Kurt did the same on the opposite side of the street. The task seemed endless and disheartening. They wanted to find her, but not in this awful place. All four men noticed a truck that had been parked along the opposite side of the street. They would reassemble from time to time and talk about what they had seen. As they talked one time, when they had been through about half the driveways, Kurt, who had been concentrating on the truck parked near the middle of the block, said, "What was the sign on that truck?"

"Reid-Carnegie," said Paul.

"Why would a Reid-Carnegie truck be parked out here in this weather? At this time of night?" said Ross.

"And what would somebody from Reid-Carnegie be doing in this neighborhood anyhow? In one of their trucks?" said Kurt. "See what you can find in that alley down there."

They went slowly into the alley, fearful of what they might see. The sole light above the side door was dimmer than the others they had seen. Paul went first, his eyes straining in the darkness as he pressed forward down the alley. This was going to be another lost hope; he knew it.

He went about twenty feet beyond the light cast by the small overhead lamp above the door. He called to his brothers softly. They answered in whispers and urged him on.

Suddenly they heard Paul croak, "Oh, sweet Jesus!" For a few seconds it seemed as though their hearts stopped beating. Then they could focus on Paul bent over in the darkness. When Ross and Conor reached Paul, they could see two figures: Molly on her back, seeming to be dead, and her assailant draped across her body.

"Oh, God, Molly!" Ross cried out. "Is she dead, Paul?"

"I don't know. I don't know," Paul said.

Ross reached across the man's body, resting his hand gently on the side of her neck. She was warm, and he felt a weak pulse. "She's alive, Conor," Ross said.

"Thank God," Conor said. "Paul, go get Kurt. Tell him to bring the car down here. We'll bring her out."

Paul turned and ran. Conor roughly grabbed the man who rested on top of Molly and turned him over. Then he kicked the man several times. "You dirty bastard. You dirty bastard!"

"What are you doing, Conor, for God's sake? He's probably dead already. The damage he did is done. Let's just get our sister the hell out of here. Let him rot in this alley."

They gently pulled the unconscious girl into their arms, but Ross cried out when he touched the blood that was now caked and drying on her dress. When Conor saw what Ross felt, he turned one more time to the unconscious man and spat upon him. "Gently, Conor. Grab her feet and hold her steady," said Ross.

They carried Molly out of the driveway just as Kurt was arriving with the car. "We have to take her to the hospital, boys," said Kurt. "With all that blood, we don't know how bad she's hurt."

"Let's go to St. Rita's," said Conor.

✳ ✳

Abramo was unconscious for most of the night. He awoke once, thinking he had felt someone touch him. Then he lapsed back. Then he was awakened again.

"Man? Please, man, wake up." He didn't know where he was or what had gotten him there. He didn't know the day or the time. He didn't remember the truck or Molly. The voice he heard was that of a child. "Man? Please wake up."

He tried to focus on her. Her face was before him: a little girl, unkempt and smudged, but with angelic face and eyes. Her skin was pale, her hair black, and her eyes blue. She touched his face with her left hand and let it linger on his cheek. "You have to move, but I can't carry you," she said. "If they find you, they'll hurt you."

Abramo was disoriented; he couldn't move without terrible pain. It felt like a horse had kicked him in the head. He couldn't move his right arm, and his back ached as he turned his neck.

Her face was now a few inches away from his. "You have to move. It's bad for you to stay here. Can you stand up?"

Abramo tried to move, but everything hurt. "Stand up. Please," the little girl said.

"I don't think I can," said Abramo.

"Can you hold on to me? I know where I can take you so they can't find you."

"I'll try," he said, trying unsuccessfully to stand.

She pushed herself beside him and draped one of his arms over her shoulder and began to crawl on her hands and knees. She dragged him with all her strength. He used his knees for leverage. His legs were all he had that weren't wounded or didn't cause him pain.

Several times faltering, she would steady herself and urge him onward. Once again she looked at him and touched his hair. She held his face before hers between her hands. "We can't stop. We have to go where you can be safe. Come on."

They moved again; both the little girl's knees and Abramo's were cut against the gravel surface and broken glass of the driveway. For about half an hour they made their way back to the alley and down two driveways. There, in the back of one of the buildings in the dark side of the alley, she took him to a small room with a cupboard on one end, a false front for another little room behind. No one would know what was inside. It was a perfect hiding place.

She dragged Abramo to a far corner, just beside the light that came through one crack in the side wall. One of the lights from the doors on the opposite side of the alley was high enough and bright enough to illuminate the corner of the small room.

Abramo was in agony. His head was spinning with flashes of light and strange patterns of colors. He knew he would lose consciousness again. "Don't die, man," the little girl said, again holding his face in her hands as she spoke to him. He heard her voice, but soon it was lost, trailed off into the darkness that settled upon his brain again.

The hours that passed were filled with drizzle and fog. It was much colder than it had been in prior days. The little girl stayed with Abramo through the darkness but left at dawn. In a few hours she returned with an old folded sackcloth that she draped over his unconscious body and tucked under his head. She held his face near hers, but he didn't awaken. She whispered to him, but he didn't respond. But he was still alive, she knew. She kissed him and held his head in her arms.

She left and returned several times during the dreary day. No one walked the back alleys on days like this. It was cold and windy, and the drizzle was driven right into the hearts of everyone outside. These were days to stay inside and whore and drink and gamble, or sleep off too much beer or whiskey in a flophouse.

Night was coming early on this harsh day. At four thirty, it was growing difficult to see. Abramo woke up again. This time he was alone, in a strange place. At first he could not remember how he got there. All he knew was that he was cold and aching. He noticed the light coming through the crack in the wall. And he suddenly became conscious of the bundle of coarse rags under his head. He touched them and found his own blood. He shivered again and waited in the darkness.

In a short time, he heard noise and was frightened. He remained still, listening to the sound of his rapid heartbeat. The wall moved and moved again. Inside, he could see a small shadow figure coming toward him. He was still, hardly breathing as the figure approached. She brought her face up to his and spoke. "Are you awake, man? Are you awake?"

"Yes," said Abramo. "I remember. You are the little girl who brought me to this place."

"I didn't want you to die," she said. "Can you move?"

"I don't know," said Abramo. As he spoke, he shivered.

"You're cold," she said, touching his face with her hands. She was so close to him that he could feel her breath upon his face.

"Where are we, *piccina*?"

"I don't know," she said.

"Do you live here?"

"I don't live anywhere," she said. She felt his face and neck shudder against her hands. Once or twice she saw his eyes close and then reopen. She knew that he would fall into a deep sleep again. "Stay awake, man, okay? I'm going, but I'll be back. If you don't make noise, no one will find you."

"I won't make noise," Abramo said.

She rearranged the flour sacks on his body to keep him warmer. Then she left. Abramo tried to remember what had brought him to this place. There were holes in his memory, and they began filling in from these most intimate moments outward. He remembered the little girl dragging and carrying him down the alleys on her back, but he could not remember finding this hideout. He struggled to remember the driveway. He knew someone had hurt him; he remembered the crushing feeling that the first blow brought to him. It felt like his head exploded. Then the second blow across the shoulders and the back brought him only darkness, that now he was living through with the help of the little girl. But why? Who was his assailant? And why? Slowly he began to remember the girl who had blood on her dress and on the white, torn pantaloons underneath. Where was she? God, who had hurt her? He remembered the shadowy figure raping her. Then he drifted off to sleep again.

Chapter 6

THE OLD WOMAN WAS the Hannons' cook for both the AOH and the whorehouse next door. She was known as Tilly, a former prostitute long past her prime, and for nearly twenty years she ran the kitchen for the Hannons. Tilly was a thick, heavy woman, crude and tough. She smoked constantly, rolling cigarettes better than any man in the AOH. She also drank heavily, but only after her day's work was done. Then she slept soundly, preferring the deathly stupor of liquor to nights awake haunted by the demons of her life. She alone was good to the orphan children. She patched their clothes, cleaned their cuts and sores, and fed as many of them as best she could.

Occasionally Tilly would let some of the children come into the kitchen to have soup. She was known for her tasty soups. The children seemed to grow hungrier as the cold weather approached. The little girl, known as Piccina to Abramo, was called Blackie by those who frequented the AOH because she was the only child among the orphans to have black hair. Of all the children on the Way, Tilly liked Blackie best. The little girl was one of those who always spoke from the heart, whether she asked for a crust of bread or whether she wanted to know if she could sleep near the furnace on a cold night. There was no pretense or guile in her. When Tilly made soup, she would allow the girl to take a second helping if she wanted it. The last two nights, the girl had a big appetite, asking for more bread and cheese. Tonight, she even drank a sip of Tilly's beer and kept a full water can for herself.

Dilworth, the former mill partner of Joe Hannon, was one of Joe's spies and enforcers in the gang. He was short and round, and as much a bully as his mentor, which meant that he was cruel to those he could dominate physically and disdainful of those he could not. And when those he could not dominate became threatening, then he was a coward. Dilworth was a natural inquisitor, comfortable with terror, skilled at setting people off balance, or turning their words inside out in order to discover hidden machinations against the gang. He was good at imagining offenses, not to himself, because he was so despised by most people on the Way that no one cared if he were hurt, but against the gang. And for those offenses there had to be condign punishments because the welfare and reputation of the gang was at stake. And Dilworth was the most ardent backstabber and throat-cutter in the gang.

Few things riled Dilworth as much as the orphans of Walnut Way. He was contemptuous of the children who were half-starved and filthy, clothed in rags, and lonely. They made him sick. The little bastards always want things, he would say. They didn't work; they didn't know anything, but they were always looking for food. Many had felt the boots of Dilworth and the Hannons on their backsides.

The second night after Molly's and Abramo's assaults, Dilworth entered Tilly's kitchen. Sometimes boredom increased rapidly on gray and dreary nights where rain was cold and steady, keeping everyone indoors. He scowled when he saw Piccina eating in the kitchen as Tilly cleaned the pots and wiped the tables. "What's she doing here?" he said to Tilly.

Tilly lied without remorse to anyone who asked her a question she didn't want to answer. It was lifelong learned behavior. And she took an especially perverse satisfaction in lying to Dilworth. She detested him, but she hadn't survived the last thirty-five years on Walnut Way by alienating those who could harm her, so she had established a phony accord with him, seeming to be a casual friend while not having any affection or respect for him at all. "She helped me do chores tonight, so I gave her some scraps," she lied.

Piccina ignored him as he sat in a chair at a table about ten feet from her. "You got any coffee?" he said.

"Yeah, there should be some left in the pot," Tilly said. "I'll get you some."

"She gonna stay in here? This place ain't supposed to have all them dirty kids coming around begging all the time."

"She doesn't beg. I won't stand for it. I'll put her out in a little while," Tilly lied again. "Here's your coffee."

"You got any sugar?" he said.

"Yeah, I'll get it," she said.

"What's in that big can she has?"

"Water. She drinks a lot of water."

"So what's in the little cup, then?" he said with an arrogant, authoritative air, tossing his hand in Piccina's direction.

"What the hell do you care about what them kids are doing?" she said, getting nervous about his persistence.

"I just want to know where Jack's money is going."

"If you have to know, it's beer," she said.

"Beer?"

"Yeah. She likes the taste. I gave her a couple shots of mine."

"I thought you said she likes water?"

"She likes them both. She has since she was a baby."

Piccina looked up at Tilly as she spoke. With a roll of her eyes and a toss of her head, Tilly signaled Piccina to leave the kitchen. Dilworth didn't notice; he was frustrated. He was in a spoiling mood, but he couldn't get past Tilly, and she wasn't easily drawn into his ploys to frame something against the background of the gang.

Piccina took some scraps of bread and little pieces of cheese and folded them carefully into an old piece of newspaper.

"It ain't right for kids to drink beer. It's a sin," he said.

"If that's the biggest sin she ever commits, she'll be all right in her life," Tilly said, wearying of Dilworth.

"Where she going?"

"I don't know. I guess she's gonna sleep in one of the flops."

"You don't know where she lives?"

"Dilworth, I got enough work to do around here. I don't have time to keep track of all them kids."

Dilworth wasn't satisfied. There was something about the little girl's cool attitude that bothered him. She seemed calm and purposeful, too sure of Tilly's affections. There was something about her that made her different from the other children. She seemed to be following some plan.

Suddenly he stood up and started for the door. "Ain't you gonna drink your coffee?" Tilly called to him.

"I'll be back later," he called back.

"Where you going? It's raining like hell out there," she said, trying to keep him from the little girl.

But Dilworth was gone. He ran out into the alley, and he saw the little girl at the far end of the driveway. He hurried after her. She seemed to be carrying something…the can of water.

Dilworth hurried as fast as he could go down into the darkness in the back alley. It took him a few minutes to get to the end of the driveway, and he wheezed and coughed as he rounded the corner, betrayed by a corpulent body long accustomed to heavy smoking. He heard something. Maybe it was more rain. Around the corner it was even darker because the little door lamps were not kept on in the back alley.

He listened. Suddenly the sound was gone. She couldn't have gone far, he thought. But where the hell was she? In a thousand places maybe? And how was he going to find her on this cold and miserable night? He knew she was up to something. But what? She just looked too cool, too determined. And that goddamned Tilly knew it.

When he arrived back to the kitchen, Tilly smirked when she saw Dilworth red-faced and blowing his breath through a round mouth and bloated cheeks. She was feeling smug. The little girl had eluded him, and he could hardly catch his breath. Little round-ball bastard, she thought contemptuously as he spat the cold coffee out on the kitchen floor.

In a while the little girl returned. "Man? Can you hear me?"

"I can hear you," Abramo said, his eyes still not open. He was getting colder now.

She held a cup before him. "Take some of this," she said. She reached for his head, but he flinched. Then she brought the cup to his lips and he drank. It was beer. She did it again. Then she opened a piece of cloth and took out some bread and some cheese. "See if you can chew this," she said as she put a piece of cheese in his mouth. He ate the cheese and took another sip of beer. He shuddered for a moment, and she worried again that he might die. "Here's some bread," she said. "I saved it. If you eat, you'll feel better." He shivered as he chewed. "Are you still cold?" she said.

"Yes," he said. He ate only a little more bread and cheese, but drank all the beer in the cup. He shivered again. She ate the bread and cheese that were left, her only meal that night. Then she held his face before her and kissed him gently.

"What's your name?" she said.

"Abramo," he answered. "What's yours?"

"I don't know. Everyone calls me Blackie."

He stared at her for a few moments. It was strange...as if he had always known her. Nothing felt more natural to him than being with this gentle, wonderful little creature. And somehow she had the instinct to know that she was what he needed.

He shivered again. "*Piccina*," he said, "I'm getting sick. Tomorrow I have to leave here...or I'm going to die."

"But I don't know how to get you out," she said, her voice agonized.

"We'll think of it," he said.

"You have to sleep now," she said. She felt him shiver again. She opened her coat and put herself against him. One of his arms encircled her; the other was stiff and useless. She fixed the coat to spread it over his torso. It was little more than patches of rags. The warmth of her made him feel good. She rested her forehead against his neck and didn't move. He shivered fewer times against the warmth of her. Finally, they both fell asleep.

Then, the police called Reid-Carnegie and told them that they had found one of their trucks on Walnut Way. "What was he doing on Walnut Way?" George Carter asked Hugh.

"He made his last stop at Nelson Concrete. It looks like he was coming back here when he was done at Nelson. They always take longer than hell to cut their checks."

"You think he's on the up-and-up?" Carter asked.

"I'd bet anything he is," said Hugh. "I'm more afraid that something's happened to him."

Later that night, Hugh was on his way to pick up Kieran and take him back to the hospital. Molly's father and brothers had been there all morning, and Kieran came home after visiting hours to close the AOH.

Hugh was puzzled by all that had happened. Something didn't fit. Abramo hadn't stolen anything out of the truck. If he were going to run away, he would have taken some of the cash from the strongbox. He had to be in trouble.

Jesus, he'd also have to go see Mrs. Reid and tell her that Abramo was missing and that her frame might not be finished. But first he had to stop at the boarding house.

Hugh parked his car and headed up to the porch of the house. He rang the bell and Isabella Chianese answered. She looked anguished and red-eyed. "Signora Chianese, may I speak to you?" Hugh said softly in Italian.

"Yes. Please," she responded, stepping aside as a signal for Hugh to enter. This time she led him to a small room that was beside the living room and that had only one door to keep it private from all the other rooms in the house. Inside, she turned toward him and said, "Please sit down, sir." She began to close the door for privacy, but then hesitated, thinking of the propriety of a woman and a man, two strangers, alone together in a closed room of the house. But she only thought of it for an instant. This was about Abramo, and she didn't care about propriety anymore. She shut the door tight.

After she closed the door, she turned back to Hugh, who was still standing. They spoke in Italian. "What news of Abramo?" she said.

"That's why I've come here," he responded. "Has he not been home the last two nights?"

"No," she said softly, lowering her eyes to the floor and turning slightly away from him.

Hugh hated what he had to ask her next. He had to know if she was lying to protect Abramo. But her red eyes and her sad appearance told him what he wanted to know. "Signorina, Abramo has done nothing wrong. All I want—"

"He is not here! There is something wrong. Don't you know that?" she said, angry and hurt, tears cascading from beautiful dark eyes.

He reached for her forearm as she spoke, almost to try to keep her from the response that he knew she would surely give. "Please, *signorina*, I know you're telling the truth."

She didn't shake his hand away, but instead turned slightly toward him. In a moment she was in his arms, sobbing, suddenly releasing all the anguish she had been holding inside her for two days. Hugh had guided her to him. Never, in all the years since Aileen died had he wanted to draw a woman into him as he had done with this lovely Italian. There had been other women, but none like this. Hugh was in love with her from the moment he saw her face. She stopped crying, still in his arms.

"He does so much for me," she said, looking down at Hugh's chest. "He talks with Gianina and the other children as though he were their brother. He repairs things for me. He helps the old men…He *must* be okay. I don't know what life in this house will be like if he is gone."

Hugh spoke then, his forehead against hers, still not releasing her, but feeling no urge from her to be set free. "He has become like a son to me, Isabella. If he's lost, I don't know what I'll do either."

"We must look for him," she said, raising her eyes to his.

"Yes," he sighed, "at first light tomorrow."

Their eyes were only a few inches apart, and she still had not moved from his embrace. Silently, Hugh bent his head toward her and kissed her lips. It was magic. All the life that had been drained out of their spirits since the loss of their loved ones so long ago was suddenly infused into them again. It was as though their lives were beginning anew, even in the face of impending tragedy. "I can't leave here without telling you this," he whispered. "My God, Isabella, I've loved you from the first minute I saw you…and I hardly know your name," he said in amazement, as much to himself as to her.

"Me too…Hugh. I was afraid I was being like a schoolgirl, yearning for someone so far above me—" He shook his head, snorting to silence her and her thoughts.

"But this is different, isn't it?" he said. "Like an inner voice telling me that you're meant for me."

"The voice I also hear," she said. This time she smiled broadly and reddened slightly.

He made a wry face. "Jesus, you must have heard that said a million times, huh?" he said, jostling her slightly.

"But I know what you mean because you're different," she said. Then she raised her hand to his cheek and let it rest against his face, imparting warmth and love to his spirit. "Take me with you? If he's hurt, I can help. I was a nurse in Italy."

Hugh smiled slightly and brightened. "You sound better every minute," he said. "Okay. Tomorrow I'll come to get you. How early can you come?"

"I can be ready as soon as it is light. Gianina will take care of the boys."

Hugh's next stop was the hard one. Mrs. Reid was probably waiting for her picture frame, and it wasn't done. Hugh knocked at the door and a maid answered. "I'm Hugh Connolly. May I see your mistress? It's very important."

"But, sir, it's so late…she'll be upset if I told her she had a caller this late."

"Please, miss, just give her my name and I'm sure she'll see me."

The girl took him into the library and asked him to wait.

For several minutes Hugh nervously drummed his fingers against the arm of the chair he sat in. Then suddenly the door opened and Anetta Reid entered, followed by the maid. She took one look at Hugh and knew that there was something dreadfully wrong. "That's all, Mary," she said to the maid, who left them alone.

Then Anetta turned to Hugh. "What's wrong, Hugh?"

"It's Abramo, Mrs. Reid. He's gone missing and…and I think some harm may have befallen him."

She took a deep breath. "What's happened?" she said.

"He was making deliveries—we made him a courier two days a week. But we got a call from the police telling us that one of our trucks was parked all night on Walnut Way. It was Abramo's truck, and there was no sign of him."

Hugh expected her next question and was shaking his head as she spoke. "Did he take anything?" she said.

"No," Hugh said. "There was money in the strongbox he could have easily taken. None of it was gone. That's what scares me."

"My Lord, you think someone could have…"

"I don't know." Hugh sighed. "But every hour we wait now is precious…and perhaps dangerous to him."

She walked over to the butler's cord and pulled it. In a few seconds the maid entered. "Mary, tell John to call the chief of police at home and connect me in here. He has the number."

As they waited, Anetta said, "Did he ever start the frame?"

"Yes, and I've seen it. It's exquisite."

She smiled slightly in satisfaction. "How much has he done?"

"All the rough work. He's doing finishing touches now…some carving."

In a moment the phone rang. She answered it. "Hello?"

Hugh could hear a voice on the other end of the line. "Charles, I need your help. A young Italian boy who is very special to me has been missing for two days. He works at the mill for Superintendent Hugh Connolly and is very well thought of. We have to find him as soon as possible. We fear he may be hurt." She listened as the chief spoke. Then she grew grim and slightly angry. "We are not entertaining those kinds of thoughts, Charles. Now, will you assist us or not?"

More talk on the line. "Fine, Charles, if you think that many will be enough. But mind you, I want this boy found soon.

"All right. Have them contact Mr. Connolly this evening." She turned toward Hugh. He nodded. "When will you be home tonight?"

"By ten o'clock."

She turned her attention back to the phone. "Send your men out to talk to him at ten o'clock. I'll put him on in a moment to give you directions. Remember, Charles, this is very important to me…I know you do. That's why I called you."

Hugh gave the chief directions and a house number, and then he returned the receiver to Mrs. Reid. When she hung up, she turned to Hugh. "Hugh, as soon as you leave, I'll call the chief of staff at St. Rita's and tell him I want a suite at the Reid Pavilion ready for when they find him. Poor boy! He must be in terrible condition."

"Mrs. Reid…I don't know how to thank you," Hugh said.

She was thoughtful for a few seconds. "Hugh, my life has been better in the last few weeks, even with tonight's news, than it has been in years. I want that boy to be safe and sound…as I know you do." Hugh nodded. "We'll find him, Hugh. I know it. Let's have faith."

Kieran waited in the windowed anteroom at the far end of the hall. He was alone, but his sons were on the way. In a short time the boys found him. Conor, who had borne the wrath of his father for letting Molly come home alone, was somber and quiet, tormented by guilt and by the lashing his father's tongue administered for his neglect. And seeing Molly, now clean and dressed in hospital white, with graphic evidence of the wounds administered by her attacker, was anguish he could not bear. Kieran knew his eldest son would bear the scars of guilt throughout his life, and that maybe that guilt would be enough to make a man of him.

"Did she wake up?" Conor asked.

"No," Kieran said coldly. "The doctor said she has lost a lot of blood and was hurt and exhausted. He wasn't sure…"

Conor closed his eyes. If she were to die, he'd made up his mind to leave Youngstown and never set foot in Ohio again. He would go somewhere where he could work, live, and die quietly, never to be heard from again.

Kieran had left her wardroom because the doctor asked him to leave. Now he saw the doctor walking toward him down the long corridor, looking grim and chagrined. "Mr. Harty," he said, "she's taken a turn for the worse. Her blood pressure has dropped, and we're having a hard time controlling the blood loss. We have to take her to surgery or she'll die."

Kieran was stunned. It couldn't be happening again. That same malevolent hand was drawing her from life, just as it did in those two terrible days long ago when Cara died. And all he could do was watch as doctors tried and failed again and again as he slowly and inexorably lost her.

"What do you wish, Mr. Harty?" the doctor asked.

"If we have no choice, then do it," Kieran said.

"We'll take her downstairs as soon as we get her ready. I'll give you a short time to be with her alone after your sons look in on her."

"We have to let Uncle Hugh know," Kieran said to his sons.

"We stopped by his house on the way here, but he wasn't home," said Paul.

"He was here earlier today, Dad," Ross said.

"Go downstairs and call him; the receptionist will let you use the phone," Kieran said to Ross. "Come back up as soon as you're done."

The two boys went in to the room and stayed just a few minutes. Then Ross returned and joined them. Finally, Kieran went in. He looked at his sleeping child and felt a chill. It was like seeing Cara again. And the best thing that had come from him and Cara was going to die. The grandchildren she would give him were only mirages—the kind God uses to punish fools and sinners for dreaming sweet dreams.

Kieran lowered his head and began to cry silently. He held her hand and felt the warmth of it. He tried to imagine touching her and not feeling that warmth, not feeling the lifeblood coursing through her. He asked God to spare her. He needed her more than anything. Why give her to him only to take her away when she made his happiness complete?

He kissed her hand and began to cry again. A hand clutched his shoulder, and he knew that it was Hugh standing silently beside him. Neither man spoke as they prayed their own prayers and thought their own thoughts. Finally Hugh said, "Let's go, boyo. The doctors and nurses are waiting to take her. Remember one thing, son: When it takes the likes of you and me praying together, it's bound to work. She'll come back to us."

They both kissed her and walked out of the room and down the dimly lit corridor. "Did you see her face, Hugh? Who would do that to our beautiful girl?"

"Those forsaken by God, Kieran," sighed Hugh. "Some people hate all things beautiful and clean…and want to destroy them."

They all sat quietly in the waiting room, the boys sleeping and Hugh and Kieran lost in their own thoughts. After a while a nurse came into the anteroom and asked for Hugh Connolly. "What is it, nurse?" said Hugh.

"You have a telephone call, sir. You can take the call at the office one floor down. I'll take you there."

"But it's almost midnight. Who could be calling so late…" he said softly to himself. He followed the nurse to the supervisor's office.

Inside the office, Hugh answered the telephone. "Hello?"

"Hugh, this is Anetta Reid."

"Mrs. Reid, is everything okay? Why are you calling so late?"

"Did the police come out to see you?"

"Yes?"

"And they will begin the search for Abramo tomorrow?"

"Yes, at daybreak…We're all going," Hugh answered, still puzzled at her call.

"Then come to get my car. It's a sedan and should hold several men…and it could help retrace the path that Abramo took. I'll have Tim make it ready for dawn."

"Thank you, Mrs. Reid. I'm not sure they'll need it, but if we do, we'll come get it."

"So tell me, Hugh, what are you doing so late at the hospital? Your housekeeper said you had a family emergency?"

"It's my niece, Mrs. Reid. She was…assaulted the other night, and she…well, they couldn't stop the bleeding. They've just taken her back to surgery."

There was silence on the line for a moment. "Why didn't you tell me you had all this on your mind?"

"I…uh, didn't want to burden you with my troubles, Mrs. Reid. I—"

"We're supposed to be friends, Hugh. It's high time I've had some burdens of friendship."

"I appreciate that, ma'am. She could use the burden of prayer now," Hugh said.

"You mean she could die? Is it that critical?"

"Yes, ma'am, I'm afraid it is."

Again, silence on the line. "Was she in a ward?"

"Yes."

"Well, when the surgery is done, she'll be taken to the Reid Pavilion. I'm ordering a suite to be made ready that will accommodate her family. What's her name?"

"The girl's name is Molly Harty...but you don't have to—"

"Is that with a 't'?" she said, ignoring his comment.

"Yes."

"All right. I'll order the suite. Meanwhile, the automobile is waiting."

"Thank you."

"I've had thanks enough." She paused. "Hugh, when did this crime happen to your niece?"

"Two nights ago, on Walnut Way. The same time that the truck..." Hugh stopped and was silent. Suddenly a thought occurred to him that Molly's rape and Abramo's disappearance had happened at the same time. His heart began beating faster. God, even the thought of it made him sick.

Mrs. Reid sensed what he was thinking. "Hugh," she said, "that boy could have nothing to do with hurting your niece. He does not have that in his heart."

"Thanks for saying that, ma'am."

"I'll have my doctors consult with yours. We'll get this girl the finest care available. We'll get her through this."

A few minutes later, Hugh labored up the stairs to the waiting room. His eyes were unaccustomed to the darkness. He called to Kieran. "Over here, Hugh," said Kieran.

"Put on the light, Kier."

"What?"

"Put on the light."

The tone he used was surprising to his friend, but he did his bidding. The boys, who were dozing, awakened immediately. Hugh stepped to the center of the small room, empty except for the Hartys and himself. Kieran advanced to the center beside Hugh. "What's up, boyo?" said Kieran, barely audibly.

"I have to find out something." Hugh turned to his nephews. "Boys, when you found your sister, did you see anyone else?"

The three young men looked at each other sheepishly. "Tell me, boys," Hugh said in a tone he never used with his nephews.

Ross answered first. "Yeah, Uncle Hugh…there was a guy."

"For God's sake, boy, why didn't you tell that to someone?"

"He looked like he was dead, Uncle Hugh," Paul blurted out. "When Conor kicked him he never made a move."

Hugh's eyes narrowed as he looked toward Conor. "You kicked a senseless man who had no defense, Conor?"

"What the hell's going on, Hugh?" said Kieran. "What have you found out?"

Hugh turned back to his nephews without answering his brother-in-law. "Where was this man when you saw him?"

Again the boys looked at each other. Ross answered again for them. "He was lying across Molly's body, Uncle Hugh. We just thought it was the guy who…attacked her."

"What did he look like?" said Hugh.

The boys didn't answer. "What did he look like, damn you all!" shouted Kieran.

Finally Conor answered softly. "He looked like a dago."

Hugh stepped backward as though dazed. He turned his back to the Hartys and put his hands up to his eyes and took a deep breath. Kieran had never seen his friend so disoriented. "Hugh?" Hugh turned around toward them again. "What color was his hair?" he said calmly.

"Dark…probably brown or black," said Conor.

"How big was he, Conor? Big like you?"

"He was slender, Uncle Hugh," Ross answered, trying to protect his older brother from the wrath of his uncle, or the even more fearsome wrath of their father.

"Was he tall?"

"No…about my height, I'd guess. He looked normal."

"Did you notice anything else about him?" asked Hugh.

"His coat was torn," said Paul, "and he had blood on the back of his head."

Hugh's eyes closed as he stood, suddenly afraid of losing his balance. He seemed to stumble a step. "My God, Hugh, are you all right?" said Kieran, suddenly grabbing him for support. "Come sit down here, man," he said, steering him into a seat.

Kieran stepped back away from them all and said, "Now tell me, all of you. What was this discussion about?"

Hugh took a deep breath. "I think the man that the boys found with Molly was the Italian kid that's been missing…Abramo."

"So, where is he now?" said Kieran.

"I don't know," said Hugh. "We're going to begin searching for him tomorrow. The police and Isabella and I."

"His landlady?" said Kieran.

"Yeah." Hugh sighed.

"Jesus, Connolly, you and I have a lot of talking to do," Kieran said.

"I know, son. But it'll be a lot easier if Molly pulls through and we find that kid alive."

Kieran then turned back to his sons. "So, did you just leave this man in that alley like a dog?"

"But, Daddy, we thought he was the rapist," said Conor. "That why I was kicking him. I thought he had done Molly."

Kieran's face reddened, and his sons became afraid. "Let me get this straight: You stomped a defenseless, unconscious man and left him to die among all them savage bastards on the North Side, right? You know what the Hannons and their gang do to helpless people they find up there?"

"But we thought he was the rapist!" said Paul.

"Did it ever occur to you that he could have been protecting your sister?"

"But he was lying on top of her," said Conor.

"So where did the blood on his head come from? Do you think Molly could have done that to an attacker?"

"It never occurred to us that he could have been helping her," said Ross.

"It never occurred to you," Kieran echoed. He looked like he'd been struck. "And that is a sin that I'll pay for when I see God." He shook his head. "It never occurred to you."

Silence settled in the room. Two nurses and a nun supervisor had come down the hallway to see what the commotion was about. They had heard Kieran's outbursts in the last few minutes. The nun, a small but imposing woman, had put together what she knew of Molly's story and the argument she had just heard and understood the situation.

She walked to the center of the room. "Gentlemen, I am Sister Mary Agnes. You have all said enough. Now you must pray to God for forgiveness and for mercy on your sainted sister. She has survived the surgery, but she is not yet out of danger. The doctors are still attending to her now, but she will soon be brought to the Reid Pavilion. You may wait for her there. I will escort you."

"The Reid Pavilion?" Kieran said. "Sister, isn't that the place—"

"Your daughter's medical expenses and hospital bill have all been taken care of, Mr. Harty. Please come with me."

"What do you mean, Sister?" Kieran said to her back as she walked out the door.

"Kier," said Hugh, waving his friend to silence, "I'll tell you about it. Come now, boys," he said, turning toward them. "Let's go see your sister."

The little girl woke up and touched Abramo's face to see that he was alive. He was still warm and breathing. His chest was wet from the perspiration that the little girl's body had induced as she slept next to him. "I'll bring some food," she said.

"*Piccina*, see if you can talk to someone. I have to leave here today."

"I'll find someone," she said. "But first I'll get something to eat."

"Can you get water? I'd like to drink some water."

Early that morning, Hugh was awaiting the police as they came to his door. He was dressed in a turtle-necked sweater and leather jacket with no tie. He had boots and thick twill trousers on. One of the policemen asked if he had a car. Hugh answered that he did.

"Good. The more the better," said the officer.

"There will be a woman coming with us," Hugh said.

The officer looked at him skeptically. "Begging your pardon, sir, but that's not a good idea."

"If he's hurt, he'll need immediate medical care. She's a nurse."

"But the neighborhoods we're going through are full of crime, especially Walnut Way."

"She will be with me every moment...and I have a gun."

"Do you know how to use it?"

Hugh smiled grimly. "I won't shoot you, son."

"Okay, sir, but please, let's all be careful. You call out if there's the least bit of trouble." He paused and took a deep breath. "Well, let's go then."

"I have two stops to make. Follow me and then one of your men can drive my car, and I'll drive Mrs. Reid's car."

"Mrs. Reid? You mean from the North Side?"

"That's the one. Now let's go."

"Okay," the officer said. "My captain will join us a little later."

The small caravan drove to Isabella's house. When Hugh rang the doorbell, Gianina answered. "Hello, young lady, is your mother home?"

"Yes, sir," she answered in English. "Please come in."

She escorted Hugh down a hallway into the back kitchen. As they entered, the back door opened, and Isabella came in from outside. She was startled to see Hugh waiting in her kitchen. She smiled broadly and didn't say a word. Instead, she gave Hugh her hand. He took it and held it. He too was smiling.

Gianina had never seen this—at least not with her mother. There was a connection between her mother and this handsome American.

Isabella turned toward her daughter and said, "*Cara mia*, see the boys off to school. Make sure they have breakfast…and you, too."

Gianina, not knowing Hugh could understand Italian, said, "Mama, do you like this American? He seems so important, so rich. He has his own car."

Isabella looked at Hugh and smiled. He answered in Italian. "Not so rich and not so important, signorina. But someone who likes your mother very much."

Gianina was mortified, but Isabella and Hugh laughed gently. Isabella kissed her daughter and spoke in more somber tones. "*Cara*, we are going with the police to look for Abramo. Signor Connolly is a dear friend of his."

"Mama, Abramo won't die, will he?"

Isabella looked at Hugh and he answered. "Signorina, if you say your prayers for us, they will tell God how much we all need Abramo."

Chapter 7

CAPTAIN RORY GROGAN WAS a huge man: six feet two and two hundred eighty pounds of controlled rage. He was known as a fair and honest man, though he had been also known to look the other way from stag parties with prostitutes and booze and gambling, or autumn crap games that were finishing up the summer season. His tolerance for such sins was insured by steaks or cases of whiskey delivered anonymously to his back porch.

But he was also a good cop who believed that the law protects little people as well as great ones. He was kind but fierce. His anger was righteous, and he hated evil men, be they Ku Klux Klan, the Irish gangs, or the Mafia. His rages were legendary among those on the police force. In his younger days he had once cleared a bar of ten men who had beaten up a little Jewish tailor and had stolen his money.

He would surely be chief of the vice squad some day. But insiders did not consider him a prospect for chief of police because of his rough edges and lack of political skills. But he was a cop's cop, the one they would all want covering their backs in a gunfight.

Rory walked up to Hugh and introduced himself. They shook hands, and Hugh said, "Thanks for coming. We need all the help we can get." Rory turned toward Isabella. "Captain Grogan, please meet Signora Isabella Chianese, Abramo Cardone's landlady…and a personal friend of mine."

Those words told Rory the whole story between Isabella and Hugh. He shook her hand and bowed slightly. "Pleased to meet you, Mrs. Chianese."

After a few seconds, Hugh spoke. "Captain, I heard something last night that made me think this whole thing through again. My niece, Molly Harty, was assaulted two nights ago in an alley off Walnut Way. When her brothers found her, there was a man, injured and unconscious, on top of her. The brothers, my nephews, thought he was the assailant. They just took their sister to St. Rita's and left the man there in the alley, still unconscious. I now believe that man was not the assailant at all. I think he was Abramo Cardone."

"Two days ago?" said Grogan. "God Almighty, Mr. Connolly, do you know what could have happened to him up there on the North Side?"

"I know, Captain. But if by some miracle he's still alive, I want to find him and see that he gets well."

"And this is an Italian kid?" said Grogan, trying to make sense of what motivated Connolly to care about Abramo.

"Yes," said Hugh. "Does that make a difference?"

"None to me," he said and paused. "But I'm glad to hear none to you, too."

"So, what do you think? Search Walnut Way first?"

"Let's go," said Grogan. "But Mr. Connolly—"

"Call me Hugh."

"Hugh…you keep tight hold of that lady friend of yours."

"She'll be with me every minute. I have a gun and know how to use it."

"A gun, huh?" His tone became stern. "Guns make policemen nervous, Hugh—even in good hands. Just don't get crazy on me, okay?"

Hugh nodded.

When the search party arrived at Walnut Way, the sun was up but hidden behind a veil of clouds. Winter was coming early to November. With lanterns, they trudged through driveway after driveway. Rory Grogan, perhaps because of his instant liking for Hugh and Isabella, seemed to be taking a personal interest in the search. He walked along with the rest of his crew and looked disappointed that they had found no one.

On both sides of the street, there were driveways and alleys. The five policemen plus Rory, Isabella, and Hugh wearily waded through trash, mud holes, weeds, and strewn garbage. The hours passed, and they grew tired. Residents of Walnut Way looked nervously at them, only to realize that this time the police were searching for someone else. Groups of ragged children watched from a distance and then scattered into hiding as searchers approached.

"How come there are so many kids up here?" Hugh asked Rory.

"Those are the orphan gangs. A lot of poor people and whores have them, and then they die…or just abandon them. The kids are left to fend for themselves. They feed each other and become scavengers. Some work in the kitchens of the bars and whorehouses. Then if they're good-looking, they become whores themselves when they're about thirteen, fourteen.

"Some of the boys—those that have it in them—learn to steal...and kill. Then they join the gangs. It's them that give the North Side a bad name."

"Jesus Christ," muttered Hugh. Isabella held tightly to his arm.

"How many more alleys do we have?" Rory asked one of his men.

"I've sent Justin and Dick over on the back sides of the buildings. When they're done, then we have about a dozen more."

"Okay," Rory said, turning to Hugh, "if we don't find anything, then we have to go one-by-one to each of these places and question everyone in them."

"The Hannons own that AOH up there," Hugh said, pointing to the middle of the block on the opposite side.

"You know damn well we're gonna question those guys," said Grogan. "That gang does about all the deadly crime in this whole area."

They broke their search for lunch. Hugh, Rory, and Isabella went to a small restaurant on the North Side that was clean and far enough away that they could breathe fresh air. As they sat in the restaurant, the two men made small talk. Isabella was quiet.

Hugh held her hand beneath the table, sensing the waning of her spirits after seeing all the human debris of Walnut Way. Rory, after a lull in the conversation, also sensed her feelings. "I'm sorry you had to see all that, ma'am, especially the kids. But you know, miracles happen. Sometimes you get a kid out of those streets that's special...they just have something in them that's drawn to goodness."

"They have God," she said. "But why don't they all? They are children…some only babies. Why don't they all?"

Hugh looked at Rory, but neither of them had an answer. Isabella had asked the fundamental question of human existence. They finished their meal and went back to work.

The afternoon was gray and cool, and the search produced no results. They found the dead body of an old, grizzled man, who reeked of whiskey and urine, in one of the back alleys and who probably died during the night. Rory called the police van to take the body down to the morgue. All the others were drunks and derelicts sleeping off binges only to begin new ones after the sun went down. And finally, the search was complete, though nothing was recovered.

They stood in a small group on the sidewalk of Walnut Way. Isabella stood behind Hugh with tears in her eyes, crushed by the futility of it all, weary and devastated by the filth and vermin and the horrible visions of children living like animals. Somewhere Abramo was all alone, either dead or dying, and they couldn't help him.

"Okay, before it gets dark," Rory said, "let's question these people. We'll split up. Terry, you go with the lady and Mr. Connolly. The rest of us will go in two teams."

"Rory," said Hugh, "I'd like to start down there. That's the area where they found my niece."

"You mean around the AOH?"

"Yeah."

"Okay, but you be damn careful. And hold on to Madam Isabella. Terry, you keep that gun of yours at the ready. And don't be afraid to defend yourself with that billy club—if you catch my meaning. If any of us find something, call the others right away. Hugh, I'm sending another man with you. I'll check on you in a while."

As they began to scatter, Rory called Terry back to him. "You let those bastards know that unless they want the police swarming all over them like flies on horseshit, they'd better answer those questions sharp."

When Isabella and Hugh walked into the AOH, she gasped. The fetid smell of smoke, sweat, stale beer, and whiskey was overwhelming. Then she saw the children, dirty and unkempt, hair matted, in clothes little more than rags. Hugh held her hand as they walked in behind Terry. "Are you going to be all right?" he asked.

"Oh, Madonna, look at these children, Hugh. Who could treat them like this?" Hugh squeezed her hand.

Terry walked over to a large, scowling man and said, "Are you the owner of this place?"

"Yeah, I am. What about it?"

"Have you seen—"

"We ain't seen anything or anybody," the owner said.

"Mister, you have a choice: either you cooperate or there'll be police all over this place like hungry vultures. Now which is it?"

"Who the hell are you?" the owner said to Hugh.

"He's a superintendent at Reid-Carnegie, Pa," said a man behind the owner. It was Joe Hannon. "His name is Connolly."

"So, you're the guy who let them break my boy's arm, and then fired him when you couldn't use him anymore, huh?"

Hugh laughed softly. "Mister, if you believe that story, you'll believe that pigs can fly. That kid shot off his mouth and got his arm broken in a fair contest."

The owner glanced back at his son. "He's lying, Pa. They'll say anything to save their asses."

Just then, one of the other Hannons started toward Hugh. Terry stopped him by placing the tip of his billy club in the front of his neck beside his Adam's apple. "Don't even think of it, or it'll be the mistake of your life," he said in a menacing tone.

"What's your name?" asked Hugh, knowing he was talking to Jack Hannon.

"Jack Hannon. What's it to you?"

"We're looking for a young Italian kid: medium height, black hair, about twenty-eight years old…Have you seen anybody like that?"

"We don't allow no Italians in this place." Hannon looked at Isabella. "Unless they look entertaining, like your lady friend there."

"Don't make me use this, Hannon." Terry brandished his billy club. "We have other guys outside."

"I know what you got outside: five cops and that gorilla captain, this guy and that whore of his. You think that's gonna be enough to fight your way back out of here?"

Hugh lunged at Hannon, but Isabella screamed, and Terry caught him by the shoulder and pulled him away. Isabella pulled him further back toward her and whispered, "No, my dear, no. Remember we are here to find Abramo. He will say those words about me again, the moment we leave this filthy place."

Throughout the time the men were arguing, some of the children drew near to Isabella. A couple of them touched her hand, and some touched her garments, her dress, and her sleeve. "Lady?" one little girl said.

"Yes, *piccina*?" Isabella answered.

"You're rich, ain't you?"

"No, *cara*, I am just a working woman."

"He's rich," the girl said, pointing to Hugh. "He has a car."

"He's not poor, but he is not rich," said Isabella.

The men had stopped talking and heard the last few words Isabella spoke to the girl. Then they turned back to Hugh and Terry, defiant and scowling. "If Captain Grogan finds out you know something about that young fellow, and you didn't tell us the truth, he's gonna be real mad. In fact"—Terry pointed the billy club at Jack Hannon—"he might want to question you all by himself—you and him, private. Like to spoil your whole day."

"You tell Rory Grogan I said he fucks his mother, okay? Tell him Jack Hannon said that about him."

Terry raised his billy club, but this time Hugh held his arm. "Let's go, Terry. We can argue all night with these bastards and won't get anything out of them."

Both Joe and Jack Hannon smirked. They had won. Isabella and Hugh followed Terry and the other officer as they made their way toward the door. Suddenly, a child's voice rang through the silence of their departure. "I know someone who says 'piccina.'"

Isabella and Hugh turned toward the voice, that of another little girl, from the edge of the room. She was loveliness covered over with dirt and sores, about eight or nine years old. Her black hair, rare among these children, was matted and filthy. There was dried blood behind one of her ears. Her hands and fingernail were dirty, her clothes rags, her shoes poorly fitted men's shoes.

"What did you say, *cara*?" said Isabella.

"I know a man who says, 'piccina.'"

"Where is this man, little one?" said Hugh softly.

"I can't tell you," she said.

"But why? We are his friends."

Isabella, by this time, was on her knees before the girl. She touched her face gently. The child turned her head into the caress, never having been touched in her life with tenderness. "I'm afraid."

"Afraid of what, *cara mia*?" Isabella said.

"I'm afraid they'll hurt him some more," she said.

Isabella gasped. Hugh knelt down this time. "My dear," he said, "is this man alive?"

She nodded. "But he's sick."

"Do you know his name?" asked Hugh, his heart pounding so that he could barely catch his breath.

She nodded again, then hesitated. "You won't let them hurt him?"

"No, my dear, we will take him to the hospital to get well." He swallowed hard. "Do you know his name?"

"Abramo."

Isabella made a soft cry and covered her mouth with her hand. "Can you show us where he is, angel?" she said.

She looked at Isabella, struck by the beauty of the gentle woman, and nodded. "Jesus, Mary, and Joseph," said Terry as he ran out the door to call the others.

"Give me your hand, *cara mia*. Lead us to Abramo, so we can help him," said Isabella.

"Where you going with her, lady? She's mine. She's my dead sister's daughter," said Joe Hannon.

"We're going to let this little girl show us where my friend is," said Hugh.

"She ain't going no place," said Jack Hannon. "That's my granddaughter, and she ain't going with you or anybody else. She's staying right here."

Just then, Rory came into the bar, flushed and breathless. "Did you find him?" he said to Hugh.

"This little girl can show us, but he says she has to stay put," Hugh said, pointing to Jack Hannon.

Rory turned toward the Hannons. "The hell you say, Jack Hannon? Here's me doing police business, and you're obstructing justice big as life…and calling the citizens' guardians bad names. Now you don't want to try to stop us from doing the people's justice, do ye, Jack Hannon?"

As he spoke, one of Hannon's younger sons, who had a small dragon insignia pinned to his shirt, stealthily reached for a thick ax handle that was resting against the back side of the bar. But Rory, always on his guard, caught the movement in a quick glance and swung his billy club in a short, stinging arc that landed on the forearm of the boy, who shrieked in agony as the club struck. "Jack Hannon, I'm surprised at you. You ought've taught these sons of yours not to use violence against the peace officers of the people. And him being a Ku Kluxer and all—a goddamned patriot, right?"

Rory turned toward Isabella and the little girl. "Lead us to him, child…and God bless you." Then he turned and glanced at the remaining five officers who had by now all come to the AOH. He nodded to them to be on guard. Then he made one last menacing look at the Hannons, daring them to do anything more to keep them from Abramo.

The little girl led them down the back stairs of the AOH that brought them to a corridor that led to the driveway outside. They went down the driveway to the alley and took a series of turns that brought them to the small room where Abramo rested. The girl moved the cupboard front and went inside. Isabella and Hugh and Rory followed.

Inside, they saw Abramo, shivering and vacant-eyed. "Isabella, is that you?" he said weakly.

She rushed toward him and kissed him, laying her hand on his forehead. "Oh, *caro mio*, God has given you back to us."

The two men crouched down on either side of Isabella and watched as she tearfully caressed the young man. "Abramo, we have to move you, but we don't know what injuries you have. Will you tell us so we can be careful as we get you up?" said Hugh.

"My shoulder mostly," he said. "I don't know…maybe my neck."

The men cleared away the sackcloth and lifted him up so he could fit through the narrow opening into the outside room. Rory kicked out part of the wall and left a hole large enough that Abramo could be carried through. The child watched as the men carefully made their way to the street with their passenger.

Rory ordered Terry to follow Isabella and Hugh to Mrs. Reid's house and then to drive them in Hugh's car to the Reid Pavilion at St. Rita's. "Doctors will be waiting for you to arrive," Hugh said to Rory. "Mrs. Reid put them on notice that they should be expecting a call when we found him."

"I'll have the YPD Dispatch alert them that we're coming," said Rory.

Then they went to Abramo. "You're in good hands, son," said Hugh. "They're going to fix you up and put you in a nice place. Then we'll be waiting for you."

"Where's the *piccina*? I don't want to leave without her," Abramo said.

"We'll bring her," said Rory. "Go ahead, boys," he said to two of the policemen. The siren was on, and the car drove down the hill toward St. Rita's Hospital.

"We'll bring the little girl to the hospital, Hugh," said Rory. "You can tell Mrs. Reid about Abramo."

"Okay. See you later. Let's go, Terry."

❀ ❀

When they rang the doorbell to the Reid mansion, the butler ushered them into the library. In a few moments, Anetta Reid entered. She knew instantly from looking at Hugh that the news was good. "Saints be praised, Hugh Connolly, did you find him?"

"Yes, ma'am. He's injured, and we won't know how bad off he is…he may need surgery. But thanks for all the help you gave us. Your car is back."

"Never mind the car. Where did you find him?"

"That's the miraculous part of it. A little girl kept him alive and safe for three days. Those gangs on Walnut Way would have surely done him in if she had not hidden him away, and then fed him."

"Who is the little girl?" she said.

"Jack Hannon says she's his granddaughter."

"Nonsense! No one with Hannon blood would be an angel of mercy as this girl was. How old is she?"

"About eight or nine, I'd guess."

She was silent for a few minutes. She had noticed the lovely woman who accompanied Hugh. She was obviously Italian, and she seemed to be more than a casual acquaintance. Anetta also noticed that the woman had looked several times at the large, tinted picture of Brendan. "And who is this guest in my house, Mr. Connolly?" she said.

"Mrs. Reid, may I present Signora Isabella Chianese, Abramo's landlady—and a dear friend of mine."

"Welcome, Mrs. Chianese. Mr. Connolly has never mentioned you in all his visits to me these last few weeks," Anetta said in a soft, amazed voice.

"I…didn't know if you'd be interested."

"Friends are always interested, Hugh Connolly. Now come here, girl, and let me get a closer look at you." When Isabella stepped before her, Anetta could see all that Hugh saw in her. There was warmth, humility, and intelligence, and not even a hint of falseness. And the beauty of her face, especially her eyes, was remarkable.

Anetta could see from Hugh's beaming face that this girl was special in his life. "Mrs. Chianese, I am a crotchety old harpy, but have had reason to enjoy my life more lately than I ever have since the death of my husband. Connolly here is one of the few people I can tolerate and trust—or even like, for that matter. But I think you will be the same." She nodded to signal the matter was all but settled. "I think we will be friends."

"Madama, I will be honored to be called your friend," Isabella said.

"Good." She turned to Hugh. "Are you going back to the hospital?"

"Yes, when we leave here."

"All right. Call me when you get back home tonight for a report on our patients—no matter how late. How's your niece?"

"They said she'll live. When I talked to her father at noon today, she was stable. But I'll let you know how both are."

"Now then, my dear," Anetta said to Isabella. "As soon as this turmoil stops, I would like Hugh to bring you here for dinner some Saturday night. It will be a pleasure to learn more about you…if Connolly will mind his manners and let us talk." Isabella smiled. "And I'll let you know some dates. The choice will be yours. But know that I look forward to seeing you soon."

They left Mrs. Reid, and Terry drove them down to the hospital. When they arrived, Hugh and Isabella walked to the Reid Pavilion. There they met an officious receptionist who sat at a desk before the beautiful wooden doors that were the entrance to the pavilion. "We are here to see Abramo Cardone and Molly Harty," Hugh said.

The woman opened the doors to let them through. Inside, both were astonished at the beauty and luxury of the pavilion. A nurse approached them and asked who they wished to see and then led them to the suites of Molly and Abramo, which were one unit apart.

When they entered Molly's suite, her brothers walked toward them. "How's your sister?" Hugh asked.

"They said she's gonna make it, Uncle Hugh, but…" Ross looked at Isabella and didn't want to continue. "My dad's in there," he said, gesturing behind him.

Hugh hurried to the room where Molly lay, sleeping peacefully. Isabella followed Hugh, and he held her hand part of the way. "Kieran, what's wrong? Is she okay?" Hugh said.

Kieran stood up to face him. His eyes were red, and he looked drawn and tired. "She's all right, Hugh. Except…" He stopped and couldn't talk anymore.

Hugh put his arm around him and said, "What is it, son? What did they say?"

"She'll probably never be able to have children," Kieran answered, still not noticing Isabella standing behind Hugh.

"No chance?"

"Almost none, they said."

"But otherwise?"

"Otherwise, she's okay. They stopped the bleeding and sewed her up, but whatever inside her was torn…She won't have children."

Hugh looked down at the floor and was silent for several seconds. "I'm sorry, Kier. I know you wanted that little girl the likes of Molly and Cara. But she's been our blessing all her life, and now, at least, she's still with us."

"Yeah, I know. But it's a lousy piece of luck, isn't it? Why do all these good women keep running into such misfortune? First Aileen, then Cara, and now Molly?"

Just as he spoke those words, Kieran noticed that they were not alone in the room. He looked behind Hugh and beheld the beautiful woman standing there quietly. Hugh sensed a change in Kieran's posture and turned back to Isabella.

Kieran looked at his old friend and brightened a little, his eyes smiling as they had not in days. "I've known you fifty years, Connolly, and you went and did this all by yourself...and never told your oldest friend what you were up to?"

"It wasn't like that, boyo. It happened quick as lightning."

"Before you could tell me anything about it, right?"

"That's it," Hugh said sheepishly.

Kieran kept his gaze on Isabella. "Introduce me to your lady."

"Isabella, this is my oldest and dearest friend and also my brother-in-law, Kieran Harty. Kieran, this is Isabella Chianese." Hugh hesitated for a second, looking at his friend who had not yet taken his eyes off Isabella. "Son, this is the woman I love."

Kieran shook his head in wonder as he gazed at Isabella. "Where did you find this girl, Hugh Connolly? She's lovely." And as he spoke, he kissed her on the cheek. "Hello, my dear."

"Hello, Signor Harty," she said, smiling.

"That will be the first and last time you address me as signor, young lady. From now on, it's Kieran."

Hugh put his arm around his old friend. "Listen, son, let's count our blessings, huh? If God wants her to have children, she will. But you know that we would have settled for anything just to see that face come toward us again smiling."

"I know you're right, Hugh. But she doesn't know it yet…"

"You talk to her, okay? She'll feel better when you let her know what she means to us."

"Where are you going now?" said Kieran.

"Abramo is right down the hall…Anetta Reid's doing again."

"How is he? I heard those bastards beat him up pretty bad."

"Yeah, they did. And the only reason he's alive today is because of some little girl up there who decided to hide him and feed him. How about that?"

"Whose little girl?"

"Someone nobody knows. She was one of the orphans over there at Walnut Way. But Jack Hannon says that she's his grand-daughter."

"A Hannon saving someone's life out of the goodness of her heart? I don't think so."

"You'll see her soon. Rory Grogan's bringing her here… Remember, Kieran, you be the first to talk to Molly when she wakes up."

Rory Grogan was attending to the report on the rape and beating of Molly and Abramo. He was trying, with the help of some experts, to decide which charges to bring against the Hannons. As he worked, Sergeant Terry McFadden came into his office. "Captain? Uh, we have a problem."

"What problem?" said Rory.

"We can't find the little girl."

"You mean the kid from Walnut Way?"

"Yeah. When you said we would bring her to the hospital after that Italian kid, I went back to the AOH with a couple of the boys, and I thought we'd just get her and take her with us. But no one knows where she went. She's disappeared. And we looked all over hell."

Rory was quiet for a few seconds. "She's probably hiding...or they've done her in," he said. "I'll kiss your ass if she's Hannon's kin."

"So, what are we going to do?"

"We're gonna find that little girl, goddammit."

Chapter 8

It was evening at St. Rita's Hospital, and visiting hours were over except for the people in the Reid Pavilion. The doctors told Kieran that Molly's vital signs were normal, and she should be coming out of the sleep of anesthesia soon.

Kieran was amazed at the number of doctors attending Molly's and Abramo's two rooms at the pavilion. Hugh hadn't told him how the cost of Molly's treatment was to be forgiven, but he was prepared to pay it all himself…if only they would let him do it slowly over the next year.

Molly stirred, and he looked up from his reverie. She was waking up. In a few minutes a nurse came into the room and took her pulse and respiration and temperature. "She's coming along fine for a postoperative patient, Mr. Harty," she said. "In a short time she'll talk to you, but don't be surprised if she doesn't remember your conversation later—it's a side effect of the anesthesia. She's a healthy young woman, and there's every reason to hope for a full recovery. If she's in any discomfort, don't hesitate to call a nurse. The doctors have left orders for continued medication."

Several hours later, Molly finally spoke. Kieran had assembled the boys with him to listen to her first words. "What happened to me, Daddy?"

"You went to surgery, my girl. They couldn't stop the blood flow."

"Am I going to be okay?"

"Yes, lass, you are."

"Who are these ugly men with you," she said, smiling weakly, her eyes closed.

"Bless you, Molly," said Conor.

"Hello, Conor. How are you doing?"

"Fine, girl," he said with tears in his eyes. "Welcome back to us."

She knew the look on Conor's face because she had seen it all her life. She also knew that Conor would never change. He would always be a small man in a tall, lanky body who would always need his omissions and transgressions forgiven as though he were a naughty child. He was not evil, just weak and self-centered. "It's all right, Conor," she said, closing her eyes.

Ross grabbed her hand. "Moll, do you feel this?"

"Yes, Ross."

"And me, Molly? Can you hear me?" said Paul.

"I hear you both," she said. "Who's running the AOH?"

"The place is fine," said Ross. "Eddie is handling it."

"Then we'll probably make some money today, huh?" She smirked, still not opening her eyes.

For the next hour she dozed and awoke, looking more alert each time. Finally, they decided to leave her and return the next day. Two doctors plus the surgeon came down to talk to Kieran. "Mr. Harty, I'm Dr. Shanfield. I'm very sorry about your daughter," said the chief of staff.

Kieran swallowed. "I'm glad she's alive, Doctor. Thank you for that." He gripped his daughter's hand. "We'll learn to deal with the other thing."

"She's a lovely young woman," said the surgeon. "I'm sure some fine young man will feel lucky to have her…and that some lucky children might have her as an adoptive mother."

"Let us know if there's anything we can do for you, Mr. Harty," said the third doctor. "We'll each be looking in on her as she recovers." He smiled. "So, you're a friend of Mrs. Anthony Reid?"

"In a manner of speaking," said Kieran. They glanced at each other, but said nothing more about it.

"You may stay here if you wish. I can have the staff bring up food and a daybed for you. Of course, if you'd like to go home, you can see her tomorrow. Meanwhile, she's recovering well physically, and after a good night's rest, she should be more alert tomorrow."

The boys went home, and Kieran stopped at Abramo's room. Hugh and Isabella were still there waiting. Michele della Malva was also waiting. Hugh came over to Kieran as he entered the suite. "How is he?" said Kieran.

"The doctors said he'll be okay," said Hugh. "They're the same people who attended Molly. He'll just need some time to recover."

"That's good news," said Kieran.

"How's Molly?"

"She'd come awake then doze off. They said she'd remember nothing tomorrow, so we didn't talk much."

Hugh nodded. "So, she still doesn't know?"

"No," said Kieran.

Isabella came over to them. "Kieran, you haven't eaten all day. Will you come to my house and have dinner with us?"

"Thanks anyway, Isabella. But I think I'll go home and shower off the day's troubles. It'll be nice to have a peaceful early sleep in my own bed."

"Some other time this week, then," she said.

"I'll see you tomorrow, boyo," said Hugh.

After Kieran left, Hugh and Isabella stayed an hour and then went back to the boarding house. Michele stayed in the suite in a daybed.

During the night, Abramo awoke. Michele came to his bedside and looked down at him. "Zi'Michele," Abramo said in greeting.

"My boy, thank God you are okay."

Abramo was silent for a few minutes, suddenly aware of the head restraint and the pain he felt at all his wounds. He tried to sort out what had happened to him. His memory was erratic. He knew he had been in trouble, but he couldn't remember the events that caused it. Of all the images that came in disconnected parts to his consciousness, only two emerged clearly into his mind. "What happened to the young girl who was raped?" he said in Italian.

"She's here in the hospital, two doors away."

"She's alive then?"

"Yes."

"Is she okay?"

Michelle shrugged. "She cannot have children. When they took her to surgery, she was so damaged that they had to do what they could to stop the bleeding…and those things mean she will never have her own children."

Abramo shook his head, as if to deny the sound of Michele's words. "And the *piccina*?"

"I don't know where she is. I was told the policemen were bringing her to safety."

"Have you seen her?"

"No."

"I want to see her."

The next morning Kieran walked into Molly's suite. She had been bathed and fed, and she looked clean, if battered and swollen about the face. He bent over the bed to kiss her. "How are you, my girl?"

"Okay, Daddy." She seemed subdued and preoccupied.

"Any pain, Moll?"

"Not much."

Kieran could tell by her short answers that the discussion between them was going to be difficult this morning.

"Daddy?"

"Yes, Moll?"

"What did the doctors tell you about me?" Kieran looked down, away from her gaze, and didn't speak. "Daddy? You'll have to tell me sooner or later."

"Well, it's about the operation…"

"What about it?"

"Well…you were bleeding a lot, and they had to stop it."

"And so they did, didn't they?"

"Yes…but there was…" Kieran sighed.

"More to it?" she said.

"Yeah."

She looked away from her father. "And I'll never have children, will I, Da?"

"Not likely, lass," he answered softly.

She turned back and gazed at him for a few seconds. "What am I going to do, Daddy?"

"What do you mean, child?"

"What will my life be like? Will I die a fat old barmaid?"

"For God's sake, no! Your life will be the life that God meant for you to have."

"You've gone religious on me, have you, Dad?"

He snorted, nodding his head. "When I was praying for you to live, girl, I did."

"You mean God just stood by and watched me? Like it was meant for me to be raped?" Tears were rolling down her cheeks. "And he meant for me not to have children? What did I ever do to God to deserve such a life?"

"I don't know why this happened, Máille. But I know that none of it was your doing. It just happened. Why did your mom die? And Aunt Aileen? Neither of them deserved it. God knows Uncle Hugh and I needed them both."

"But they both had loving husbands, didn't they?"

"As will you, girl," her father said.

She began to cry again, almost silently, with the tears streaming down her cheeks the only evidence of her feelings. "Who will want a girl who is not a virgin? Not one of the men I have ever seen around me."

"You don't give them enough credit, Máille. There will be some, as there always have been, who will want you for a wife."

"But none of them would know I was damaged goods…and that I couldn't give them children."

"You are not damaged goods, Moll! Those men forced themselves upon you."

"It won't matter, Daddy. I'm no longer a virgin. And if it was forced, then I'm so much the worse for it."

"It'll matter to the good ones, Moll…And some may want you only for children, but the very best will want you only because of you, with no thought of children or anything else. Only you. And that will be the beginning of God's restitution to you."

❊ ❊

Hugh Connolly's phone rang early at the mill that morning. "Hugh, this is Rory Grogan. We have a problem here."

"What's up, Rory?"

"We can't find the little girl."

"Oh, Lord," sighed Hugh. "What happened? She was right there beside us."

"Terry said she slipped away in the excitement. She must be hiding. That's all I can think of."

"But why would she hide from us? You don't believe that bullshit about her being Hannon's granddaughter, do you?"

"No, but those kids never really believe we'll keep our word to them. Besides, she's always been dirt under everybody's feet. Why should she trust us?"

"What are we going to do? Abramo keeps asking about her. He's restless and upset."

"I've put a couple of guys on it. She should turn up in a day or so. I'll keep after it."

"Thanks, Rory. If you find that girl, you're gonna make a lot of us rest easier."

At noon, Hugh went over to Isabella's house to have lunch with her. When he entered the hallway, she introduced him to the two old men who had boarded with her for eight years. Hugh shook the hand of each one. Both had been dozing in chairs in the living room.

After he greeted the two men, he followed Isabella into the kitchen. Then, when no one could see them, he grabbed her arm and gently pulled her toward him. She came willingly into his arms. As he kissed her, he tried to imagine if he had ever felt that way before. He knew he hadn't, and he wondered why. Aileen was his in body and spirit, and he loved her with his whole heart. So why did kissing Isabella seem like a new and wonderful experience? Her lips were warm and soft. Her body felt pliant and full in his arms. Was there anything in heaven as wonderful as this?

When they came apart, she was smiling, almost to herself. "So what's all the smiling about, young lady?" Hugh said.

She shook her head but didn't answer. "Come here," he said, grabbing her again and bringing her back into his arms. She was still smiling, and he loved it. He shook her slightly with both his arms locked behind her. "Tell me or I won't let you go."

"I can't tell you," she said.

"Why the hell not?"

"I'll be embarrassed."

"Let me be the judge of that."

"I know when you kissed me, you were thinking."

"Thinking what?"

"Something."

"About you maybe, huh?"

She shrugged. "Maybe about me," she said more seriously.

"Always about you," he said, still holding her.

"Is that true? No memories of someone else?"

He shook his head. "Only new memories. You must know that," he answered. Then she kissed him quickly and broke away, turning and walking toward the stove.

"Can't a hard-working man get something to eat around this place?" he said.

She stopped in her tracks, closed her eyes and snorted, and then turned back toward him. He grabbed hold of her again. This time she looked surprised and curious as she stayed in his arms looking up at his face. "Will you marry me in January?" he said.

She shrieked softly, almost a gasp, and smiled through her tears. She stepped back from him, still not taking her eyes from his. She just stared back at him as though not believing what she had heard him say. "Isabella? I don't ask that question every day."

"Oh, yes," she said, coming back into his arms and kissing him. "Oh, yes."

After a long and passionate kiss, when they were both breathless, he smirked and stepped back. "If I'd known I'd get that kind of reaction, I'd have asked you the first night I saw you."

"Shame on you, Hugh Connolly! This is a sacred thing."

He chuckled. "It's more sacred than you think, lass…because you make it so."

"I love you," she said.

"And I you, girl," he said. "Tell me—just in case I can't find out for myself before January—do you look as wonderful with no clothes on as you do with?"

She stepped away again and laughed, heartily this time, and reddened slightly. "Well, do you, girl? You might not know it, but these things are important." He held out his hand to her, and she came back into his arms. "So, what's your answer, before I give you half of everything I own?"

She was beaming now. Then she nodded reassuringly, blushing again. And as she did, he grabbed her and held her tight as he twirled her off her feet around the kitchen.

He kissed her quickly. "Damn, it would be nice to get some sustenance here…even just a crust of bread."

She huffed in mock disgust. "You keep interrupting me," she said. "I've set the table. Sit here."

They talked breezily through lunch, but she sensed something about his behavior that was different. "What is it you want to tell me, Hugh?" she said as she brought fresh coffee to the table.

"Jesus, you dagos are scary," he said. "How did you know I had something to tell you?"

She shrugged. "When you love someone, you know," she said.

"Rory Grogan called me this morning. They can't find the little girl."

"Piccina?"

"Yes. He thinks she's hiding."

"But she would have come with us. If she's hiding, it would only be to avoid the Hannons."

"You think she would have come with us?"

"Do you remember when I touched her face? And she turned her cheek toward my hand? I know no one had ever touched her like that before." Isabella faltered. There were tears in her eyes.

Hugh understood. And he also marveled at his own good fortune: finding this gentle creature, who in one gesture could reach out and touch the heart of a poor child. He gave her his handkerchief and held one of her hands. He stood up and walked around the table to her. She stood up, curious about what he would say. "My dear, I'm the luckiest man in the world," he said.

In all the commotion with cars full of police and an ambulance and curious neighbors and on-lookers, the orphaned children scattered into hiding. Piccina was very careful to leave as soon as she knew Abramo would be safe.

But she was troubled. Now she was alone again. And once, out of the corner of her eye, she saw the ominous figure of Dilworth staring at her. She was running with tears in her eyes because she knew now that Abramo would forget her when the rich man and the beautiful dark lady were with him. Rich people would visit him, and girls who were beautiful. He would eat good food. He would be clean, and his wounds would heal. He'd wear nice clothes and laugh with the beautiful rich girls he knew.

She stopped and found a small walkway between two buildings. In the back of one of the buildings was a door to an empty little room. She entered and sat down in the dark. For the first time in a long time she began to cry. It was strange. She had learned not to cry, because it never did her any good. In fact, crying made her vulnerable. Few of the other children would feel sorry for her. Few would care about her troubles, and most would make fun of her and find ways to hurt her.

But crying was bad in another way, too. She had come to know that tears were wet prayers that were never answered. Crying only reminded her that no matter how hard she tried, nothing good would happen to her. She had heard Tilly and some others talk about God. But God didn't want her to be happy. No matter how good she was, God didn't care.

She tried to like somebody else, but there was no one... except Tilly and Abramo. She helped him and cared for him. Now he was gone. And God would not know that she missed him. He would be with rich people, with rich ladies who looked like the pretty black-haired one. He would get better, and he would laugh again.

But the little girl he called Piccina would be here with Tilly and Dilworth and Joe and Jack, and God wouldn't care. And if she cried, God would not know it. If God wanted her to be happy, then he would have made Abramo remember her. He would have made Abramo love her.

But no one would ever love her. And someday, she'd be like Tilly, she thought. Someday she'd be a whore, and someday she'd smoke cigarettes, and someday she'd drink whiskey, and someday she'd be fat and smell funny and be always drunk.

And someday Abramo would have a beautiful brown-haired wife and beautiful brown-haired girls, and he would have a house and a car and would never come on this street again. Now Abramo was happy to be home, and he would forget the girl he called Piccina. He would find another girl, a clean one, one with curly hair and pretty eyes and new shoes. And he would love her. Someday he would forget the little black-haired girl who loved him. Someday he would not remember her name. And someday, always, there would never be anyone to love her.

Dilworth had a lantern, and he led a small gang of men back into the alley. He had followed her this time. He knew just where she was. Damn, he was right all along. That little bitch was up to something. She fed that goddamned dago and kept him out of harm's way, and nobody knew it. That bastard dago was the guy who broke Joe's arm, and she fed him. The dago was the one who stopped him from fucking the red-haired Irish girl, too—that kept him from getting on her after Joe was done. And Blackie kept him alive.

They quietly walked down the narrow corridor between the two buildings. Dilworth shaded the lantern so they wouldn't alert the girl but still had enough light to find the door. When they found the door, he gathered them silently outside it. And on his signal, they broke through.

Piccina screamed hysterically and would not stop. Finally, Dilworth ordered one of the men to gag her and carry her out. She was going back to Joe. He'd be glad to know that Dilworth was looking out for him. Jack would also learn how valuable a man Dilworth could be.

When they arrived in a back room of Hannon's AOH, they stopped. "Go up and get Joe," Dilworth said to one of the gang. "And be careful—just knock on his door, 'cause he's probably in there with one of them whores. Tell him I got a surprise for him."

A few minutes later, Joe came into the room, scowling and stuffing his shirttails into his pants. "So what the hell's your surprise, Dilworth?"

The men standing behind Dilworth parted, and Joe had a clear vision of Piccina, gagged, bound to a chair, and eyes flowing with tears.

"Well, saints be praised!" said Joe Hannon. "What have we here? A spy? A traitor? A lying little bitch!"

"She's all that and then some," Dilworth said. "She knew she did wrong because she left that place where she hid the dago and got her ass down to that narrow alley back of Delaney's flop. She was hiding in the dark when we found her."

"Just like she done something wrong, ain't it?" Joe said, staring at the little girl. "Take the gag out," he said as he advanced toward Piccina. "Take them bounds off her, too."

He stood tall over her. "So tell me, girlie, why'd you help out the guy who tried to do your Uncle Joe harm? Who broke my arm? A fucking dago?"

She didn't answer, and Joe was getting angry. There was always something about this Blackie that made his blood boil. She was not talkative or surly, she seldom laughed or smiled, but there was something about her face. More like her eyes—like she thought she was smarter than everybody else. She was sneaky, and she knew the alleys along Walnut Way better than any of the orphans who lived there. And she was hard to con, almost like a flophouse whore or a bar girl at the AOH.

"So tell me, Blackie, did you give that dago my food? Food that we gave you out of the goodness of our hearts? See this arm, how crooked it is? This is what that bastard dago did. The same bastard dago you took care of."

She had stopped crying and was just looking at him. She stared at him, straight into his eyes, as though she had nothing to fear. There was that look, Joe Hannon thought, that wise-ass, fuck-you, I don't owe you anything, ain't you terrible look.

"Why?" he said.

She didn't answer again, and instead he saw the look. It was the same look that he had seen from those bastards at the mill: Connolly, Tom, the Jew, Wroblewski, and especially the dago, Cardone. And now was he to get it from some fucking orphan who ate crumbs from his table?

Hannon's left hand slapped her, lashing out like a thick snake, and sent her sprawling across the room. Some of the men in the gang were nervous now. They had seen Joe Hannon in his uncontrolled rages before and knew the pattern. It was as though he heard voices as he acted, and each punch, each hit was just a prelude to something more brutal.

Some of the older ones had watched Joe's fury get so intense that he kicked and stomped and smashed things into his helpless victims. Some had seen him kill niggers they caught on the North Side, and some old drunken dagos, Greeks, or Germans who were found sitting on the front steps of the flophouses on the Way. The Ku Klux Klan always helped in getting rid of the bodies.

But this was different. This was Blackie. All of them knew her, and she was only a little girl.

Blackie stood up after she rolled against the wall. Her lip was cut and bleeding, puffed already by Hannon's blow. She still didn't speak; she didn't cry. And still she had the look. This time Joe feinted as though he was going to slap her again, and she ducked. Then Hannon kicked her and caught her with the broad side of his shoe, fully on one buttock, and sent her crashing into the wall. This time there was blood pouring into her eyes, down her forehead, down her cheek. Now there was another cut on her mouth, and one on her nose, which was swollen and bloody.

Now everyone, even Dilworth, had had enough. None of them were interested in witnessing another of Joe's ritual assassinations. Even the legendary Jack Hannon had never beat a child to death, and especially not one of the orphans of the Way. They were almost like pets to the members of the gang, and as close as anything they had to family.

"Joe," Dilworth said, putting himself in front of Hannon. "Don't ruin a good thing."

"What the fuck you talking about?" said Hannon.

"Look at her, Joe," Dilworth said. "In about five years, she's gonna look good. She may even have some tits. You know what a good-looking twelve-year-old can bring at one of our cathouses here? There are guys that'll pay fifty bucks a night to fuck her first; you know that."

Hannon glanced at him. "Yeah," he muttered. Joe was always trying to prove himself a worthy successor to his father. The gang would be his someday. Lately, after his loss to Abramo, he began to posture as a man with a good head for money. Using Blackie in the whorehouses would be a smart move.

The little girl stood up again, her eyes blinking because of the blood pouring into them, her nose bleeding, but she wasn't crying. As distorted as her facial features were by the cuts and the swelling and the blood, she still had that look. For a moment, Hannon almost lost control again. He was about to go after her to inflict one last blow to salve his anger. "Joe, remember, you don't want to screw her up. She'll be a cash cow for quite a few years…if you don't make her ugly."

Hannon, in his dull rage, wrestled with his common sense. What Dilworth said was true. And he had already given her two blows she would remember a long time. "Yeah…all right. But she's gonna be taught a lesson, Dilworth. You take her down in that little cellar where they used to keep the old beer kegs. I'm gonna make sure she remembers this. A few weeks in there will teach her that you can't fuck with Joe Hannon."

Then he left the room, striding through the gang members who were relieved and fascinated by his callous, cruel performance.

"Go get Tilly," Dilworth muttered to the gang. "She has to be fixed up a little before she goes into that cellar."

Chapter 9

KIERAN'S DAYS SEEMED LONGER and grimmer since Molly's troubles began and their world seemed to come apart. The boys were morose and quiet; Molly was distant and withdrawn, speaking in short sentences and only then in response to direct questions.

As he walked through the Reid Pavilion toward her suite, Kieran was met by Dr. Shanfield. He was led into a small conference room and asked to be seated on a couch. The doctor sat opposite him in a large leather easy chair.

"Mr. Harty, I've checked the surgical incisions, and everything seems to be healing nicely. I changed the dressings, and there's no evidence of bleeding or infection. For a woman of her age, there's every reason to believe her recovery will be rapid and...uneventful."

"Thank you, Doctor, that's good to hear," Kieran said softly.

The surgeon noticed that Kieran was not as heartened by the news as he expected. In fact, he looked troubled. "But you're worried about something else, aren't you?" said the surgeon.

"Yeah," sighed Kieran, avoiding the doctor's gaze.

"Her state of mind after the assault?" Kieran nodded. "Mr. Harty, I have not had many rape cases in recent years, but in all the cases—every one—the women were depressed and tormented by the event. As men, we can't imagine the pain and sorrow and sometimes even guilt these poor women feel when something like this happens. She'll need patience and, most of all, love from the people she cares about. Her body will heal more easily than those invisible spiritual wounds left by the assault.

"In a way, she has to heal herself. She has to come back to us, but in her own good time. We can't force it. All you can do is be what you have always been to her: forbearing at first, but normal, accepting her back into your lives. Remember, no doctor or medicine can heal the wounds in her heart. You—all her loved ones—are the medication she needs."

Kieran glanced back at him and nodded in agreement. "Thanks, Doctor."

"She'll be here for a while yet. We'll be checking on her surgery, but we'll also be monitoring her mental state and trying to observe any signs of serious trouble. I'll be in touch soon. Remember, you're what she needs. All of you will help heal her."

Later, after a difficult discourse with Molly, Kieran sat alone in the suite. Hugh and Isabella had visited earlier, but they got no more response from Molly than anyone else. Her brothers tried to engage her, but they, too, failed. Even Ross couldn't get her to talk freely.

It was very quiet that evening. Molly had drifted off to sleep, so Kieran decided to go down to Abramo's room. As he entered, he could see Hugh and Isabella and a huge Italian man, almost as tall as he, but far heavier. He remembered seeing him in Abramo's room before, though they had not been formally introduced.

Hugh introduced the man as Abramo's uncle. They shook hands and exchanged pleasantries for a few minutes. Then Kieran walked over to Abramo's bed. "How do you feel, son?" he asked.

"I'm okay," Abramo answered. "How is your daughter?" he said, not smiling or bright.

Kieran was getting used to tepid reactions from these two patients. "Her wounds are healing fine," he said. Abramo glanced at him knowingly. He understood the words left unsaid about Molly's mental state. "Mr. Cardone—"

"Abramo," he said.

"Abramo…I hope you know how much I appreciate your saving my daughter's life." The three other people in the room were absolutely quiet, listening intently to what Kieran might say. "I owe you a debt of gratitude forever. And, Mr. Cardone, I want you to know that you are welcome in my house always—an honored guest—from this day forward. And if there's anything I can ever do for you, if I know what it is, it will be done."

"Thank you, sir. But I really was late to…keep them from your daughter."

"You put your life at risk to save a stranger, my daughter. That was as honorable a thing as I can imagine."

Abramo shrugged. "Thank you," he said again.

"Well, get some rest, lad. I'll look in on you tomorrow. I hope to see you walking around here soon."

"Maybe tomorrow. That's what the nurses say."

Kieran squeezed Abramo's forearm gently and walked toward the doorway. He stopped to talk to Hugh, who motioned for him to walk outside so they could talk more freely. "So, how's my niece?" Hugh said.

"She's about as talkative as this kid," he said, gesturing over his shoulder toward Abramo's room.

"They still haven't found the little girl," said Hugh, "and he can't stand being cooped up in here if she's not with him. Hell, he's talking about going back up there to look for her himself."

"And Molly's still feeling terrible because she can't have any kids. I swear, the worst of it is the kids, even more so than the rape or the surgery."

"I believe it," said Hugh. "She's got a mother's instinct. That was going to be her life."

"You know what she called herself yesterday?" Kieran said with tears in his eyes. "'Damaged goods.'"

"Jesus Christ," Hugh muttered.

"I think she feels guilty...responsible somehow."

"Rory Grogan told me he's in charge of both these cases, Molly's and Abramo's. He wants to talk to Molly soon to see if she can identify the rapist."

"He can try any time. I don't know how cooperative she'll be."

Abramo had been sitting up for two days. The cuts on his head and neck had been stitched and were healing after the surgery. The slashes on his knees and shoulders were patched and braced so he would heal properly. The concussion was healing; there were headaches, but no loss of motor skills or memory or vision or hearing impairment. Even the nurses were surprised at the remarkable progress he had made. He briefly walked around his room and in the hallway outside his door.

Toward the end of the second week of his recovery, he was sitting in his room in mid-afternoon alone. He had been reading some of the books Isabella had brought him, but often it seemed he couldn't concentrate. His mind would wander. He wondered about Molly and Piccina. He wasn't aware of any visitors to either suite today, since most visitors to one of the suites were usually visitors to the other.

He put his book down and stood up. He steadied himself and walked to the mirror. Presentable enough, he thought. Quietly, he made his way out to the hall and walked down to the small placard on the door: Miss Máille Harty.

The door was open, so he walked into the anteroom. At the far end, there were another two doors, one of them leading to a room with a hospital bed. He saw her move, so he walked hesitantly into the room. "Signorina?" he said softly. There was no reaction; she had been crying. "Signorina?" he said again.

She frowned and then pushed herself up on her elbows. For a moment they just stared at each other as though they were each trying to remember who the other one was. "How are you, signorina?" he said softly, noticing the red eyes.

She nodded. "I'm okay. How are you?" Her tone was cold.

"They may release me early next week."

"I haven't heard when I'll be released."

They stared at each other again, each not knowing what to say. "Are you eating well?" said Abramo.

"Well enough," she said. Again silence. From time to time she would look directly at him and turn away. He did not advance any closer than where he stood, about six feet away from her.

"Well, signorina, I must go. I'm glad you are healing properly. Perhaps I will see you again." She didn't respond.

He turned and started for the doorway.

"Mr. Cardone," she called to his back, "thank you…for saving my life."

"I'm sorry I didn't…" He stopped, a pained expression crossing his face. "I'm sorry I was late."

She was silent again. They looked at each other for a few moments; there seemed nothing more to say. He turned and walked away.

Back in his room, Abramo sat in a chair that was near a window overlooking the downtown. He didn't expect the meeting between him and the girl to be so formal and disheartening. For a few minutes he picked up a book, but he soon put it down. Finally, he put his face in his hands and tried to cope with the feelings that roiled within him. He couldn't keep back the tears that gushed forth into his hands as they shielded his face.

Why was God still torturing him? What manner of God would bless him above all other men, give him Angelina and a baby daughter, and then snatch them both away? Why give him anything at all if the loss of it brought such anguish? And why, if there were not a capricious and malevolent God, would he be alive today after saving the life of a girl who was now so unhappy? And why would his own life be spared in a place where mortal danger was all around him only to lose the angelic little girl who saved him? Where was she? If she were the messenger of God in his life, why was she so poor and wretched, dirty and starving, longing for love and a gentle touch?

What was this give and take? The beautiful Irish girl, who should be grateful for her life, was so tormented she could barely talk to him—as though he were the one who had hurt her, as though the memory of his face was inextricably bound to the vision of what her childless life would be.

He sobbed quietly and held his face against the light of the room. His hands were the dam against the tears that flowed so easily and quietly. Just then, Isabella walked into the room, followed by Hugh. Abramo didn't hear them as they came, and in a moment, Isabella held him in her arms as he cried again against her shoulder. "Oh, my dear heart," she said softly in Italian as she clung to him.

Hugh stood beside them with his hand on Abramo's shoulder. They stayed that way for several minutes until his sobbing subsided. "We'll find her, son," Hugh said softly.

The maid, Mary, came into Anetta Reid's sitting room. "Mr. Connolly's down in the library, ma'am," she said.

"Tell him I'll be right down…and bring some tea and cakes."

Anetta began to look forward to these frequent visits from Hugh Connolly. Ostensibly, they were for a report on the two young people, but Hugh seemed to like talking to her, and she began to feel warm and maternal toward him, especially now that his life was involved with the Italian girl and Abramo.

As she entered the library, Hugh stood to greet her. "How are you, Mrs. Reid?" he said.

"I'm fine, Hugh." She sat down a fixed him with a firm look. "Hugh, my name is Anetta, and few people have called me that since Anthony died. You and I have become good friends...do you think you can call me that?"

Hugh looked at her, marveling at the changes that had occurred within her in the last few months. Surely more than he understood, perhaps more than she understood. "I would be honored to call you by name...in private, like we are now. But in public I'd probably just revert to Mrs. Reid. Is that okay?"

"It's fine. Now, tell me about our two patients."

He shook his head and didn't look happy about what he had to report. "It's the same story. Physically, both are young and healthy enough to recover quickly. But for as much as they progress physically, they seem to get worse emotionally."

"Both of them? Still?"

"My niece is so despondent, she hardly talks. She thinks of herself as 'damaged goods,' and since she can't have children, she feels that no man would ever want her. I'm afraid she'll never trust a man enough to think he would want her just for herself."

Anetta shook her head. "And what about Abramo?" she said quietly.

"He's another one. He waits every day to hear if they've found the little girl."

"And you've heard nothing?"

"Rory Grogan has assigned two men to Walnut Way, but they've found no trace of her. We don't even know if she's still in the district. The Hannons, of course, say they know nothing of her whereabouts and piously accuse the police of not working hard enough to find her."

"So Abramo's despondent, too?"

"Yes. Isabella and I walked into his room last night and he was alone, crying. He longs for the little girl...and when he tries to talk to Molly, she'll have nothing to do with him."

"He was married once, didn't you say?"

"Yes. He's a widower," he said with a wry smile. "They seem to be all over these days."

"How did his wife die?"

Hugh looked up at her and started to speak but didn't. He shook his head slightly, as though restraining himself from telling.

Anetta suddenly knew that she would not like what she would hear, but now she had to know. "How did she die, Hugh?" she said softly.

"Abramo was impressed into the Italian army. Soldiers from an insurgent group came into the town while he was away..."

"Go on."

Hugh took a deep breath. "His uncle told me this story...They raped and murdered his wife and their baby daughter. Abramo never saw the little girl. She was born and dead before he had a chance to return home. All this happened over five years ago."

"Oh, my Lord," Anetta whispered as she brought her hand-kerchief to her face. "My Lord, that poor young man. I never knew he was living with such terrible memories."

"And now he wants the little girl who saved his life, that nobody else wants, and either she is being kept away from him or is hiding. And I think, Anetta, he wants Molly too, and she will hardly talk to him."

Anetta wiped her eyes again. Her voice seemed strained and tense. "That poor boy," she whispered. "I had no idea."

"It's something he never talks about."

Mary came in with tea and small cakes. Anetta poured two cups and gave one to Hugh. He enjoyed the warmth of it after the cold air outside had chilled his spirits, already depressed, as he rode home from the mill.

"Hugh? Do you really think Abramo cares for Molly?"

"I think so," Hugh said. "And, you know, Molly is one of the sweetest and most warm and gentle girls imaginable, and yet something comes over her, especially when she sees him, and she talks to him like he's some alien who will do her nothing but harm." He stopped to think about what he was saying. "So basically we have three people who love each other and who, for reasons nobody seems to understand, can't be together. Molly doesn't trust Abramo to love her for herself, the little girl who saved Abramo from certain death can't be found, and the love that those two kids could give that little girl would be a joy to behold. And yet none of them can get near each other."

They were both silent and thoughtful for several seconds, each drinking tea and minding their own thoughts. "Hugh," Anetta said finally, "I'm going to have a meeting here on Thursday night. I'd like you to be here, too. Bring Isabella if you can."

"A meeting?"

"Yes. I want to get to the bottom of this. That little girl is the key to the happiness of three people, herself included. After all Abramo's been through and all Molly's been through, they deserve each other, and the life that that little girl can give them."

The next night, three doctors came together to see Abramo late in the evening. "Mr. Cardone," the chief of staff said, "we think you're doing fine. The pace of your recovery is excellent. At this rate, you should be back to normal in a few months. Just make an appointment to visit us here at the hospital once a week, and we'll monitor your progress. Mrs. Reid has been apprised of your condition and she's pleased. If you have any trouble—such as severe headaches—please let us know immediately. If you feel okay tomorrow, you may go home. I've been told that your land-lady is anxious to nurse you back to health herself. You'll probably recover faster at home than here."

Abramo took a deep breath. "Thank you for all you've done. Thanks to everyone."

Again the pavilion was quiet. Abramo stacked his few books and clothes in a suitcase. He packed his shaver and toothbrush into a small overnight kit. He was ready to leave.

He thought of Molly, as he did most hours when he was alone. She was healing also, physically. The swelling on her face was gone. The scratches were less raw and sanguineous. She was as beautiful as he imagined she would be when he painted her in his mind's eye without the bruises, the cuts, and the swelling. He had been to see her daily since their first awkward meeting, and each meet-ing was as reluctantly civil as the first. She was uncommunicative and distant. He exchanged a few words with her and then he left. Tonight would be the last time he'd see her.

As he walked down the short hallway to her room, Abramo thought of how strange his life had become. Of all the women in this world other than Angelina, this was the only one he was attracted to, the only one he cared about. And yet, as easy and natural as it was with Angelina, it was awkward and tense and uncertain with this girl. And he had given up on God. If God had a plan, it was a mystery to him; if God had a plan, it would be like all the others, designed to lead him to envision happiness and then watch helplessly as the dream was shattered. Molly would be wretched; he would be wretched; and Piccina, wherever she was, would be wretched. He was convinced now that some people were permitted to know happiness only to feel more intense grief when it was taken away.

He walked into the anteroom quietly, through the door that led to Molly's bed. Inside, he was startled to see Kieran sitting in the large easy chair beside her bed. The room was nearly dark. Kieran had left a small light on only to be able to move around the room. "Abramo," Kieran said, "how are you?"

"Okay, signore. I'm going home tomorrow."

Kieran stood up and smiled at the young man. "I'm glad for you, son. I wish you all the best."

"How's the signorina?" he said.

"Her name is Molly, lad, and I want you to call her that." He sighed. "Her wounds are healing…on her body, that is. Otherwise, she's just the same. Come, I'll wake her."

"No, please. Let her rest. She doesn't have to see me."

"All she does is rest. It won't hurt her a bit to see you." He turned to his daughter, who he wasn't sure was really sleeping. "Moll? You have a visitor."

She opened her eyes but made no movement. "Hello, sign… Molly, how are you?" Abramo said hesitantly.

"I'm okay. How are you?" she said softly, with no brightness or warmth.

"Abramo got some good news tonight, Moll," her father said. "He's going home tomorrow."

"Oh?" she said, smiling half-heartedly. "That's nice. I'm glad for you."

"I've come to say good-bye…and to wish you well. Do you know when you'll go home?"

"Maybe in a few days, the doctors said…they're not sure."

"Well…God be with you, signorina," he said. "I wish you health…and a happy life."

He turned abruptly, walked toward the anteroom, and out into the hall. "Abramo," Kieran called to his back, "wait a minute. Please."

Abramo stopped and turned back to him but said nothing. "Abramo, I'm so sorry about the way my girl treats you. This is not her true character. She's a kind and decent girl who never tries to hurt anyone. I know she doesn't seem to care if she hurts you. I'm sorry for that. All I can say is that she is not that way."

"I know that, signore. I have seen the real Molly. I know what she is like. I'm sorry for her anguish. I wish I could do something to help her."

"Son, all you've ever done is help her. She would not be in that bed and healing if it were not for you. And I'm ever grateful. Please come to my house when she returns home. I'm sure there will be a time when she'll know how much you deserve a good welcome."

✻ ✻

Later that night, Hugh walked into the AOH. Kieran saw him at the bar and motioned for him to sit at a table. Then he joined him. "So how are things, boyo?" said Hugh.

Kieran shrugged. "She's healing fine. You have to look hard at her to know she'd been beaten up, wouldn't you? She looks like she did before."

"But...?"

"But she won't talk to anybody...me, Ross." He rolled his glass between his palms. "Abramo came down to say good-bye. He's coming home tomorrow, right?"

"Yeah. Isabella and his uncle are going to get him."

"Well, the poor kid's been over to see her a dozen times, and she won't give him the time of day. Hell, she acts like he's the rapist."

"Yeah." Hugh sighed. "That kid just can't make a buck. They can't find the little girl who saved his life, and the girl whose life he saved won't talk to him. I hope he doesn't like the taste of booze 'cause what's happened to him will drive anyone to it."

Kieran didn't say anything for a few minutes. Then he said, "Hugh, I'm going to give you some money for that kid. He won't be able to work for a while."

"It's all right, boyo. I still have him on the payroll, though he doesn't know it. As far as I'm concerned, he was doing company business and got hurt on duty. All Anetta Reid would have to hear is that we laid Abramo off without pay." He chuckled. "Jesus, the whole executive staff would be fired."

"But I have to give him something," Kieran said.

"What he wants, you can't give him."

Kieran glanced at him in surprise. Hugh made no sound, but nodded. Kieran leaned back in his chair. "You mean Molly?"

"I'd bet my next paycheck on it."

"But how do you know?"

"I just know."

Kieran looked away for a moment, his thoughts his own. "Has he said anything to you about her?"

"No. But what do you think makes him keep coming back to her? Even when she will barely talk to him?"

Chapter 10

HUGH WAS SUDDENLY HAVING trouble managing his life. He hadn't been involved in precinct politics in weeks. He'd begun to let his work at the mill back up on him, and he would stay late into the evenings to try to get caught up-to-date. He longed to see Isabella every night, but because of his responsibilities to Molly and Abramo, he would see her for minutes at a time a few odd nights a week. He had visited the hospital almost daily when Molly and Abramo were there, he stayed late at the mill, he visited Anetta Reid, and he visited Isabella.

He had not seen Kieran in two days. So, he stopped at the AOH on the way home from work. Inside, it was crowded for a Tuesday night. Kieran was at the bar helping Eddie fill the drink orders. Hugh was concerned about his old friend. Kieran looked drawn and tired. "How're you doing, kid?" he asked when he got to the bar.

Kieran snorted. "Trying to make a buck," he said.

"How's Molly?"

"She's okay, I guess. She's hardly been out of her room in three days."

"So, she's no better?"

"Not a bit." He sloshed whiskey into a glass and shoved it toward a patron. "Abramo has been over here three nights. She refuses to see him. She hardly talks to the boys…even Ross." He rubbed his thumb against the whiskey bottle and his voice grew soft. "She's bitter, and I'm afraid she's going to think all men are alike."

Hugh rubbed the back of his neck and let out a sharp breath. "This is crazy. I've never seen so many good people be their own worst enemies. This is the damnedest turn of events."

"I wish I knew what to do," said Kieran. "I feel so bad for her." His mouth thinned. "I can see her doing more harm to herself, brooding about what a horrible life she's going to have."

"Can I talk to her, Kieran?"

"Of course you can. Why do you have to ask?"

"Because I may tell her some truths she doesn't want to hear."

Kieran considered the statement for a moment and then nodded. "You're the only one in the world she might listen to."

Hugh stood up and brushed off his vest and pants. "Well, son, we're going to find out soon." He walked to the entrance of the house at the back wall of the AOH and trudged up the stairs. What would he say to her? At the top of the stairs he turned left without hesitation down the hallway toward Molly's room. He had spent many a night at the house in a back bedroom, especially after Aileen died.

He stopped at the room, knocked, hesitated a few seconds, then opened the door and walked in. Molly was startled to see him suddenly in the middle of her room. She was sitting in a large, old stuffed chair, reading a book by the light of a floor lamp. "Uncle Hugh?"

"How are you, Máille?"

"I'm all right."

"The hell you are."

She was startled by his gruff tone. He, above all people, never spoke to her in any way that was rough or offensive. "I'm getting well," she said weakly.

"You can talk that way to other people, my girl, but you can't buffalo me. You're getting worse, and you damn well know it. Your body's healing, and your heart's turning to stone."

She had tears in her eyes now. Yet she grew resentful when she heard men talk of things they never had to experience and heartaches they never had to bear. "You don't know anything about my healing."

"You're healing in spite of yourself," said Hugh. "I know you're doing everything you can to turn yourself into the banshee that rapist hoped you'd be. You hurt your dad, you hurt your brothers,"—he took a deep breath and said more quietly—"and you hurt the man who saved your life."

She thumped her book on her lap. "How did I hurt him? I was civil to him. I thanked him. What more does he want?"

"You know it's more than civility that he wants."

She hesitated for a few seconds. "I know what he wants," she said, voice quavering. "But he doesn't understand that I can't give him what he wants."

"The hell you can't. You just won't give yourself a chance…or him."

She was crying now, arguing through tears. "A chance to have my heart broken?" she said shrilly. "To let him think that I can give him what any other woman can, only to have to tell him some day that I can't have children…and then watch him walk away from me for someone younger, and fertile, someone normal? Does he know, as I know, that every person on the East Side will know that I've been used? That he's just the second one in line? Do you think none of that will matter to him?"

"First of all, did he ever treat you like he wants to use you? There are whores all over town that he can use. So, why does he still come over every day? Because you're so damned pleasant? You're so convinced he'd abandon you just because you can't have children that you're willing to deny him—and yourself—any chance for happiness."

"Happiness? He can't be denied it if he never had it to begin with."

Hugh felt his anger begin to seep out of him. "Máille, this is the one side of you I thought I'd never see, this self-pity…or is it self-contempt? You don't have any idea of what he wants, and you deliberately keep yourself from knowing it because you're afraid he might walk out on you."

He drew up a footstool next to her chair and sat on it, leaning in close to her. "You know what he wants? Why he kept coming to your room at the hospital? Why he comes here every night only to have you slam the door in his face?" She stared at him in silence. "He wants you, not children. He knows you can't have children."

Suddenly, she was stricken. "What?" she said, sitting upright in the chair as though poised to stand up.

"He knew from the beginning. His uncle heard your dad and me talking, and he told Abramo. It was an innocent bit of truth." She turned her head away from him and closed her eyes. "And I'll tell you something else you don't know," he said. "When he was married, he had a child. And did you know that his wife didn't just die of disease in Italy? She was killed." He waited until she met his gaze before continuing. "She was raped and strangled by marauding soldiers when he was in the army far away from their village. And the child was killed along with her mother. They were dead and buried before he ever knew about it. He never saw the baby born, and he never saw her or her mother die." He took her hand in both of his and squeezed it. "This man lost a wife—and a child—and still comes to you, of all people, knowing all the while you can never give him children."

Molly shrieked and began to sob. She pulled her hand free and covered her face, turning away from Hugh's gaze. In a few seconds, Ross and Paul were at the door. Hugh waved them away. He stood up and tried to turn her toward him. She struggled against him, but finally relented and fell into his arms crying. "Oh, my God, Uncle Hugh, I didn't know. I was just feeling sorry for myself."

"And well you might, my dear. And well you might," he muttered.

They stayed together and talked for another half hour. When Hugh left her, he walked back down to the tavern.

"Have you done any good, Hugh Connolly?" Kieran said.

"When you hold a mirror up to someone, it hurts. We'll know soon enough," Hugh said wearily. "I'll see you tomorrow, huh?"

After Hugh left, Kieran sat in the tavern waiting for two lone drinkers to leave. He was tired and didn't want any more customers that night. He started from his lethargy when Abramo walked into the room. "Signor Harty, how is Molly?" he asked as he approached the bar.

Kieran thought for a few seconds, staring into the face of the young Italian. Maybe this was the time to find out how well she really was. Maybe this was the time to do something different. "Come with me, son," he said, standing up and urging Abramo toward the doorway to the house.

Abramo seemed puzzled, but he followed Kieran up the stairs. At the top of the stairs, Ross and Paul met them. "What's going on, Dad?" they said in unison.

Kieran didn't answer. Instead, he pointed down the hallway. "It's the second door on the right. Knock once, then walk in," he said.

"Daddy, what in God's name are you doing?" Ross said.

"This man has seen your sister's nakedness and has never once dishonored her—in word or deed. He has more right to speak to her than anyone. He saved her life."

Abramo hesitated, put off by the question the boys asked their father. "Go on, man," Kieran said, and Abramo cautiously started down the hallway. As he walked away, Kieran turned toward his two sons. "Now, you boys either go to your rooms or come downstairs with me...but whatever you do, leave them alone."

Abramo's heart was pounding as he reached the door. He knocked, hesitated, and then entered the room. She was sitting, curled up on the chair, her eyes red and tear-filled, her face streaked with the dry traces of salty tears on her cheeks. She didn't look up or show any sign of acknowledging his presence.

He sat opposite her on the bed facing her from about four feet away. He said nothing. Instead, he watched her intently as she sat, still not making eye contact with him. He was amazed that she didn't protest, didn't even react to his intrusion into her most private chamber. They sat for almost ten minutes saying nothing. From time to time, she would shudder from crying and take deep breaths, but the crying was silent, and the tears flowed in silence.

Finally, she spoke, without looking at him, without lifting her head from the back side of the chair. "Well, he accomplished what he came for." She sighed.

"Who?" he said.

"Uncle Hugh."

"Was he here tonight?"

"You know he was here."

"Why would I know that?"

"Didn't you come with him?"

He frowned, perplexed by her questions. "I came alone, a few minutes ago."

Her eyes narrowed. "And you didn't know he was coming?"

"But why would I?"

"You didn't talk with him about what he was going to say to me?"

"To you? Why would he ask me about what to say to you?"

"And you didn't plan this?"

"Plan what? Signorina, I don't know what has happened, but I did nothing with Il Signor Connolly."

"And you just decided to come here?"

"I have come for the last three nights, as you well know," he said. "Il Signor Connolly knew nothing of that."

Finally, she raised her head and looked directly at him. She studied his face. He really didn't plan anything with Uncle Hugh, she thought. He was telling the truth; he looked that way every time he talked. He was always telling the truth. "Why do you keep coming back after the way I treat you?" she said softly.

He sighed. "I don't know."

"I'm sorry I acted the way I did...to you especially. I'm thankful for your saving me."

"I know," he said.

She stared at him. He avoided her gaze. He sat on the bed looking down at the floor, or around the room. "You know I can't have children?" she said.

"Yes," he said.

"You always knew?"

"Yes."

"And that doesn't matter to you?" she asked, studying his movements and body language.

He hesitated for a few seconds, unsure where their conversation was going. "No," he said.

"Why didn't you tell me about your wife and baby?"

"It would have done you no good," he said, looking directly at her now.

"And yet you let me say the things I did, act like I did..."

"You were hurt. And you were sad," he said. "It was all right."

She looked away. "Abramo," she said, using his name for the first time, "I don't know how I will be when another man touches me—"

"You will be as you always would be," he said and paused, "if it is an act of love."

In a moment, she was out of the chair and in his arms, crying again. He kissed her forehead, then her eyes, then gently her lips. He had forgotten the wonderful feel of a woman in his arms, but this feeling was new somehow. This was a feeling only Molly could create. This was the new gift that she brought to his life.

She released her hold of him and stepped back away from his arms. "You know that everyone who…" She looked down and put her hand to her forehead. "That everyone who sees us will know that I was first had by someone else, not you?"

"Is there no difference between those who raped you and me?" He placed his hands on her shoulders. "You did not give yourself to those men. They beat you, tore your undergarments, and forced themselves into you. That was not an act of love."

"So, your not being the first doesn't matter?"

"With me, it would be your first act of love."

"Love?"

He smiled slightly. "Would someone who does not love you take the abuse you give me?"

She smiled, a full wide smile that lit up her face and made it beam. "You love me?"

He shrugged playfully. "I can't help myself. Maybe if you loved me back, it would help."

"But I do love you," she said, still smiling. Then, just as suddenly, she grew serious again. "I had to believe you were real and not a mirage, Abramo—conjured by the devil to give me hope, let me dream, and then vanish. Uncle Hugh told me to learn to trust you."

"Your uncle is a good, wise man."

"Now will you say it? Tell me that you love me?"

"I love you, and have loved you from the first moment I saw you."

Then she was in his arms again, this time kissing him fully and passionately. When they separated, he said, "I can't do this. This bedroom is too great a temptation. Let's go downstairs."

She took his hand and turned toward the door, but faltered slightly. He caught her but winced as he held her. "We are still not completely healed."

"We'll go slow," she said. "Just hold my hand, will you?"

Kieran sat brooding at a table in the AOH, wondering if his tactic—letting Abramo walk into Molly's room—made sense or was foolhardy. Maybe the boys were right to be outraged. Maybe Molly would resent it more. He had excused himself by believing that it was a reasonable response to crumbling circumstances.

The bar was empty, and he was all alone in the quiet, dim light of the AOH. Then he heard voices, vibrant, fresh, and joyful—voices with the musical tone of a young girl who he knew once to be happy and glowing and beautiful.

Molly walked through the door followed by Abramo, who was holding her hand. They looked happy, and they looked like they shared a secret. "Daddy, we have something to tell you," Molly said.

Two days later, Conor was going to drive the new truck out on its first deliveries. Molly asked if he would give her a ride to the boarding house where Abramo lived. Conor was glad to do anything that Molly wanted because he thought by degrees he'd assuage the guilt he felt over what happened to her.

On the way, Conor said, "You really like this guy, Moll?"

"Yes, Conor," she said.

"But them dagos are so different from us."

"They're not that much different. The have the same love of family and friends as we do." She touched his forearm with her hand. "Give him a chance, Conor. I know you'll like him."

"Yeah," sighed Conor, agonized at the prospect of having a brother-in-law who was a dago. The guys at the Crab Inn would have a jolly time with him on that one. "Moll? How long are you gonna stay? I'm coming back this way around two o'clock. I can stop to get you."

"Well, that would be fine. I might be staying longer, but it would be nice to know that I have a certain ride," she said.

When he left her off at the house, she rang the doorbell. Isabella answered the door, startled to see the lovely young girl on her doorstep. "Hello, Mrs. Chianese, I'm Molly Harty…Remember me? A friend of Abramo's?"

Both women were struck by the beauty of the other. Isabella had always admired the glorious combination of red hair and green eyes and the milky white skin that Molly had. She believed that all men in their hearts desired such women, so beautiful and confident, so intelligent and poised, so fluent and natural with the American language.

"Signorina Harty, welcome. Please come in."

Molly entered the old but spotless house. It reminded her of the rectory at St. Mary's, polished wood everywhere, a statue of the Blessed Virgin, and soft comfortable chairs scattered about the rooms with end tables and floor lamps nearby.

When they were inside, the two women looked at each other and seemed awkward together. They both started to speak at the same time, then laughed. There was so much for them to say that they hardly seemed to know how to begin. Both knew that each was going to have a large part in the life of the other.

They stared quietly, their eyes and other senses drinking in all that they saw of each other. Isabella came toward Molly and hugged her, kissing her on one cheek. "Your uncle has told me much about you." Isabella touched her cheek with her hand, and Molly felt the warmth of her spirit go deep within her. "You are most welcome here, my dear."

Just then, Abramo came into the room. He was startled to see Molly and more surprised to see the two women in what had been an embrace. "Signorina Harty has paid us a visit, Abramo. You may go into the little room. I'll close the door so you can talk."

"But you don't have to—" Molly began. Isabella interrupted her.

"Yes, I do. You will want to talk. These doors will close, and you can have privacy." She turned to Abramo and said in Italian, "Take your lady to the room. I will make coffee and bring it to you."

The moment he began to speak, Isabella waved his words away. Then she turned to Molly and clasped her hand. "This house is your house, my dear."

Isabella escorted them into the little room, the same room where Hugh told her he loved her. Abramo was troubled, and Isabella knew it. If anyone could comfort him in his travail, it would be this lovely

Irish girl. She nodded to them both and left the room, closing the door behind her.

Molly didn't expect him to be so melancholy. He had told her only two nights ago that he loved her, and said the words that were the most joyous and musical she had ever heard in her life. Yet, today the troubles of the world seemed to haunt him. Even the beauty of their love was not enough to assuage the longing he felt for the little girl. She had prior claim to his heart. Without the little girl, the love between Molly and Abramo was not solely Molly's to nurture. In spite of all the magic Molly could work in Abramo's life, and though Abramo loved Molly and would live a life of happiness with her, Molly knew that the little girl was the key to the final perfection of their love.

They stood apart. She held a small purse in both hands before her. "How are you, my love?" she whispered. He nodded, looking away from her. He wasn't ready to face her. He had not known she was coming that morning. "Please, my dear, I can't stand to see you like this. Please? Let me share this with you."

"There is nothing you can do, except to be here so I can hear your voice," he said, still not making eye contact with her.

"They'll find her, Abramo. They'll bring her back to you."

He lowered his head and groaned softly. "Where is she, Molly? Why does God do these things? Let us see the happiness and blessings of our lives, and then keep them away from us? She needs us, we need her. Where is she?"

Molly crossed the few steps between them. "Abramo, I think God knows what we need. Look at us. He knew before we did that we needed each other. You know she's meant for no one but you—for us. We'll find her."

Isabella brought coffee and sweet rolls. She glanced at Molly and knew she was having a hard time. "They will find her, Abramo," Isabella said, caressing his forehead. He said nothing. She turned to Molly. "Your uncle will come here this evening. Will you stay for supper with us?"

Molly turned back to Abramo. "I'm not sure, signora. But thank you."

Abramo reached for Molly's hand as Isabella left. He looked at her for a moment and smiled weakly. "Maybe they will find her," he said.

"How are you feeling? How's your shoulder…and your neck?" she said.

"They are better each day. Soon I will finish Brendan's frame."

"What?"

"The picture frame for Mrs. Reid. Did you not know?"

She shook her head. "No. Can I see it?"

"Yes. But how are you feeling? How's your…" He stopped, and for the first time in days, he smiled. "I don't know how to say it…that part of you," he said in amazement.

She also smiled. It was so strange for her, being playful with someone she loved. It was so different from being playful with Ross or one of her other brothers, or her father or Uncle Hugh. This kind of play was better; this was total communication. It was almost like a touch or caress. There was no comparable feeling when it was done with someone else. "I don't know how to say it either," she said. "Maybe we'll ask the doctor."

"You ask him," he said, smiling. "Do you want to see it? It's downstairs."

"Yes. Will you help me down the stairs?"

"Of course. Let's go."

Outside, the room was empty, so they walked to the basement entrance and slowly went down the stairs. She would stop occasionally, and Abramo would turn back to see that she was all right. Once, when he turned toward her, she kissed him. He smiled. "Did I kiss you when you came here?"

"No," she said. They were now at the bottom of the stairs.

He stopped, still holding her hand, and looked troubled. "I'm so sorry, Molly. You above all others I should kiss." He shook his head. "I'm driving myself crazy."

"It's all right, Abramo," she said. "I know she's on your mind always."

He rested his forehead against hers. "What am I going to do?"

"You know, I asked my father those very words when I found out I couldn't have children, 'What am I going to do?'"

"And what did he say?"

"He said I should do what God wants."

Abramo snorted. "I never know what God wants. I can never understand why he gives and takes away from me."

"I don't know either, Abramo. But I can't believe God would not give you this little girl who means more to you than anything else in the world," she said, her eyes flooded with tears.

He knew immediately what she was thinking. "Oh, no, *cara mia*. You are the best part of my dreams, my happiness." He put his forehead next to hers as he held both her hands.

"I know you love me, Abramo, but I also know you need her for our happiness. Without her, we…" She cried again.

"Molly, she saved my life. She saved me for you. She has given me all of my happiness." He paused for a moment. "I need her in my life, Molly."

She nodded. "I know you do, my love. I know. I just wish I knew why, if God was going to make me the happiest of all women, why it has to be so strange and hard."

After a few moments of silence, he kissed her again. Then he led her to the small room where he had the frame. He had carved the last of the bas-relief of laurels across the frame on both upright sides. Now all he was doing was oiling the wood with a pale, light oil that gave it a blond and golden look that shimmered softly in the light.

Molly drew a quick breath when she saw the frame. "It's the most beautiful piece of woodwork I've ever seen, Abramo. I had no idea you could do this." She turned to him and grabbed his hand and held it. "Oh, God, it's exquisite."

"It will be done by Christmas. Mrs. Reid would like that," he said.

Suddenly, he heard someone running down the stairs. Isabella entered the room, flushed and looking frightened. "Abramo, Captain Grogan is here to see you," she said.

Abramo looked at Molly for an instant. "Maybe it'll be good news, Abramo," Molly said softly.

They all started toward the stairs. "You go on ahead," said Molly. "I'll catch up."

"No. I'll wait. We'll go together," he said.

"I'll put him in the little room," said Isabella, walking up the stairs ahead of them.

Rory Grogan waited with Isabella in the small room. In a moment, Abramo and Molly walked in. Rory was surprised to see them together. "Captain Grogan," said Abramo.

Rory looked first at Abramo and then at Molly, sensing immediately that they had become more than casual friends. "How are you both feeling?" he said.

"We're recovering well," said Molly. "Is there any news of the little girl?"

He shook his head. "I've had two men questioning people all along Walnut Way…as a matter of fact, all over the North Side. No one has seen her. We can't figure out how she could have slipped away."

"Could she be hiding?" Molly said. "The Hannons certainly didn't like it when she took care of Abramo. Maybe she's afraid to face them."

"Hiding from them and not us? Yeah, she could be," said Rory.

"Then she will not stop hiding unless we go look for her," said Abramo.

"But where will we look…and how will she know that we're looking for her if she's hiding? We've been all over that neighborhood. Maybe she's someplace else on the North Side."

"I don't know," said Abramo, turning his back on them and pacing back and forth in the small room.

Molly turned toward Abramo, who had his back to both her and Rory. She studied his back for a few seconds then turned back toward

Rory. "Please find her," she whispered to Rory with large tears in her eyes.

And those few plaintive words from the young girl told Rory that the little orphan girl was not only the angel of happiness to Abramo, but also to this girl, who needed her so their lives could all begin together. "I'll find her," Rory said, clutching the hand of the girl.

Then he walked over to Abramo. "Son, I know what this little girl means to you…and I know what you mean to this young lady. We'll find her, and then we'll find for sure the man that violated this girl here. I swear we'll get to the bottom of all this."

When Rory left, Abramo and Molly walked into the kitchen to talk to Isabella, and to wait for Hugh to come there from work.

Anetta Reid was angry, and her meeting was going to be a time when her anger would be controlled with great effort on her part. Hugh and Isabella were there, as were Judge Samuel Tolland, Chief of Police Charles Rowntree, and Captain Rory Grogan. The mayor was not there because Mrs. Reid detested him for his Ku Klux Klan sympathies. His name would not be mentioned in her house.

"You're about to see a sight you can tell your grandchildren about," Hugh whispered to Isabella, "Anetta Reid in high dudgeon. Even God trembles before of her."

The door opened, and Mrs. Reid made a magisterial entrance, looking as fierce and righteous as only she could look. "Please be seated, gentlemen…and Mrs. Chianese," she said. She then waited as coffee and brandy were brought in by John, the butler, and Mary, the maid.

When they left, Anetta began after a few seconds of hesitation. "Gentlemen, I want you to know how distressed I am that this little orphan child has not yet been found. Almost two weeks have passed since she was reported missing."

"But Anetta," said Judge Tolland, "you know how difficult it is to keep track of anyone on Walnut Way…much less the many orphaned children."

"I am only interested in one child at the moment, Samuel. One little girl…and evidently all the safety resources of this city are unable to discover her."

"But we've had two officers on the case for a week," said Chief Rowntree.

"Then two are obviously not enough, Charles," Anetta said coldly through tensed lips.

"Anetta, we just don't have the resources to—"

"Don't lecture me on community resources, Samuel," she snapped. "We have mobilized posses in years past to go on fools' errands looking for drunken hunters in the woods. And you dare tell me you don't have the resources to look for a missing child? Right here in the city? Has it ever occurred to you that harm could have befallen her? And that that's the reason why two policemen have had no success in finding her?"

"Anetta, why are you so concerned suddenly for this one child? An orphan?" said Judge Tolland.

"For your information, this little girl saved the life of a young man who is very dear to me. And I want her safe in this house tomorrow."

"But what do you intend to do with her, Anetta?" said Judge Tolland.

"I intend to feed her, bathe her, clothe her, and have Dr. Shanfield examine her. Then I will have her sleep in one of the front bedrooms upstairs."

"But you certainly can't consider being her permanent guardian. She'll have to be put up for adoption or taken to the orphanage in Canton."

"She certainly will not! She will stay in this house under my care until she is adopted by a suitable young couple who loves her."

"And where will you find this willing and acceptable young couple?" said the Judge.

"Aren't you forgetting something, Samuel? You're talking about a child who sleeps anywhere she can at night, who gets scraps of food as handouts, who is often hungry, who is dirty and dressed in rags. No matter who decides to adopt her, chances are very great that her conditions will be much improved over what they are now, which are deplorable. Let's just find her first…give her a good meal, some clean, warm clothing, and a restful sleep. Then when she's had some time to be a healthy, normal little girl, we'll talk of adoption."

"I'm sorry, Anetta," said Chief Rowntree. "I just can't justify keeping more than two men on that search for a little girl. Why, she might have just run away." He waved his hands in a feeble motion. "To Niles or Poland or Canfield—"

"And how was she going to get to those places, Charles? Fly? What you may not be able to justify is your job when a new mayor takes office next year. And I guarantee you that he will be guided by people who have given a good deal of financial support to his campaign. Unlike that fool of a mayor who appointed you, with my blessings I might add, the new mayor will not be an honorary member of the Ku Klux Klan. He will have principles—and he might be reminded that a chief of police must do something sometimes to help the people of Youngstown, and not merely attend parades and civic functions."

Hugh squeezed Isabella's hand. She could see his smirk out of the corner of her eye. She was in awe of the gloriously righteous dowager.

"Please, Anetta, I'm sure we can work something out." The judge glanced back at the ashen-faced chief of police, who nodded in agreement with the judge. "We'll get whatever we need in the way of human resources, and we'll do an extensive search. As soon as we can."

"Tomorrow, Samuel. I want that child in this house tomorrow night."

"But what if we don't find her?" said the chief.

"Damn you, Charles! Can a little girl who is barely mobile elude the entire Youngstown police? All right. It seems that what you lack in manpower and initiative is also matched by your lack of imagination. Therefore, I will go myself to Walnut Way tomorrow to look for the little girl."

"I can't allow that, ma'am. That would hinder the investigation," said the chief.

"How dare you, Charles Rowntree! You will have to arrest me if you're so determined to keep this wretched investigation going with the same results as before. But so help me God, I will never look upon your face again as long as I live if you say another word about stopping me."

Judge Tolland was out of his chair now, and he seemed frantic about getting the chief to accommodate Anetta Reid. He looked with dismay at the chief and tried to placate Anetta. "Please, Anetta, I'm sure Charles was only thinking of your safety."

"He should be thinking of the safety of that little girl," she snapped. "Captain Grogan has been exceedingly helpful in all of our work before. I will expect him to be with me first thing in the morning...nine o'clock. I'd also like Mr. Connolly and Mrs. Chianese to be with us. They have seen and talked to the little girl recently."

"But surely you don't expect to trudge through all those wretched places on Walnut Way, Anetta," said the judge.

She turned toward Hugh. "The child was last seen in the AOH, was she not?"

"Yes...until she led us to Abramo," said Hugh.

"All right. We'll begin there. Samuel, I'd like you to be there to lend some authority to this effort. Chief," she said formally now, "you may come or not...as you wish."

Judge Tolland nodded in resignation. "I'll be here at nine o'clock, Anetta. Captain," he turned toward Rory, "why don't we make this the rendezvous point. We can all go from here."

"You and Mr. Connolly and Mrs. Chianese can come in my car, Samuel. I want all of us to see the living conditions of those poor children on the Way."

Chapter 11

IT WASN'T UNTIL NINE thirty that Rory Grogan came to pick them up. Then they drove to Anetta Reid's house. "Judge Tolland will join us on Walnut Way. I just talked to him," Anetta said.

Hugh, sitting in the front seat with Rory, and Isabella and Anetta sitting in the backseat, drove to the AOH on Walnut Way. Rory kept the motor running and got out of the car to talk to the other policemen.

Hugh, watching all the police cars, said, "You must have put the fear of God into Charley Rowntree, Anetta. This place is swarming with police."

"If he would have done this when she first was missing, we might not have had to worry about the child," she muttered.

Rory went up to one of his sergeants, one he liked and trusted. "Terry, that's Anetta Reid in that car. She's here to see to it that we do our job right. God help us if we don't find that little girl. Judge Tolland is also on his way here. You get the picture? If we want a halfway decent Christmas this year, we damn well better find that child."

"We got every door and window of that place covered, Captain. When Joe Hannon makes a getaway, we'll know it."

"Whatever you do, kid, make sure you nail him down. I want to look into his eyes about that little girl. And if I see one thing amiss, I'm gonna beat his fucking head in."

"Remember, boss, we want him to hang, so you can't have all that much fun," said Terry.

"Yeah," muttered Rory. "Okay, just get the scouts on it. The rest of these men are gonna be all over this Way like flies on horse shit."

As Rory walked back to the police car, Judge Tolland's car drove up. The judge was met by Rory and Hugh outside their car. "She's really here?" the judge said.

"You could have bet your house that she would come," said Hugh.

"All right," said Rory. "Maybe we can get off to a good start. I don't intend to be nice to these bastards."

"It all depends on Mrs. Reid," said the judge. "We don't know how she'll take to tough tactics. She could erupt any minute."

"We'll be careful," said Rory. "Ready, Hugh?"

"Yeah, God help us," said Hugh.

The somber party walked through the main door of the AOH. Inside, there were about twenty men drinking early for lunch. There were also about seven or eight children scurrying about, some bringing beer to tables, some going in and out of the kitchen. A few of the smaller ones were sitting and watching as people drank, ate, and talked loud.

Isabella knew what to expect. Anetta was unprepared for the stench, the sour smell of sweat and spoiled beer and urine and putrid food. She nearly gagged as they walked inside. Isabella held her forearm to steady her. The little group was supported, at a distance, by police in blue uniforms who ringed the room near the entrance.

Anetta, as she recovered from the initial shock of smelling the foul odors and seeing the filthy bar and tables, took notice of the children. They were as pathetic as any she had ever seen. The ragged clothes, the dirt and body sores, the greasy, matted hair, the old, ill-fitting shoes. Some of the girls wore shoes that had been taken from men mysteriously found dead in the alleys, or from derelicts who died in the flophouses.

Isabella, who had seen the children once before, was still not prepared for the sight of hungry children dressed in dirty rags and looking pasty and malnourished. She scanned the room looking at the children, ignoring the men and the few adult women who were staring back at the intruders.

"Isabella," whispered Mrs. Reid, "did Piccina look like these children?"

"Yes," she said softly.

"My God! How can they treat them like this?"

Rory walked up to the bar, leaving Hugh and the judge and the two women behind. As he neared the bar, Jack Hannon walked out of the back room, wiping his mouth on his sleeve, chewing the remainder of the food he had been eating.

Hannon glared at Rory. "What do you want now?" he said. "How come you're always bringing women when you come?"

"That's our business," Rory said. "We're looking for that little girl, the one they call Blackie."

"How many times I have to tell you guys? No one has seen her. We're the ones who should be mad at you cops. Why the hell ain't you found her? That's my granddaughter."

Rory ignored the last comment about the granddaughter and walked away from the bar. Then he scanned the group of patrons and addressed them. "We're looking for an orphan child that's known as Blackie, and we want to see that girl real bad. Our patience is wearing thin here, and we're beginning to worry that the child might have met with some misfortune. Lord have mercy on the misbegotten bastard who has harmed that little girl! So, if someone were to tell us about that child, we'd be obliged."

He scanned the crowd but got no reaction. Instead, he got nervous fidgeting and coughing. "Has no one seen the little girl then?" he said.

"How many times you gonna ask?" said Jack Hannon. "We can't help it if you guys can't do your jobs right."

Rory turned and took two steps toward his adversary. He raised an index finger toward him. "Jack Hannon, there's not much that prevents me from taking this place apart board by board. So, you watch your mouth."

The door behind him opened. Sergeant Terry McFadden and two other officers walked in, leading Joe Hannon in handcuffs. "He was in his car, heading out of town," Terry said to Rory.

"What are you running from, Joe?" said Rory.

"I ain't running from nothing. I was just making a delivery."

"Out of town delivery, huh?" said Rory.

"Yeah. That's right."

"What were you delivering?" said Rory.

"A case of beer."

"That's damned good service you boys provide," Rory said. He turned toward Terry. "Is there any beer in that car?"

"No," said Terry.

"Now, why would you go and lie to me, Joe Hannon? And why are you hell-bent on getting out of town so early in the day? You wouldn't be running from something would you, Joe?"

"I told you I made a delivery."

"Oh, you made it, did you?" Rory glanced at Terry, who shook his head imperceptibly. As Rory was talking, two of the children came forward and touched Isabella and Anetta's dresses. Anetta was startled. "They touch us almost as though they don't believe we're real," she said softly to Isabella.

Hugh saw the two children touch Anetta and Isabella's sleeves. He studied them for several minutes. They were undernourished but not starved. Some of them had patches sewn onto their garments to cover holes. Who fed them? Who sewed the patches on their clothes? Who would feed Piccina?

While Rory was preoccupied with the Hannons, Hugh turned toward the two children who had approached Isabella and Anetta. He motioned toward Isabella to bring one child closer to him. Both Anetta and Isabella were intrigued by what Hugh would do. "Come here, child. I won't hurt you," he said, holding a quarter toward the little girl. She came closer. "Here," he said, "give me your hand." She extended her hand, and he folded the quarter into her palm. "Will you eat today?" he asked.

"Yeah," the little girl said.

"Who will feed you?"

"The old lady," the girl answered.

"What's the old lady's name?" Hugh asked.

The girl hesitated. Then the little girl who was with her, hoping to get her own quarter, answered for her. "Tilly," she said.

Hugh motioned toward the other girl, and she came forward. He gave her a quarter also. "Where is Tilly, little one?" he asked.

"Over there," the girl said, pointing to a doorway behind the bar. "Thank you, my dear," Hugh said as he stood up.

Both women gave him a questioning look. "If our girl is alive, maybe Tilly has been feeding her," Hugh said softly.

Hugh walked up to Rory. "Can I talk to you a minute?"

"What's up?" Rory said.

"There's a lady named Tilly who works here. She feeds these kids and does things for them."

"You think she might know Piccina?"

"Why don't you and I go in there and talk to her, Rory… before we have to hang all these bastards?"

Rory nodded. Then he started for the door behind the bar. "Hey! Where you going?" said Jack Hannon. "You got a search warrant?"

Rory grinned and turned back to the little group standing in front of the policemen at the door. "Meet the Honorable Judge Samuel Tolland," Rory said, pointing to the judge. "We're hungry. We want to see what you've been eating," he said as he and Hugh walked through the door.

Inside the door another young child stood by as they walked in. "Where's Tilly?" Rory asked him.

"Back in the kitchen," the boy said, pointing down the long hallway.

"Take me to her, son," Rory said.

"I can't. Jack don't want no people coming back here."

"It's okay. I'm a police officer here on an investigation," said Rory.

The boy led them downstairs to the kitchen where Tilly and two small girls were working. Tilly was startled to see Rory and Hugh standing before her. No one was ever permitted to be back in that part of the house except orphans or gang members who helped Tilly.

"Are you Tilly?" Rory said to the woman as the children hurried away.

Hugh studied her for a few seconds. She had to be in her fifties, but seemed older. She looked tough and hard, but he could also see in her eyes the something it took to care for the orphaned children.

"Yeah," she said.

Suddenly Dilworth appeared at the door, looking directly at Tilly, admonishing her silently to hold her tongue. When Rory saw him, he swung his baton and caught the little fat man in the stomach, doubling him over and making him howl in agony. Rory reached down, yanked him up by the collar, and slammed him back against a wall. "I saw you upstairs, didn't I? What's your name?"

"Dilworth."

"Dilworth what?"

"Just Dilworth."

"He works at the mill," Hugh said. "He's one of Joe's henchmen."

"What are you doing down here, Dilworth?" Rory tightened his grip on Dilworth's collar. "You didn't come down to try to intimidate a witness, now did you?"

"No, I was going to try to help," Dilworth said weakly, his feet barely on the ground as Rory held him up by the throat against the wall.

"Help, huh? Well, let me tell you what will help me. See, if I find out you've been lying…or if you know something about that little girl…or if you've made threats to my witness here,"—he tossed his head in Tilly's direction—"then I'm gonna go back upstairs and tear you apart in front of God and everybody—limb by limb—and you're gonna wish you died long since, boyo. Like maybe a milk horse would've run your sorry ass down in the street to spare you a death in agony. And that's gonna help me plenty." Then he slammed Dilworth against the wall for good measure.

Tilly was frightened as she had never been. Dilworth was always someone full of menace, someone whose look askance would be a warrant for a beating or a throat slashing by the gang. And now this terrifying giant was dangling the feared little back-stabber like a kitten against the wall.

Rory's grip had been tightening steadily against Dilworth's collar, and now the little man was wheezing for breath. Rory gave the collar one last twist and threw Dilworth down to the floor in front of him. Then he walked out the door and called to Sergeant McFadden. "Yes, sir," said the young man.

"You take this, uh…this vermin back upstairs…and keep him there till we come back. Mind you, keep him away from Joe or Jack Hannon. And don't let another son of a bitch come down them steps. Understand?"

"Yes, sir," said the sergeant.

Now both Hugh and Rory confronted Tilly. "Rest easy, ma'am," said Rory. "All we're looking for is the truth. Mr. Connolly here has some questions he wants to ask you."

Rory looked at the surprised Hugh and motioned for him to begin. "Have you worked here a long time, Tilly?" Hugh said.

"All my life," she said warily.

"You cook for the Hannons and the AOH, right?" She nodded.

Hugh was silent for a few seconds. "Tilly, I know you've had a rough life, but there's something in you that makes you be kind to these kids. I've seen the patched clothes. And I know you find a way to feed them."

"There's never enough to go around...not for all of them," she said.

"Tilly...we're looking for a little girl. We call her Piccina, but I think you call her Blackie," Hugh said softly. She seemed startled. "Have you seen her, Tilly?"

"No...I...I know who she is, but..."

"In the last few days...Have you seen her?"

She looked troubled and nervous. She looked at them, then looked away, then looked back again as she walked a few paces to the side. "Tilly? This is really important," Hugh said.

"You men want me to put a noose around my neck," she said finally.

"You think the Hannons will get you, Tilly?" said Rory.

"What do you think?" she said disgustedly. "Just you coming down in this here kitchen means I'm gonna be out on the Way." She shrugged. "Where do you think old whores sleep at night?" Her voice cracked. "Where do they eat except out of them garbage cans?" She broke down and cried, falling into a chair.

Both Rory and Hugh were filled with remorse for what they were doing to this pitiful creature. "My girl," Rory said softly, "there is no noose around your neck, and there never will be. The Hannons are finished. This Way is going to change so you won't recognize it. There is nothing the Hannons will be able to do to you."

"Oh, yeah? What about the gang? What about Dilworth? You think they're gonna become choir boys just because you get rid of the Hannons?"

"I tell you, Tilly, the Way is finished. There won't be a gang because, so help me God, I'm gonna put them in jail or they're gonna go straight to hell where they belong."

"Tilly," said Hugh, "that little girl is special to us. If you tell us where she is, I'll see to it that you will never go hungry or lack a place to sleep again."

She snorted doubtfully. "You know how many times I've heard them kind of promises?" she said.

"Please, Tilly?"

She marveled at them, just standing there asking, saying please. No threats, no anger, no beatings with the billy club. They just stood there and asked like two gentle schoolboys. "I don't know where she is," she said.

Hugh's eyes fell closed, and Rory turned instantly toward the door. "But," she said, calling back their attention, "I think I can help. I know she's alive."

Rory looked at Hugh, and both men turned back toward Tilly. "I send food over every night. Joe Hannon keeps her locked up in a cellar close by. I think it's down below the Jenkins flop. There's a kid upstairs named Brigid who brings it over to Blackie. She can take you to her."

"God bless you, girl," said Rory, taking in a deep breath.

"Why is she locked in the cellar, Tilly?" said Hugh.

"Why do you think? Because she kept that dago kid alive and away from the gang, that's why. They didn't kill her because she'll be a good moneymaker when she's about twelve years old. That's the one good thing Dilworth did in his whole goddamned life, keep Joe from killing that kid by convincing him that she'd make him some pimping money."

"Tilly, I'll talk to you again," said Hugh. "Okay with you?"

"Yeah," she sighed, feeling strange at being asked instead of told. "See you later."

When they returned upstairs, Rory called Terry McFadden to him and said, "Ask one of these kids to point out Brigid for us. Bring her back to one of these nearby rooms behind the bar. And do it quiet-like. I don't want none of these bastards to know what we're doing."

Hugh walked directly across the room to Isabella and Anetta. He nodded to Isabella and grabbed her hand. He stood in front of Mrs. Reid. "She's alive, Anetta. Someone's going to show us where she is."

"But how, Hugh? What happened?"

"It's a long story. I'll tell you both later, huh? Right now I'm going to get that little girl. It's a bad place, Anetta, and hard to reach though it's nearby. If you'll stay here with the judge, we'll be back soon. Come with me, Isabella," he said, turning toward her.

As they walked out, the judge came over to Mrs. Reid. "They've found her, haven't they?" he said.

"Yes," said Anetta.

"Have you ever seen anything like this in your life?" he said.

"No. Nor will I again," Anetta said.

"Look at these children…who on earth could do this to them?" said the judge.

"No one cares about them, Samuel. They've never known a mother's touch, or the lap of a father or other loved ones. They are left to grow up in a pack…like animals."

"I am going to do my level best to see that this kind of place never has children around it again," Tolland said.

"I'm going to do something about it, also," said Mrs. Reid. "We'll talk more about it later." She walked over to a chair and sat down.

Meanwhile, in an anteroom of the bar, Hugh and Rory and Isabella confronted a young girl named Brigid. She was about the same age as Piccina, about eight or nine years. "Come here, child," Hugh said, holding a dollar before him. "Tilly told me we should talk to you because you are kind to Blackie." She nodded. "Here," he said, placing the dollar in her hand, "this money will buy you a pair of shoes."

She looked warily at him. "I don't want it," she said.

"Why not?" said Hugh.

"What you want for it? I can't do the things you want yet… I'm only eight years old."

Hugh looked at Rory first, then Isabella. "No, little one, I don't want you to do anything...and I don't want to touch you. I just want you to show me where they're keeping Blackie."

"I can't. Joe will kill me if I take you there. Dilworth will find out, and I won't have no place to stay...or get any food from Tilly."

"Don't you worry, child," said Rory. "If you help us find Blackie, we'll see to it that no harm ever comes to you."

She shook her head to herself, as if trying not to hear Rory's words. Isabella touched Hugh's hand and knelt before the little girl. When the girl came near, she began to listen, began to stroke Isabella's blouse as they talked. "My dear," said Isabella, "you are a good friend to Blackie...and to Tilly. You are a nice little girl, and these men will never let anyone hurt you." As she spoke, the child's hand touched her face, as though not believing that Isabella was real. "We promise you, we'll help." The girl stared at Isabella. "We promise," she whispered again, tears in her eyes.

Finally, Brigid nodded. Rory then called one of the officers to join them, leaving Terry behind to make sure the Hannons were confined to the barroom of the AOH.

The little rescue party followed the girl outside and down the back alley to the Jenkins flophouse. It was dark even in the daytime. They descended through a narrow stone stairwell that was darkened by slimy black stones. At the base of the stairs, there was a corridor that led to a small room. Rory held a flashlight. "Is there a light in here, child?" he said.

"On the wall, by the door."

Rory groped the doorway at shoulder height and finally found the switch. When he turned it on, Isabella gasped. The place was like a dungeon, small, filthy, and rank with the smell of human excrement. There was a single door about six feet in height, set into the far wall. "Call her, little one," Rory whispered to Brigid.

The little girl walked to the door and knocked. "Blackie? Blackie, can you hear me?"

They heard a muffled, weak voice on the other side. Rory turned down the door handle, but it was locked. "I'll kill that son of a bitch," Hugh muttered aloud to himself.

Rory turned to Isabella. "Talk to her, madam...so she won't be scared." Then he turned toward Brigid. "Where's the key, child?"

"Dilworth has it."

"Dilworth?" Rory said, his voice raised. He turned to Hugh. "He knew where she was all along—he and Joe Hannon."

"Piccina?" Isabella called. "Piccina? I'm the lady who talked to you before, Abramo's friend. Can you hear me?"

A small voice answered yes. "Stand back away from the door, my dear. We will find a way to get you out."

"I'll get her out of that goddamned hole," Rory said, and he kicked the door with the heel of his foot.

"Here, let me help," said Hugh. He kicked also. Then the other officer kicked it. It was showing slight signs of giving way. Then Rory stepped in and kicked it four times quickly. Finally, they heard a cracking sound. A few more kicks by all three men, and the door split down the middle.

"Piccina?" Isabella called as Rory pulled away the pieces of broken door. As the light from the room entered the dark hole,

Piccina came forward. Isabella beckoned her with open arms, and the little girl fell into them crying, shielding her eyes from the brightness of the light.

All three men were overcome with pity for the child. After a few seconds, Hugh noticed her face. It was bruised, and her lip and nose were scabbed. Her forehead had a cut along the hairline. "My God, Rory," he said. "They beat her."

Finally Isabella held her at arm's length to see her face. She made a soft cry of dismay when she saw the cut and hugged the girl again.

"Let's get the hell out of this ugly place," said Rory.

Hugh walked over to Piccina. "Come, child, we're going home." He stooped to pick her up. Rory took Brigid's hand and, behind Hugh and Isabella, walked out of the building.

When they entered the back room of the AOH, Hugh put Piccina down and held her hand. In a few seconds, they were in the crowded barroom. He turned and gave her hand to Isabella, who led the pale, wretched little girl up to Mrs. Reid. "Piccina, this lady's a dear friend to all of us. She wants to be your friend."

"Do you know Abramo?" the little girl asked.

"Yes, my child, I know him very well," said Anetta.

"Can I see him?"

"If you come with Mrs. Chianese and me, we'll feed you and bathe you and give you new clothes, and we'll all see Abramo tonight. Will you do that with us?"

"Abramo didn't forget me?" Piccina asked softly, tears streaming down her face.

Anetta Reid, an aging aristocrat, rich and pampered all her life, who had never for a day been dirty, was so taken by the filthy, beaten, bloodied little girl that she began to cry, and pulled the child into her arms. "No, angel, he did not. Come with us now. It's time your luck changed." She nodded to Hugh, and he picked Piccina up again and started for the door.

"Captain," Judge Tolland said to Rory, "will you join Mr. Connolly and me outside?" Rory nodded and followed them onto the street. On his way, Rory beckoned to Sergeant McFadden and instructed him to drive Mrs. Reid, Isabella, and the child to Mrs. Reid's house.

Hugh placed Piccina between Isabella and Mrs. Reid once the women were seated in the car. "Go on ahead," said Hugh. "I'll be along later. I want to talk to Rory and the judge."

Rory and Hugh and the judge had a private conference. "Rory, go back in there and arrest those Hannon bastards," the judge said. "Charge Joe with attempted murder, rape, assault, and kidnapping. Charge the father with conspiracy, child brutality, obstructing justice, harboring prostitutes, and anything else you can think of. Get as many of those miserable bastards in jail as you can…and you needn't be gentle about it. They are going to rue the day they come into my court." He started to turn back toward his car.

"Judge, before you go," said Hugh, restraining him by gently touching his arm.

"Yes, Hugh?"

It was strange, but Hugh felt that what they had witnessed had somehow formed a bond of respect, perhaps even friendship, between the three of them.

"How many fire stations are there on the North Side?"

"I don't know," said the judge. "How many are there, Rory?"

"Two," Rory answered, puzzled by Hugh's question.

"Do they always have a full complement of firemen at the ready?"

"Except on Sunday," said Rory, suddenly beginning to sense what Hugh was thinking.

"You know," said Hugh, "wouldn't it be a shame if on a quiet Sunday, firemen were too few in number…and too slow to respond to a large fire on the North Side?"

Both men now understood Hugh's intent. "You mean like a sudden fire on Walnut Way?" said the judge.

"Yeah…maybe. I mean if there were no orphaned children around to be hurt, and suddenly there were a large fire, say like around the AOH and other Hannon flops and whorehouses."

"I'll tell you one thing," Rory said wryly, "if misfortune such as you fear befell the Hannon gang and all they own, there'd be a damned sight fewer throat slashings and backstabbings around here in the next few years."

"It would be a terrible thing, such a fire, wouldn't it?" said the judge.

"That's what I was thinking, too," said Hugh. "Rory, I'd make damned sure none of the torches for hire around town ever find themselves on Walnut Way on a Sunday, wouldn't you? Knowing that the two Hannon ringleaders were both in jail?"

"Yeah," said Rory, "especially those unfortunates who hate both the Hannons and the Klan, huh? All them Mediterranean types who are skilled craftsmen with a box of matches? And who have been mocked and beaten and hated by the gang for years?"

"Yeah. Those are the ones," said Hugh.

"Rory," said the judge, "I'm going to issue a court order to remove all orphaned children from Walnut Way—today. We'll keep them in the second floor of the city warehouse downtown. We'll feed them and clothe them and keep them out of harm's way. That way you can concentrate on persuading the Hannon gang that the laws of this society are made to punish transgressors."

"I'll make sure that they respect the law, Judge," said Rory.

"Well, Gentlemen, here's hoping that no, uh, Act of God will cause a terrible conflagration amongst these dens of iniquity," said Hugh.

"Amen," said Rory.

Chapter 12

When Anetta and Isabella drove away with Piccina, Hugh and Rory were standing alone in the street on Walnut Way. "So, what do you think Mrs. Reid would have done if we had not found that little girl?" Rory said.

"She would have cut the balls off a whole lot of politicians and police officials," said Hugh.

"I can believe that," said Rory. Then he took a deep breath. "Well, are you coming?"

"Hell, I wouldn't miss this for the world," said Hugh. "But before we go, Rory, can we find reason to arrest Tilly and get her out of this place today?"

"Why would you want to do that?"

"I want you to take her to the woman's reformatory so they can clean her up and feed her. Then I'm going to set her up with a job and a place to stay."

"I can do that," Rory said. "Anything else?"

"How much you want to bet that it was Joe Hannon that raped Molly?"

"I'd bet my next paycheck on it."

"Well, then, let's go in and make these bastards repent, boyo."

Rory put his hand on Hugh's shoulder and looked him in the eyes. "Son, you're looking at the Wrath of God. And the worst day those sons o'bitches ever had is gonna seem like a birthday party compared to today."

Hugh was thoughtful for a few seconds. "You know, Rory, I think we're going to be friends."

"I'd like that, Hugh."

"Don't forget, we're supposed to be at Anetta Reid's at seven o'clock, so if you're gonna kick some ass, we'd better get going."

Hugh and Rory walked back into the AOH and signaled to the other police to watch the doors. Between the Hannon gang and some regular patrons, there were about twenty people in the room.

"So, what'd you guys do with my granddaughter?" Jack Hannon said.

It was just the spark that Rory needed. He took his huge billy club and threw it into the mirror behind the bar. There was a great explosion of glass as the mirrors shattered and cascaded onto the bottles on the bar. The bottles tumbled over each other and crashed together, spilling whiskey and glass all over the floor. It seemed to come in waves, like an avalanche that was deafening as well as destructive.

"You're out of your fucking mind, you lunatic," said Joe Hannon. "Daddy, call up Judge Evans and get this guy the hell out of here."

"Shut up, Joe," his father said. The other people in the room, gang members and customers and two women of easy virtue were startled by the crash, but sat still in their seats, almost like frightened statues.

"Good thinking, Jack," said Rory. "See, you don't want to call in your markers too often on them crooked judges…and this kid doesn't know that, does he? In fact, he doesn't know that his ass is in a sling, either, huh? Like he thinks he's gonna get away with this one, but he doesn't know that he's under arrest for, let's see, kidnapping, attempted murder, assault, and probably rape.

"You know, Jack, you better take a good look at this demon child of yours, and then say good-bye, because you're never going to set eyes on him for the rest of your life. In fact, he might even hang if we get the right jury."

"You're full of shit," said Jack Hannon. "I know a lot of judges in this town. Do you think you can make all them charges stick?"

"Yeah, Jack, because the one thing you couldn't do was buy them all. And one of those ones you couldn't buy—like Sam Tolland—is going to sentence this piece of dogshit either to the gallows or to life in the pen, same place you're going."

"We'll see, you fucking gorilla," said Joe Hannon. As Rory looked toward him, Hannon spit in his face.

The room was silent. Rory wiped the spittle from his face with his sleeve and glared at Joe. "Thank you for that, son. You've given me the inspiration I was seeking." He looked to Terry McFadden. "Take them cuffs off him."

Suddenly Joe was afraid. Terry roughly pulled his hands up and unlocked the handcuffs.

"All right, now, Joe. This is for Blackie and all the other kids you abused around here."

Joe tried to sucker punch Rory, but the officer was waiting for a cheap shot. Joe swung and missed, and Rory countered with a punch low on the groin of the big man. Joe groaned, but stood back up to face his assailant. He tried to kick Rory, and again the policeman stepped aside and countered with another blow to his neck. Then he caught Joe as he reeled away from the neck blow and hit him squarely in the face. Blood gushed from Joe's nose. Then Rory hit him with a backhand punch across the mouth and drew blood from his mouth and his lips. Finally, he ran Joe into the bar and dragged him through the shelves of bottles and plates and beer barrels. By this time Joe Hannon's face was a mass of blood and saliva, so swollen and distorted that he could barely breathe.

Then Rory turned toward his father. "This is your own devil child, the fruit of your loins, who beats little girls, rapes good women, and has brutalized and killed God knows how many Negroes who were just passing through. And if he lives, and is not hanged, then he'll get more of that down at the pen. God have mercy on both your souls.

"And by the way, you're under arrest too, Jack, for white slavery, conspiracy, assault, child molestation, and selling illegal booze. Damn, it'll be a shame to close this place!" Rory said with a grin.

Jack's face was almost purple with anger, but he didn't move. "You ain't closing nothing."

"Who's going to be here to run it anyway? You two pieces of dogshit are gonna be in jail, as will that other piece of shit, Dilworth. Cuff these assholes, Sergeant." He handed Joe over to one of the officers and turned toward Dilworth on the other side of the room. "And now, you little round-ball bastard, I charge you with kidnapping, white slavery, conspiracy to murder, and child molestation. You'd better get a good look at these Hannon bastards, because you ain't gonna see them for the rest of your days."

"How come you're charging me with the same charges you did for them?"

"Because you're going to hang, too, asshole. Because it's gonna come out that you're Joe Hannon's right-hand man, who cut uncountable throats in the last ten years, and then you'll go to your eternal damnation with them."

"But I didn't beat that kid, or fuck that girl."

Suddenly both Hugh and Rory were listening. "You didn't beat Blackie?" Hugh said.

"No," Dilworth said and pointed to Joe. "I talked him out of it."

"And which girl didn't you fuck?" said Rory. Now Dilworth was afraid. He had said too much, and he knew it. But he could also see the murderous squint-eyed rage on Rory's face, and he was terrified of what this crazy giant would do to him.

Rory stepped forward and grabbed him by the front of his collar with both hands. Now he was whispering ominously, pulling Dilworth's face up to his own. "I said which girl didn't you fuck, Dilworth?"

"That red-head girl."

"The one Joe Hannon was topping, right?"

"Yeah."

"The same girl the dago kid tried to help in the alley?"

"Yeah. And Joe tried to bash his fucking head in. It's true, I swear it."

Rory stopped a moment, releasing his grip on Dilworth's collar and turned back around to look at the two Hannons, handcuffed and scowling, surrounded by a retinue of Youngstown's finest. "You can't go on the word of that little bastard," Joe Hannon mumbled through swollen lips.

"Maybe you don't think so, but a jury sure will." Rory turned around to face Dilworth again. "I don't know why you kept Joe Hannon from killing that little girl, but it'll do you some good if you've been straight with me, understand? You may not hang for it."

"Yeah," muttered Dilworth, frightened both by Rory and the Hannon gang, "but living all my life in jail don't sound too good neither."

"Use your head for once in your life, Dilworth. You gonna let these scum put a noose around your neck? You ever see someone die on the gallows? If you did, you'd be spilling your guts to me right now."

"What more do you want?"

"Not much, only the truth about the AOH and the gang…and the Harty girl and Blackie and Abramo." Rory paused and looked away. Then he came face-to-face with Dilworth again. "But if you think you're gonna lie to me and somehow come out okay, then you're crazy. It's either you or them, boyo. And if you choose to lie to me—even a little white lie—I'm gonna lead you through the bowels of hell, and you're gonna end up worse than those two dogshits over there."

Rory released Dilworth and turned around and walked to the center of the room, addressing everyone in the AOH. "Now we have the names and whereabouts of each of you heathens…and we're gonna remember them well. If one of these orphans comes up missing, or if we find bodies of some of God's unfortunates around here, all you worthless sons o'bitches are gonna join that dogshit family over there in hell. Everybody understand me? This Walnut Way is gonna be a test to see which Youngstown police officers can prove how tough they are. Watch what happens to the Hannon gang and make sure you don't let them take you down with them."

Anetta was energized as she had not been in years. The little girl sat between her and Isabella in the car and said almost nothing as they drove. She had obviously never been in a car before, and the ride probably seemed long to everyone but her.

When they arrived at Anetta's house, Judge Tolland, who was behind them, got out of his car. Anetta said, "Will you come back this evening about seven for a small private gathering? Since you had so much to do with finding this girl. And, by all means, bring your wife. I'm sorry for the short notice. It's just that there would have been no gathering if we had not found her."

Samuel was surprised. Anetta Reid's invitations were rare things, especially since she made it a point to request his wife's attendance. "I'd love to meet her," Anetta said, clasping his hand.

"Yes," he said, responding to her softer tone. "We'll be here." Then he walked away dumfounded.

Anetta and Isabella brought Piccina into the mansion. The girl was amazed and intimidated, but the touches of Isabella and Anetta reassured her. They went directly into the dining room.

The cook and a kitchen maid joined John, the butler, and Mary, Anetta's personal maid, wanting to see the little girl.

"Bring her some hot broth and some warm ham and some cheese with warm bread," Anetta said to Mary and the maid. They both stared at Piccina, marking her mangy, dirty condition. "We'll wash her hands and face before she eats," Anetta said, anticipating their questions. "When you're half starved, food is more important than anything else."

She turned to her butler. "John, have one of the girls prepare a bath upstairs," she said. "Then call Dr. Shanfield and ask him to come to the house this afternoon to examine the child. Mary, call Mrs. Easley at the children's store. Tell her I want her to bring out several dresses and all manner of shoes and clothing. Tell her that the child is slight and about eight years old. We will also need several outfits and shoes for play…and especially some warm clothing for outdoors. After you do that, Mary, I want you to join Mrs. Chianese and me as we give this child a bath. We may want to cut some of her hair, also. That way, she'll be ready for the doctor and the dressmaker."

"Anetta," said Isabella, "while she eats, I'll go home and get a few nightgowns of my daughter's from when she was young. When she's out of the bath, we can dress her in those until the dressmaker comes."

"All right. John, make your calls to Dr. Shanfield and get Tim to make the car ready to drive Mrs. Chianese home and bring her back as soon as she's ready." She paused. "By the way, John, I'm having some friends here tonight. We'll need to begin preparations for our guests…perhaps twenty people."

Only John remembered any commotion in the Reid house such as this. He had been with the Reids for thirty-four years and remembered days prior to the turn of the century when Anthony Reid invited the governor and many other dignitaries to numerous balls and dinners. But noise, much less excitement, had been nonexistent in the Reid mansion for two decades. Now, suddenly, there would be more people in the house on this single day than there had been in the past two years. John looked at Mrs. Reid. Her old spirit was back again. She was bright, energetic, and full of—dare he say it—warmth.

When the maid brought the warm broth and ham and cheese and warm bread, the little girl ate carefully, knowing she was being watched. But she had never been taught to use a knife and fork, so eating was a struggle until Mrs. Reid cut up her meat into small, bite-sized pieces, easily gotten with the fork. The child ate in gulps and spilled her soup several times, uneasy with the large spoon provided.

Once, Piccina stopped and looked up at Mrs. Reid. "Did the pretty lady go for Abramo?" she said.

"No, my dear, not yet. Abramo will come this evening. Don't worry, Mrs. Chianese went to get you a nightgown to wear for when the doctor comes."

"I'm not sick," she said.

"I know you're not, my dear, but I just want to be sure you have the proper food to eat to make you healthy. And I want him to look at those cuts on your face." She touched the side of her face that was still slightly swollen. "Is it sore here?"

Piccina nodded but didn't speak. She continued to gulp her meat and bread. "My dear, you don't have to eat it all if you're full. We'll have more food tonight that you'll like. Would you like some cake?"

The child looked curiously at Anetta. "I don't think she knows what cake is, ma'am," said Mary.

"Oh, dear," Anetta said. "Bring her a small slice of cake, Mary."

Piccina gulped down the cake in a few seconds. As she ate, she watched the old lady. Never had she seen anyone like her. She was firm and imperious, but gentle and kind. She had cut up the meat for her and had helped wash her face and hands with Isabella. And she was going to let her see Abramo tonight.

The pretty lady returned and said, "How are you, Piccina? Mrs. Reid's food was delicious, was it not?" Piccina nodded. "Piccina, have you ever had a bath?" Isabella said.

"No. Tilly gave me a shower sometimes."

Isabella looked at Anetta. "We're going to give you a bath, child," the old lady said, "and make you look clean and beautiful."

"But first, Piccina, we're going to cut your hair, just a little of it. Then we're going to wash it and make it clean and shiny," said the pretty lady.

Piccina nodded. She not only liked these gentle ladies, but she was beginning to trust them. They had given her food that was better than anything she had ever tasted. And they said they were going to make her hair pretty and shiny. And they said they would help her see Abramo soon. Yes, Piccina liked them both. She liked the soft touches of the pretty black-haired lady with the same color hair as hers—Isabella, she reminded herself. And the old white-haired lady, Mrs. Reid, had kind eyes, and her touch was also warm and gentle.

Upstairs in the huge bathroom, Isabella smiled at her. "Piccina, we're going to wet your hair and clean off all this blood and dirt. Don't be frightened by the water and the brushes. When we put the shampoo in your hair, we'll tell you to close your eyes so the soap won't burn, okay?"

"Then when you open them again, your hair will be clean and smell wonderful," Mrs. Reid said, "but first Mary's going to cut a little of your hair."

The three women coached each other about what to cut and where. Finally, they agreed that the split and matted and unkempt hair should all be cut because it was not salvageable. And so the hair was closely cropped to form a black halo that cradled the girl's head. Suddenly, she seemed like an angel in their midst. Each of the women smiled with delight as they brought the mirror to Piccina. At first she didn't believe that she was the girl in the mirror. But when she shook her head, and the image shook also, she began to believe that she really was that pretty little girl.

"Are you ready for your bath now, Piccina?" said Isabella. She nodded, less anxious this time. "I'm going to take all your clothes off, and we're going to give you clean new ones, okay?" Again she nodded.

When they took off the layers of rags, they unveiled the dirt and the foul odor that were hidden beneath them. And as they finally got all her clothes and shoes off, they could see large bruises fading into yellow patches against her pale skin, one on her buttocks and one on her shoulder. "Where did you get those bruises, child?" Mrs. Reid said softly.

At first she didn't answer, knowing subliminally that one did not tell on the Hannons. She was in a quandary, and she looked at Isabella. Isabella nodded, assuring her that it was all right to tell the truth. "Joe," she said finally.

Mrs. Reid took a deep breath. "Mary, go tell John I want him to call Chief Rowntree and ask him to come here at seven o'clock tonight."

As they washed the girl, the women could see angry red marks on her knees, now scabbed and worn into red welts. "Oh, Piccina, where did you get these cuts on your knees? They are the same as those Abramo has."

"They're from the alley," she said. "When I was carrying him, the glass and stones cut my knees…his too. He was trying to help me crawl." Isabella touched her face and shook her head, trying to keep the tears in her eyes from cascading down her face. She looked back at Anetta, and the older women also shook her head in wonder.

The changes in Piccina were those that people beheld when they watched stone being carved into a Michelangelo sculpture. Her fingernails and toenails had been cut and scrubbed clean. Her hair was washed and rinsed. Parts of her that had never been cleaned and seldom touched had been cleaned and washed. Finally, she was rinsed completely and then emerged from the water. She was dried, powdered, combed, and dressed in one of the nightgowns Isabella had brought. "Look at her," Anetta said to the other women. "She's positively angelic."

Isabella brought Piccina to see herself in a full-length mirror. The child seemed strange, almost as though she knew this was all a dream, and she would soon wake up in a filthy corner of one of the back rooms of the whorehouses on Walnut Way. She turned toward Isabella. "That's me," she said.

"That's you," said Isabella.

There was a knock at the door, and one of the maids stepped in. "Dr. Shanfield just got here, ma'am," she said to Anetta.

"Show him up to the large guest bedroom, June," Anetta said.

In a few moments, Dr. Shanfield joined Anetta and Isabella and Piccina in the guest bedroom. "You have a child you want me to examine, Anetta?" he said.

"Here she is, Evan," she said, turning to give him a look at Piccina.

He looked at the child then looked back at Anetta. He said nothing. Piccina stood silently looking up at him. "Come here, child," he said softly, patting the bed. "I'll examine you up here."

Piccina did as she was told. The doctor removed her night-gown and began to run his hands over her arms and legs, moving each limb carefully. Then he looked at her upper body and noticed the bruises. "This child had been beaten," he said, frowning, turning toward Anetta.

"That's why we called you, Evan," she said with a huff.

"I know you didn't beat her, Anetta. But where did she come from?" While he was speaking, he was feeling, turning, stretching, and pulling on the little girl's limbs.

"She's an orphan who lived on Walnut Way," Anetta said.

"But why do you have her?"

"This child saved the life of Abramo Cardone," she said, nodding slightly to Isabella.

"Then this is the little girl we've heard so much about?" he said, turning to Piccina and smiling. "What do you intend to do with her, Anetta?"

"I certainly do not intend to send her back to that awful place where we found her," she said indignantly. "She will live here with me until suitable adoptive parents will have her."

He nodded. "And I don't suppose you have any such parents in mind," he said with a smirk, knowing that there was more to the story than he was being told. "These terrible cuts on her knees... they are just like Abramo's," he muttered, shaking his head.

"In the process of saving Abramo, she dragged him along the ground and in so doing cut her knees."

"You really saved Abramo's life, my dear?" he said to Piccina. She nodded.

He continued his examination, listening with his stethoscope, looking into her mouth and ears and eyes and nose and vaginal and rectal areas. "Well, she has a calcium deficiency," he said. "Her baby teeth are not in very good shape. And her left leg is slightly turned. She'll have to wear a brace for a while...several months," he said.

"Can it wait until after Christmas?" Anetta said. "I want her to get used to being here, away from Walnut Way."

He nodded. "It can wait a little. Meanwhile, she needs meat and milk and cheese and ice cream as a regular part of her diet. I'll send a dietician round to help you plan menus for her."

"She doesn't even know what ice cream is," Anetta said.

He shook his head. "We should have a dentist and a pediatrician look at her after Christmas. But I think with good nourishment, she'll begin to fill out. She's underweight now, of course, but she's in remarkably good shape for someone who has lived through what she has. There are no hair lice, which is remarkable, and her genital and anal areas are free of infection. She'll be okay with your care, Anetta," he said, smiling easily for the first time.

After the doctor left, the dressmaker came. Piccina had never seen such clothes in her life. She was fitted with slippers and nightgowns and dresses and jumpers and shoes and coats. "These few play clothes she can wear the next few days…and the velvet jumper. I'll have the others done in a week. I'll hire some extra women to help me," the dressmaker said.

"She will need some outdoor wear as soon as possible," Mrs. Reid said. "And I want the boots done as quickly also."

"Yes, ma'am."

When everyone was gone, Anetta ordered tea for the bedroom. Then she turned to Piccina. "This will be your room for a while, dear," she said. "Would you like to take a nap?"

Piccina didn't understand. Isabella interpreted. "Piccina, let's try your new bed." She turned back the covers and urged the girl into the bed. "Mrs. Reid and I will stay here with you. If you want to sleep, that's okay,"

"You won't leave?"

"No, my dear, we won't leave. We'll be here talking."

She settled back against the pillow. In all her life she had never touched any clothes as fresh and clean and soft as the blankets and pillows on the bed. She felt safe and content and comfortable. "I'll see Abramo tonight, huh?"

"Yes, dear, very soon," said Isabella.

The two women settled into their chairs and began to sip the tea that John and Mary had brought them. "All she thinks about is Abramo," Mrs. Reid said quietly.

"Abramo's the same. He thinks of her constantly and worries about where she is."

"But how does Molly take this? Hugh told me that they are engaged."

"Watching him and Molly is wonderful. They are very much in love, and they dream together. They are so fresh and promising." Isabella's smile was bittersweet. "Yet, there has been a sadness within him that will never be relieved until he has Piccina."

Anetta shook her head in wonder. "I've never known anything like it," she said.

Isabella quietly stood up to walk a few steps toward the huge bed. The little girl's eyes were closed, and she was sleeping soundly, the most peaceful and contented sleep of her life.

Isabella returned and sat down. Anetta had been watching her and marveled at her quiet grace and charm. "Isabella," she said, "are you and Hugh going to be married?"

"Yes," she said. "He asked if I would marry him on January seventeenth."

Anetta was quiet for a few moments, then she said, "I would like to do something for you."

"Oh, Anetta, you have already done so much—"

"Nonsense, this is what friends are supposed to do." She paused for a few minutes, thinking to herself. "You know, Isabella, after Anthony and Brendan died, I changed. I became lonely, harsh, and embittered, especially against those who spread lies about Brendan being a deserter from the Army. I have a Commendation of Honor from the Secretary of War for all the work he did as a counterspy. But somehow the terrible rumors stuck. People who hated us for our wealth enjoyed hearing rumors and spreading them themselves…I became a society matron with many wealthy and important acquaintances, but no friends. I mistrusted everybody.

"Then Hugh began to come here because of his position in politics. And of all the men I knew, he was different. You could see that his heart was good. And he asked me about Brendan…and believed in him. Then Abramo came with him one day and said he would make a frame for the portrait of Brendan, whom he called a hero. I tell you, Isabella, those two boys are like a son and grandson to me. And since my dear Brendan's death, I have never had a good day until I began to see all of you." She nodded toward the bed. "And now this wonderful little girl."

She paused for a moment, staring ahead as if something had been revealed to her. "You have become my family, Isabella, and there was a time when I never thought I would have a happy day again."

Isabella left her seat and walked over to the older woman and knelt down in front of her and kissed her. "Oh, my dear," Anetta said, hugging the younger woman, "you are a blessing to my life."

She held Isabella for a few seconds and then released her to look at her face. "Isabella, I would like the bishop to marry you in Saint Andrew's Cathedral, and if you intend to have a dinner and reception, I would like it to be in this house. Do you mind doing that? It would be my wedding gift to you. I would feel like my own son was marrying a wonderful Italian girl."

"Oh, Anetta, I know Hugh would be honored. But you must know that we will love you if all your money were gone tomorrow."

She touched Isabella's face. "I believe you would, my dear."

Chapter 13

ABRAMO WAS PENSIVE AS he sat in the Harty parlor waiting for Molly to finish dressing. Hugh said that he would pick them up in his car and take them with him to Mrs. Reid's Christmas party. In a few minutes, Molly walked in and stood before him. "You are beautiful," he said, looking up at her.

"You look quite handsome yourself," she said. "You'd look even better if you had red hair," she said, teasing him.

He smiled and stood up to kiss her. "So you want a red-headed Italian, huh?"

"You're what I want," she said. He raised his eyebrows in appreciation, but didn't say anything more.

"Abramo?"

"Yes?"

"I know you miss her, and I know how hard it is to go to a Christmas celebration and be happy. But many people we love or care about will be there. Will you try to enjoy yourself?"

"Yes. I can be happy as long as I'm with you."

Just then, Hugh walked in. "Hello there, pretty girl. Are you ready?"

"Uh…yes, but where is Isabella?"

"She's there already. She went over early to help Mrs. Reid get ready for the party."

"She did? But I would have helped her. I wonder why she didn't call?"

"I don't know. Ask her when you see her," he said dismissively. "Where's the old man?"

"He's upstairs shaving and bathing. He said he'll see us a little after seven."

"All right, then. Let's go."

When they arrived, there were many people there already. A woman was playing Christmas music on the grand piano. When they walked into the reception room, they saw Molly's brothers, Judge Tolland and his wife, Chief Rowntree, Rory Grogan and his wife, Abramo's uncle, Michele, and his aunt, Renata, Dr. Shanfield and his wife, James Parsons and his wife, and Gianina and her brothers.

"How did the children get here?" Molly wondered aloud. "Maybe I should go see if I could help them."

"Oh, no," said Hugh uneasily, "you stay here. I want to squire you around the room and introduce you."

He was glad that the secret of Piccina would only have to be kept a few minutes longer. He had forgotten how sharp Molly was and how easily she noticed things.

When Kieran arrived, the party was complete. Hugh introduced the young couple to all the people who did not know Molly or Abramo. With the hors d'oeuvres and drinks available, the party soon took on a festive glow.

Abramo tried valiantly to enter the spirit of the occasion, but he was having a hard time. He was almost beyond enjoyment, not caring much for party food or Christmas music or joyous sights. Molly, of course, could not be at ease while she knew how much Abramo was hurting inside. "I wonder if everything is all right with Mrs. Reid?" she said as the large mantle clock struck seven thirty.

"I'm sure it is," Hugh said, sticking close to the young couple. "Come on over to see Dr. Shanfield. I'm sure he'd like to know how you're both mending."

"I'm gratified that you're both doing well," said the doctor warmly. He turned to his wife. "They were patients at the Reid Pavilion only a short time ago—in very bad condition. Now it seems they are recovered…and engaged to be married."

Most of the guests seemed to be aligned along the walls, forming little groups, talking and laughing easily in this strange new event at the Reid mansion. Hugh had positioned himself with his back to the wall, facing the opposite side of the room where there were two large wooden French doors. Molly was beside him, facing Abramo and Dr. Shanfield, whose backs were turned toward the center of the room.

Suddenly Molly had a strange look on her face. "Abramo," she said softly, looking beyond him with her eyes opened wide.

Abramo turned slowly as he heard some murmurs from those who were seated in chairs arranged about the center of the room on opposite sides of a small aisle leading to the great doors. He caught sight of Isabella and Mrs. Reid and could not, for a second, understand what they were doing. Suddenly he realized that there was someone else with them, someone small, who they were looking at as she began slowly walking down the aisle, as though looking for someone.

She was a little girl with short black hair, a beautiful maroon velvet jumper, a white blouse, high white stockings, and black patent leather shoes. Isabella and Mrs. Reid smiled at the little creature who was walking toward Abramo. Instinctively, he moved toward her.

This child was clean and lovely, dressed in beautiful clothes, and with short hair. She wasn't the little girl in rags who dragged him through the alley, who fed him, whose body kept him warm against the night. She couldn't be. It was too much to believe, a dream too easily shattered. Yet as Abramo sank to his knees in the middle of the room, as the child drew nearer, he saw the lovely eyes that watched him through his delirium, the little hands that held his face, the small mouth that kissed him so many times to restore his health.

He held out his hands as she drew near, trying to believe she was his Piccina. And this child's eyes did what Piccina's always did: look as far into his as she could look. And this child was unsmiling, with eyes as fearful and uncertain as they were in the alley. But when their hands touched, both knew immediately that they had found each other. For a few seconds they stayed apart, eyes meeting, silent, as though unable to speak.

The little girl spoke first, holding his hands at arm's length. "Please keep me, Abramo," she said, her eyes clouding.

Piccina! His heart beat faster, and his voice faltered. Then after a few tries and a few gasps of breath, he mustered a response. "Oh, my dear angel, I will keep you forever. I love you."

They still held hands at her arms' length. "You love me?" she said, lowering her head, crying as she closed her eyes, as though not believing what she had just heard. All the times she slept in dark corners alone, all the dreary, cold days when she longed for the warmth of someone who cared for her, all the times she dreamed of a soft touch or gentle word, all the times she doubted, in her child's mind, that anyone could love a ragged, dirty, forsaken little girl…all those memories were banished now by Abramo's words.

There was not a dry eye anywhere as all the unsuspecting guests beheld the two figures holding each other tight in the center of the room. They saw her step back from him and touch his face with both her hands and then bring his face toward hers as she kissed his lips in a childlike embrace, just as she had done so many times in their hideout on Walnut Way. These were two people whose dreams of love had intermingled into one beautiful story. There would never be another night when the little girl would fall asleep wondering if anyone loved her. There would never be another night when he would be tormented by the fear that God had tantalized him, again, with the prospect of something sublimely beautiful only to have it torn away in an instant and never found again. These were two people who cared nothing about wealth or power or prestige. They were content just to have each other.

Then Abramo felt a hand on his shoulder, resting carefully and tentatively. He knew it was Molly's, and he released the little girl. "Piccina," he said, "this is someone else who loves you. And she loves me also."

Piccina understood. She nodded. "I know her," she said.

"How do you know me, angel?" Molly said.

"You're the lady Joe beat up," she said.

Suddenly every adult, especially Rory, Hugh, and Kieran, was listening to the little girl. "You saw it, Piccina?" Abramo said.

She nodded. "I saw him hit you, too," she said.

"And you saved Abramo, didn't you, honey?" She smiled and nodded again. "Can I kiss you?" Molly said.

She glanced at Abramo, sensing that he was pleased. Then she went into Molly's embrace. As Molly held her, Piccina stepped back to face her. "I love Abramo," she said, nodding as if to reassure Molly.

"I do, too," said Molly. "And I'd like you to love me, too, someday." Piccina nodded and smiled.

Kieran Harty, wiping yet more tears from his eyes, turned to Hugh. "I'm glad I lived to see this, Connolly, but I don't think I could ever go through another one."

"Nor I, son, nor I."

Anetta wiped her eyes several times during the little tableaux between Abramo and Piccina. She stood watching as everyone did and was overcome by it. Judge Tolland had made his way across the room with Hugh toward Anetta and Isabella.

As the judge approached, Anetta said, "Well, Samuel, is there any doubt in your mind who should have that little girl?"

"Not at all. There's only one problem…I can't give her to him if he's a single man."

"Why not?" Anetta huffed. "She's a starving, orphaned, beaten street urchin."

"You know why not, Anetta," said the judge.

"But they're going to be married," said Hugh.

"That would make all the difference," Samuel said.

"All right," said Anetta, "but until they're married, Samuel, I want the child with me." She turned to look directly at him. "And not in some orphanage."

The judge sighed and nodded agreement. "Anetta," said Hugh, "the bishop can marry more than one couple at the same Mass, can't he?"

"He can do anything he wants," she said.

"Could they get married with us on the seventeenth?" Hugh said. Suddenly Anetta understood. "We don't have to have a big affair here," he said.

"Hush, Hugh. It would only mean inviting a few more people, would it not?" said Anetta. "We can easily do it. Do you think they would consent to it?"

"I'd bet my house on it," he answered.

Meanwhile Isabella had brought Molly over to them. "My dear," said Anetta, "do you think you and Abramo could be married soon?"

She smiled. "Now that he has Piccina, he would do it tomorrow morning."

"Good, good. Young lady, I'd like you to be married with your uncle and Aunt Isabella, on the seventeenth of January. And you would all have a joint reception at this house."

She hesitated, looking at Hugh and Isabella for guidance. They both nodded in response. "But we don't—"

"It would be my wedding present to you both," Anetta said, clutching Hugh's hand. Molly nodded.

A little later, Rory came up to Hugh and Kieran. "Did you hear that little girl put those nails into the lid of Joe Hannon's coffin?"

Hugh walked in to the AOH at noon. Kieran was surprised to see him, because he seldom left the mill so early, especially to come to the AOH. "Is my niece around?" he said by way of greeting to his old friend.

"She's upstairs…mad at me," Kieran said, scowling as he rubbed a towel over the spotless bar.

"What'd you do now? She's usually right about things, you know."

"Well, she's not right this time, goddammit. I told her I didn't want her working. So, she's upstairs sulking. Since you've been easing Abramo into that office job, when he's gone all day she's a damned grouch—just like her mother used to be. If they can't work, they become witches from hell."

"Well then, I'm here to do you a favor, boyo."

Kieran rolled his eyes and snorted. "You've come over here to torment me, haven't you? To think I knew you when you had to work for a living."

"Never look a gift horse in the mouth, Harty. Here's me going to smooth your daughter's feathers and take her out for some fresh air, and you're mistrusting me."

Kieran crossed his arms. "You've got something on your mind, Connolly, so why don't you just tell me what it is? You know I'll find out sooner or later. And if it's one of your con games, I'm gonna cut your balls off."

"What have you been doing with that towel, Kieran? Wiping and clearing tables? So who's cooking in the kitchen?"

Kieran squinted at his friend. "What are you up to, you bastard?"

"Listen, you know Molly's going to be gone in a few weeks... and you can't run this place without more help, right? Face it: you're richer than the Pope already, and you're just going to have to spend some of it on help. If you keep counting your money every night instead of servicing your customers, someone's going to put up an AOH down the street, and then you'll be wailing like a banshee about losing business."

"You've got some balls talking about my money. You're the guy that's being married in St. Andrew's Cathedral by the bishop," he said in an exaggerated, mocking voice. "You probably own half that mill already."

"I'm ignoring those calumnies, pagan, because I'm here to do you a favor."

Kieran chuckled again, wiping the bar as he spoke. "Lord Almighty," he muttered. "Okay, what do you want?"

"Well, son, I want you to put somebody to work."

Kieran gazed at Hugh. "Who is he?"

"It's a she."

"And where's she from?"

"Now, look, before I—"

"Where's she from, Connolly?"

"From the Hannon AOH."

Kieran threw down the towel. "You're not my friend at all, are you? You're the serpent from the Garden of Eden in one of the devil's disguises."

"Will you calm yourself, man, and let me tell my story?"

Kieran paused for a few seconds. "All right. Go ahead."

"This lady used to be a whore in—" Kieran started laughing. "Will you pay attention, Harty?" Hugh grumbled. "As I was saying, a whore in one of the Hannon cat houses. When she got too old and beat up, she became the cook in the bar, before it was the AOH."

Kieran was listening to him more thoughtfully. "Go on," he said.

"Well, you see, son, those orphans on Walnut Way are alive today because of Tilly. She'd save table scraps every day and feed those kids. And she used to look after them. She'd save shoes for them from dead bums and whores on the Way. She'd use their clothes to make dresses and coats for the kids, and she'd patch the clothes they wore when they got thin. And when one of those miserable bastards like Joe Hannon would beat on one of those kids—like he did on your new granddaughter—then she'd clean their wounds and patch them up. You see how Piccina had those cuts on her face? He worked her over, and Tilly put her back together."

Kieran shook his head in disgust. "That son of a bitch," he muttered. Then he looked at Hugh. "You really think she'd work out here?"

"With you as a boss, I know she will. I've seen you show people how to act right."

"So, why do you want Molly?"

"I want her to come with me so we can buy Tilly some clothes. She doesn't have a damned thing. The Hannons didn't even pay her regularly. They'd just toss her a few bucks when they felt like it."

"I suppose she doesn't have any place to stay, huh?"

"No," said Hugh.

"She can have those two rooms at the end of the downstairs hall. There's even a bathroom down there."

"You know she can't pay you anything for those rooms?"

"Did I say anything about her paying me, goddammit?"

"You know, boyo, this lady never got a break in her life," Hugh said. "You'd be the first one."

"Tell her I'll pay her what I pay the guys…minus a token for the room. And if she steals from me, I'll cut her throat."

"Sure you will," said Hugh brightly.

"Now take my daughter out of here, so she won't be such a bitch until Abramo gets back. And convince her that people who just get out of the hospital have to get well before they go back to work."

Hugh and Molly drove downtown in his car. The East End had the stores of the working class; the West End, past the square, had the newer, larger department stores, frequented by the middle class. The clothes there were finer and more expensive. But the working people seldom ventured west.

"Let's park here and walk," Hugh said.

"What does she need?" Molly asked.

"Everything. This lady is an unfortunate, Moll. All her life, she's been trapped by circumstances she couldn't fight."

He was thoughtful as he maneuvered the car into a parking space. "But you know, Moll, without this lady, that little girl that saved Abramo would never have made it. This Tilly was like a mother to all the orphans on Walnut Way. When any of them needed something, they went to Tilly. Piccina, who they planned to make a whore at the age of twelve, was cared for, patched up, and clothed by Tilly."

"If Abramo knew that, he'd go crazy," Molly said, looking straight ahead.

"She's a good soul, kid. And your dad's going to give her a job in the kitchen of the AOH."

"Really? Where will she live?"

"In those two back rooms in the downstairs of the club. I think she'll be a real help to your dad."

"I think so, too," she said.

For several minutes they walked in silence. "What's she look like, Uncle Hugh? What's her body like?"

"She's a little taller than you, and heavier and more square."

"You want me to pick what I think she'll need?"

"Yeah. And she needs everything."

"Okay," she said, intrigued by the challenge of outfitting an adult from head to toe.

"When we're done, we'll go see her," Hugh said.

"Where is she?"

"In the women's reformatory."

They spent about two hours buying clothes and shoes for Tilly. The store clerks on the East End were unpretentious and helpful. Finally, they had what they wanted, so Hugh drove them to the reformatory.

Inside, Molly was shocked by the stark bareness of the place, so bleak and forbidding. They walked down a long corridor that showed dampness leaching through the stone walls and floors. At the end of the corridor was a desk with a guard in attendance. "We'd like to see Tilly Ednam," said Hugh. "Captain Rory Grogan gave me this." He handed a note to the guard.

The guard looked it over. "We'll have to bring her down," he said. "You can wait in the interview room."

Down at the interview room, they were seated behind a large, wooden rectangular table. Molly looked nervous. "You okay?" said Hugh.

"I'm okay," she said. "What an awful place!"

He snorted. "It's better than where she was. Although a lot worse than where she's going."

Tilly was escorted into the room. She looked at Hugh skeptically and then seemed surprised to see Molly.

"How are you doing, Tilly?" Hugh said as she sat down.

"Oh, you fixed me up with a great place to live. Jail's nice," she said.

"You won't be here long," Hugh said. "Tilly, this is my niece, Molly Harty."

Tilly stared at Molly for a few seconds. "What's she doin' here?" she said.

"I needed some help with my shopping," Hugh said.

"Shopping?"

"Yeah," said Hugh as Molly slid two shopping bags across the table.

"What're these for?"

"For you, Tilly," Hugh said.

"Yeah? And what do I have to do for them?"

"You have to work…for her father in his AOH," said Hugh, nodding toward Molly.

She stared coldly at them both. "Her father's Kieran Harty?"

"Yes," Molly said, "and he will hire you to work in our AOH."

"How do you fit into this?" she asked Molly.

"I'm getting married, and my dad needs someone to replace me at work. Are you a pretty good cook?"

"I get by," she said.

"Oh, I forgot," Hugh said as he reached into his vest pocket. He slid two packs of cigarettes across the table.

"What's with the clothes and the cigarettes? You must be expecting more than just cooking in the kitchen."

"That little girl you call Blackie is going to have this girl as a mother," Hugh said, gesturing with his thumb toward Molly. "We owe you at least that for taking care of her."

Tilly looked at Hugh and then at Molly, trying to decide if they were phony or not. Hugh knew what she was thinking. "We don't have to do any of this, you know," he said to her, reading her doubts. She nodded.

"Tilly," Hugh said, "every once in a while someone comes along that you have to trust…because they might change your life.

You did it by taking care of Picc…of Blackie." He raised his hand, index finger up, off the table toward Tilly. "Kieran Harty is the best man I've ever known…although the kid she's gonna marry," he nodded again toward Molly, "is right up there with him. There are damn few people lucky enough to be working for a boss like Kieran, but you look to me like someone who could use a break."

Tilly sat back against the chair and stared at them for a minute. Then she nodded in assent. "I'm grateful." She looked at Molly. "That little girl's sweet, and she deserves the best. I think you might be the one to do it, girly."

"Did you know her when she was born?" asked Molly.

"Yeah."

"She's Joe Hannon's niece, then?"

Tilly chuckled. "I hate to see how he'd treat an enemy if he treats a niece like that."

Molly and Hugh glanced at each other. "What are you saying, Tilly? Is that kid Jack Hannon's granddaughter?" said Hugh.

"Like hell she is," Tilly muttered.

"She's not related to the Hannons?" Molly said.

"No. Her mother was a nice kid, a whore when she was thirteen. Prettiest one on the Way. She was a dago and had black hair, just like Blackie. All the guys wanted her."

"Where is she?" Molly said cautiously.

Tilly snorted. "She's been dead about five years…when Blackie was three."

"Did you take care of the baby?" Molly asked.

"Yeah. Her mother asked me, if anything ever happened to her, would I take care of Blackie."

"How'd she die?" said Hugh.

"Them whores die all the time. You know...she really liked this one guy, a soldier—nice. They were gonna get married, but he got killed in the war. She stayed on here. Then one morning they found her in the park strangled."

"What happened? They ever find who did it?" said Molly.

She shook her head. "Nah. Some of them kids get hooked up with these nasty johns. They flash some money at the girls, then they turn into killers 'cause it's easy, and they can get away with it."

Molly had tears in her eyes. Tilly reached over and touched her hand with her own rough, gnarled hand. Molly looked at her. "Tilly, you'll see her all the time. We'll be over there to see her granddad. We won't let her forget you." Tilly smiled and nodded.

"Get your stuff, Tilly. We're gonna take you over to see your new boss," said Hugh.

Chapter 14

Hugh RANG THE DOORBELL, and John answered the door. "Good morning, Mr. Connolly."

"Good morning, John. Is the mistress about?" said Hugh, walking in as John instinctively stepped aside to let Hugh, now treated as a family member, in.

"Yes, sir. I'll call her." John and the staff, seven people in all, had been amazed at the miraculous changes in their lives. Anetta Reid had become a happy, sociable, and spirited woman. Piccina had changed the whole household. And the daily visits by Hugh and Isabella and Abramo and Molly had infused more life and happiness into the house than there had ever been. Suddenly, a queen of Youngstown society had become a grandmother to a big Irish and Italian family. And John knew that it all began with Hugh. The whole staff liked him, not only for the changes he had wrought in Anetta Reid, but for bringing Piccina and all the other wonderful characters to the house and filling it with warmth and noise and wonderful new foods and customs.

"Did she order one, John?" Hugh asked.

"No, sir."

"Good. I'll be in the library," Hugh said.

In a few minutes Anetta Reid walked in to the library. "Hugh? Is everything all right?"

"Yes. How are you, Anetta?"

"I'm fine," she said curiously.

"Is Piccina here?"

"She's upstairs with Mary. They play for an hour or so each day while Mary combs her hair and dresses her," she said smiling.

"Molly and Abramo told me to ask you if they could take Piccina out this afternoon," Hugh said.

"Why...yes. That would be fine," said Anetta, still perplexed by the turn the morning was taking.

"Good. I'll let them know."

"Hugh. It's not often you come here this early. Are you sure everything's all right?"

"Of course...but there is something. I want you to come with me."

"When?"

"Right now."

"In this weather? For what purpose?"

"The best, to get a Christmas tree."

"But I haven't had a tree in years," she said.

"Times change, Anetta. We have to have one now. So get your coat."

"What? You really want me to go with you?"

"That's why I'm here," he said brightly.

"Hugh Connolly, I'm too old to be gadding about in all that Christmas traffic out there. Besides, someone has to be here with Piccina."

"You know darn well that this staff would love to have her all to themselves a while. They'll play with her and feed her all kinds of goodies. Even John is crazy about her. And remember, Molly and Abramo will be coming by later."

"But can't you get one? I'll pay for it, and you can certainly pick one to my liking."

"Absolutely not. And if you behave yourself, I'll take you to lunch. Now come on, time's a'wasting."

"Go out to lunch during the middle of the week? Whoever heard of such a thing?"

"It's Friday, first of all—the end of the week. And it's done by all sorts of God's creatures."

"But Hugh, I don't know if we even have decorations for a tree."

"I'd bet my next paycheck that you do. Now please go and get your coat."

"Oh, very well," she huffed. She turned away and walked toward the door, muttering to herself as she went, but in her heart pleased and excited by the spontaneous interest the younger man had shown in her.

In a few minutes she returned, Piccina holding her hand and Mary frantically trying to get Anetta's garments in order so she wouldn't get a chill. "Hi, Uncle Hugh," Piccina said, running toward him for a hug.

Hugh hugged her and picked her up. "How are you, angel? You looked like you've gained some weight," he said.

"Two pounds," Mary said proudly. "Dr. Shanfield was surprised."

"Mrs. Reid and I are going to go out for a while," Hugh said to the little girl. "Will you stay with Mary and John until Molly and Abramo come to pick you up later?"

She nodded, kissing him. "Come back soon, Mrs. Reid," Piccina said.

"Yes, my dear, I'll be back soon," she said, caressing Piccina's cheek.

"Well then, let's go," said Hugh. Anetta followed, still with a perplexed look about her.

Hugh winked knowingly at Mary as they made their way out the door. He knew a place on the East Side that sold nice trees. When they arrived, Hugh stopped the car and stepped out. He then waited. "Well, are you coming?" he said finally.

"Do you really want me to pick out a tree? Aren't they all the same?" she said.

"One of these trees has your name on it, Anetta," he said, opening the car door.

She got out of the car with his help and began to walk with him up and down the lines of trees, set up to attract buyers. There was one very large tree that seemed to be in perfect shape, with long needles and bright color, but for some reason she hesitated in choosing it.

She and Hugh had evolved a gently gracious way of acting toward each other. Onlookers would have thought that this was a mother and a son: talking, taunting, laughing, teasing, touching. Anetta was amazed at how easily she adapted to the new change in her life, how natural and easy was her relationship to Hugh and all the others who were led by him through her portal. She had come to love Isabella as a daughter and rejoiced at the attentions of Gianina and the boys. And Piccina had enchanted her so much that she now dreaded the thought of not seeing her at the breakfast table every morning.

Molly and Abramo saw her constantly and would visit often together or separately. Molly would talk to Anetta about her upcoming marriage and ask her questions and advice. Abramo would fix things around the house that needed repair and would come to talk to his beloved Piccina.

One day Anetta found the two of them in the library, sitting in a chair under a lamp, reading. The child was curled up in Abramo's embrace looking at the book that he was reading from. Piccina listened intently to the fairy tale, asking questions about what happened in the story, learning about life experiences she didn't understand.

Anetta wished she had a photograph of the two of them. There was something about the way they looked, so intent on the story and yet so intimately together: his one arm holding the book and the other around her, while her hands held each of his arms in an unconscious touch of shared warmth.

Kieran and his boys would often visit and would see to it that all things around the house were stocked and supplied. Even Kieran's sons, at first uneasy around the fierce-looking dowager, responded to their father's warmth toward her and began to relate to her as individuals. They had known few old people like her. They were only accustomed to the old cranks and boozers of the AOH.

Even Abramo's Uncle Michele and his Aunt Renata would visit every few weeks and speak the language of the elderly to her. Their conversations would last several hours over coffee and refreshments. Anetta was always thrilled by some of the exotic Italian treats that they brought her—chestnuts and pomegranates and all kinds of baked goodies.

They had become friends, each learning from the other: Michele and Renata that the Irish were warm and kind and generous, and Anetta that the Italians could be wise, cultured, and interested in the same mysteries of life as she.

"Well, we've been through them all. Do you want to go to another place?" Hugh said.

"No, there's one I want," she said, looking behind her, trying to remember where it was.

"You mean that big one we saw in the second row?"

"No, there was another one," she said, still thinking of where it could be. "I think it was in the fourth row."

They went down the forth row but couldn't find it. Then they went down the third row. She stopped in front of a tree that was smaller than the beautiful imposing one they had seen before. It was full, with medium long needles and very dark green. "I want Piccina and the children to see the tree up close, to be able to touch the top if someone holds them," she said. "This will do."

Hugh walked over to the seller and paid for the tree. "Can you get it there by two this afternoon? And send another, smaller one, also."

"Yeah, when the guys get back from their other run, we'll send them right out. What's the address?"

"1435 Monday Parkway," said Hugh. "It's on the North Side."

"Everybody knows where that is," he said. "That your place?"

"No. Hers," said Hugh. "And put stands on them. How much will that be?"

"An extra three dollars," the man said.

"Okay. Here's five. By two o'clock now. Go around to the back door. It'll be easier to get it in."

Then he went back to Anetta. "Now, let's get some lunch, huh?"

"Are you sure, Hugh? You don't have to do this," she said.

"I know I don't have to. I want to," said Hugh.

"Where are we going?"

"To the Speier Hotel."

"But we didn't make reservations."

"Yes, we did," said Hugh.

They drove the short distance to the Speier dining room. When they were seated, she was quiet. "I have not been out to lunch since Anthony died," she said.

"Well, I guess we've started something," said Hugh.

They ordered from the menu and then talked about the Christmas party. "Did we invite Captain Grogan, Hugh? Do you remember?"

"We must have. He told me he was coming."

The waiter brought coffee for them. Both sipped the warm brew as they felt the cold of December leave their bodies. "Anetta," Hugh said, "there's something I…" He stopped.

"Yes? What is it?"

He shook his head. It was one of the few times in his life that he was at a loss for words. "Hugh? Is there something wrong?"

"Oh, no, nothing wrong. I wasn't even going to say anything, but…"

"But? Tell me."

"Well, it's about the kids. Mine and Isabella's…and you."

"Me?"

"Yes. They want…" He hesitated again, getting upset with himself for even starting the conversation.

"What do they want?"

"Well…Please don't take offense. There's none meant, but, well…"

"Hugh Connolly, will you please tell me what's on your mind? I'm an old lady who could die before you get around to making your point."

"Well, they've never had…" He twisted his coffee cup by the handle, back and forth. "I mean, they'd like to call you Grandma."

She closed her eyes and smiled slightly. "That's the thing you had so hard a time telling me?" He nodded. "Piccina asked me if I was like a Grandma the other day. I didn't make anything of it because I wasn't sure if Molly and Abramo would approve. She never asked again, because I'm sure she thought I didn't like it."

"Well? Did you?"

"Of course I did. Do you think I could be offended by anything that child—or your children—could do?"

"Well, these Italians do such things, you know. We Irish aren't as familiar as they are, and I thought you might consider it a presumption. You know, Anetta, there are people all over town who would say that the only reason why all of us have grown close to you is because of your money."

"Those are the same people who wanted to believe that Brendan was a traitor to his country," she said, dismissing his point.

She was quiet for a few minutes. "Hugh, not too long ago, I was waiting to die, in a dark and shaded house, closed off against the world, bitter because all I ever cared about in this life had been taken from me. Then I got to know you…and Abramo and Isabella and Molly, and of course, Piccina.

"Adults might be venal charlatans, but not those children. So I've decided to live my life trusting the love that I see around me… and being grateful for it." She drummed the table with the fingers of her right hand. "I think, Hugh, I'm going to live a long time," she said. "Being called 'Grandma' by those children would let me know that something of heaven has been slipped into my life today."

"I'm glad, Anetta. None of those kids have ever had a grandmother. It'll seem like this Christmas brought them the greatest of all presents—a renewal of their past."

While Hugh and Anetta were having lunch, and Hugh was dawdling over his food, at the Reid Mansion there was frenetic activity. The Christmas tree decorations, stored for years in dusty boxes in the attic, had surreptitiously been cleaned and restored to their former beauty and elegance. They were quickly brought out of boxes and set out for Isabella and Molly and Mary and the rest of the staff to decide which to use.

Meanwhile, Abramo and John and Kieran's boys were carefully bringing in the new frame and taking the old frame down so that the picture of Brendan could be detached from it.

Conor, who had come to like Abramo, and who looked forward to becoming his brother-in-law, had suddenly grown interested in carpentry and stood by to help Abramo as they hurriedly but carefully took the picture out of the old frame.

The library was filled with more than a dozen people, coming and going. Piccina was upstairs in her room, being entertained by Gianina while the whole staff was discussing how the tree should be decorated. Only John had served long enough to remember what Anetta liked in the way of decorations, and his memory was sketchy at best. In the end, Isabella and Molly and Mary decided to infuse their own spirits into the decorating.

Conor called to everyone in the room. "Don't look, anyone… not until we tell you."

Abramo, Conor, Paul, and Ross held the picture and lifted it above the mantle, placing it carefully on the wall, securing it so it would not fall forward. Abramo leveled the picture against the pitch of the mantle and drove in the last brace to hold it.

They all stepped down from the ladders and looked up. It was superb. "Okay," said Conor. When all the guests and staff saw the picture, they were dazzled by its beauty.

Suddenly, the back doorbell rang, and the delivery men had the trees waiting on the doorstep. In a few moments, the trees were brought inside and set up in the library and the reception room. Gianina and Piccina were called to decorate the little tree in the library. In an hour both trees were done, and the rooms were clean and filled with cookies, cakes, breads, and pies that smelled wonderful when blended with the fragrance of hot tea and coffee on the tables. The odor of pine needles filled the air, and the trees with all the brilliant, ancient decorations were placed where ceiling lamps made soft light seem to cascade down the silver and gold ribbons that wound about them.

They all drank coffee and tea and ate Christmas cookies as they mixed together, talking and laughing and enjoying the success they had in doing all this behind Mrs. Reid's back. The staff was amazed at the conviviality of all these Irish and Italians entertaining together. And they all treated the staff with courtesy and warmth. In this joyful season, they became social equals for the day.

Suddenly, they heard the front door open. Hugh and Mrs. Reid entered. In a second, John and Mary were beside them to take their coats and help them brush the light snow from their clothes. "We took longer than we thought," Anetta said to both John and Mary, noting the wide smiles and happy demeanor of her two long-time servants.

"What's that I smell, John?" she asked.

"I don't know, madam," he said smiling.

"Bring us some tea and sherry, would you?" she said.

"Yes, ma'am," said Mary.

Meanwhile, Hugh was headed toward the reception room. "Hugh? I thought we might have tea in the library?"

"That's fine, Anetta. I'd like to see something first."

Unconsciously, she followed him as he slowed down deliberately to let her catch up. He opened the double doors wide.

Anetta stepped forward a few paces and saw the tree, decorated in shimmering beauty. Then she saw the large group of people standing quietly and smiling as she gazed at their creation. "Oh, my goodness," she said, "it's absolutely lovely." She looked at all of them and shook her head. "He wouldn't finish his lunch. He ordered dessert and coffee, then a drink…It took forever," she said, brushing Hugh's arm with her hand as he stood beside her grinning like a mischievous schoolboy.

"Where's that tea, Mary?" Hugh said, winking at Isabella.

"In the library, sir," Mary said in well-rehearsed response.

"I'd love to have a cup, wouldn't you, Anetta," he said, offering her his hand to escort her into the room.

As she walked in, Anetta was amazed at the large assortment of pastries and cookies that were arranged on trays surrounding the tea- and coffee pots. "But who made…" Then she looked at Isabella, Molly, Mary, and John all standing together beaming for the way they had created those secret, beautiful delights. She smiled and shook her head in amazement. For a few seconds, she was preoccupied with the table, but when she turned to go further into the room, she saw the picture.

Without a sound, she walked over and stood before it. On her tiptoes she touched the frame and ran her hand along the base of it. She stood back, motionless for a few minutes, her back to everyone now assembled in the room. She wiped her eyes with her handkerchief, holding it to her face.

After a few moments, she made the Sign of the Cross and turned toward them, smiling through her tears. She came toward Hugh and put her hand behind his neck and drew him toward her so she could kiss him on the cheek, just as she had done so often to Brendan when he was a young man. She held out her hand to Abramo, and he took it and stood before her. She kissed him and hugged him. "Thank you, my boy. It's more beautiful than I ever could have imagined. Please let me give you something for—"

"Never," said Abramo. "He will rest now."

It was almost four o'clock in the morning as Hugh Connolly sat in his kitchen drinking coffee. What he wouldn't give to have Isabella here with him now. Just the thought of her touch made his arms tingle. Hugh poured himself a coffee royal. God, would he love to have Isabella here. He chuckled. She conjured up evil thoughts during the middle of the night. He never wished for Christmas to come and go so quickly. But if it did, then January seventeenth would come and she would sleep in his arms that night. Finally, he went upstairs to shave and bathe. Suddenly the big house seemed terribly empty, as though it longed for more life within it, more noise, more music, more joy.

He was early, especially for a Saturday, but he had to see her, so he rang the doorbell at seven o'clock. Isabella came to the door in a robe over her nightgown and in bare feet. She looked alarmed and fearful. "Good morning, signorina," Hugh said brightly.

"There is nothing wrong?" she said as she pulled him inside by his arm.

"Nothing's wrong, except that I need a cup of Italian coffee before I go to work. I'm going down for a few hours."

She rolled her eyes and smiled as she walked him into the kitchen. He studied her as she made the coffee. When she realized what he was doing, she turned to him. "What?"

"I was up most of the night," he said, "and I was thinking about you."

"I was up, too…thinking of you," she said.

Hugh smiled, pleased. After a few seconds, he said in a more serious tone, "Isabella? How much money do you owe on this house?"

"About one thousand dollars. Why?"

"Well, I was thinking last night…My house is so big…and so empty. We're going to live there, aren't we?"

She shrugged her shoulders. "So much has happened in the past weeks, I have not given much thought to it. I will do whatever you wish, Hugh."

"The children would have their own rooms, and there would be a guest bedroom besides ours. I would like you to be mistress of my house as you are of my life. It might make you…Well, Aileen never lived in that house." She smiled and touched his hand. "Isabella?"

"Yes, my dear? What are you trying to tell me?"

"Well, you owe about what? Five years?"

"Yes," she said, curious about what he would say.

"Well, how would it be if we gave this place to Molly and Abramo as a wedding gift? They won't have a home of their own otherwise. They can finish off the mortgage and then it would be theirs."

"Do you have enough money so that we could give them this house?"

"Yes."

"Then it is a beautiful thing, and we should do it."

"I was thinking: where would the old men go if we sold the house to strangers? This way Molly can take care of them as you did. And when she can't, you can help her, okay?"

There were tears in her eyes. "Don't cry," he said. "How can I think lustful thoughts if you're crying?"

She laughed. "I love you, Signor Connolly." She thought for a few seconds. "Hugh? Will you have time to ride me to Anetta's now?"

"Sure," he said, curious.

"We have to ask her about Christmas. Besides, I have made dough for pizza. She loves pizza, and I can make it for her while she's in church…I'll get dressed now," she said.

"You need any help getting dressed?" he said.

"If you help me, then I will not get dressed."

"There are worse things," he said. "I just know that between now and January seventeenth I'm never going to get you alone. God does me that way."

"It's only a few weeks away, Hugh," she crooned. "Then forever we will always be together, and you can teach me about all the lust you dream of," she said, giving him a quick kiss.

He sat quietly alone drinking coffee in the kitchen for several minutes. The door opened and Gianina walked in, like her mother, barefoot and in a nightgown. She shrieked when she saw him. Hugh laughed. "Good morning, young lady."

"Good morning, signore," she said, wide-eyed and bewildered.

"I'm waiting for your mother. I'm going to take her to Mrs. Reid's house," said Hugh.

"She'll see Piccina," she said, smiling. She poured some coffee and came to the table to sit across from him. She had grown fond of Hugh. She liked his wit, his intelligence, and his kindness. Isabella had told her much about him, and Gianina began to know him vicariously, and to like him.

"Signor Connolly…" She stopped, unable to complete what she was to say.

Hugh could see so much of Isabella in her that he had to restrain himself from being as familiar with her as he was with her mother.

"My dear," said Hugh, "since your mother and I will be married in a month, we're going to have to find a new form of address for each other."

"What do you mean?" she said in unaccented English.

"I mean that 'Signor Connolly' would hardly seem appropriate for the man who is married to your mother, who sits at your supper table every night, who sleeps with your mother in a bedroom upstairs."

"What would be appropriate?"

"I don't know," said Hugh.

"You have no children?"

"No. My wife took sick shortly after we were married. And then she died."

"Why did you not marry again?"

"I could never find anyone as special as my wife."

"But you found my mother?"

"Yes. And she is special."

"Will you love her as much as you did your first wife?"

"Yes. I will love her with all my heart."

She was quiet for a few minutes, drinking coffee silently. Then she said, "Did you want to have children with your wife?"

"Yes," he said.

"Do you get lonely sometimes since you're all alone?"

He shrugged slightly. "Yes. My job at the mill keeps me busy. I'm active in politics. But the loneliness is always there…especially in quiet moments."

"Why do you stay alone in such a big house?"

"I sometimes wonder myself. Perhaps it's because I harbored secret dreams of filling it someday. For now, it's just a place where I live, not a home."

"Why is it not?"

"Because something is missing."

"What?"

"The love of a family." She smiled and took another sip of coffee. "Could I ask you something?" he said.

"Yes," she said, curious about what he would say. She was taken by his frankness, and by the way he addressed her as an intellectual equal as he answered all her questions.

"Do you miss your father?"

"I hardly remember him. The boys don't remember him at all." Hugh didn't say anything more. Then she spoke again. "Will we be happy together?"

"We will if we want to be," he said. "I mean, we have to count our blessings and choose happiness over misery."

"But what if we argue?"

"Have you ever argued with your mother?" he asked. She nodded. "And with your brothers?" She rolled her eyes in response. "Do you think you might argue with me?"

She was thoughtful for a few moments. "If I can argue with my mother, I can argue with you." She paused again. "What will you and I be like? I mean, what will we mean to each other?"

He drew a deep breath. "All men want sons…but more than anything I wanted a daughter…someone like Aileen. So, for many years I have been lonely for my wife and for the daughter she might have given me. It just wasn't meant to be. Then, one day, I come to this doorstep." He gestured over his shoulder. "And an angel answers the door. And the angel has a daughter. And I've been thinking…all my life…"

She looked into his eyes for a few seconds. "Would you want me as a daughter?"

"More than anything else in the world," he said softly.

"But if I'm your daughter, then you're my father."

He grinned. "That's usually the way it works."

"And if you're my father, then I can call you 'Papa'?"

He nodded. "And that would be music to my ears."

Gianina leaped up from her chair and into his arms as he stood up to meet her. He kissed her on the forehead, and she in turn kissed him on both cheeks.

At that moment, Isabella came back into the kitchen, startled by the display of affection between them. She held her hand, palm vertical, pointing toward her daughter in consternation and curiosity, a gesture seen a thousand times in the homes and on the streets of every Italian neighborhood. "Look at you—nightgown, bare feet."

"Oh, it's okay now, Mama," Gianina said, glancing at Hugh and beaming. Hugh, too, was grinning broadly.

"What's okay? What are you two grinning about?" she said, sensing the playful happiness between them.

Hugh grabbed Gianina's hand and took one step toward her mother. "Signora Connolly, may I present Signorina Gianina Connolly, my daughter."

Isabella brought both hands to her mouth in amazement. She looked at Gianina, and her daughter nodded. She and Hugh had forged a family just by talking over coffee. Gianina hugged her mother, who gave a love tap to one of her buttocks. "You'll catch cold," Isabella said, embracing her daughter.

"I have to go, Papa," Gianina said, turning toward Hugh. "I'll see you tonight, won't I?"

"Yes, my girl. At supper."

When the girl left the room, Isabella shook her head in wonderment. "How did you do that?" she asked.

"Magic," he said, raising his index finger before her. "You think you dagos are the only ones who know witchcraft?" She swatted his shoulder gently. Then he grew more serious. "After you left, she walked in, not knowing I was here. Anyhow, we were drinking coffee, and she started talking and asking questions. One thing led to another, and I became 'Papa.'"

Hugh and Isabella brought the fresh pizza that Anetta liked so much. During tea and pizza, they settled into casual conservation, Anetta leading the subject. "My dears, will all of you and your family be my guests for dinner on Christmas? I'll invite Molly and Abramo and Kieran and the boys, and Abramo's aunt and uncle…and, of course, we can watch the children open their gifts. Piccina doesn't know what Christmas really is, so we'll go to Mass, and then we'll have dinner about two o'clock. Is that all right?"

Hugh looked at Isabella, and she nodded. "Well, if we're coming, we want to help," said Hugh. "That's what families do, right?"

"Can I help you make some of the food?" Isabella asked.

"If you would make some of this pizza and those dainty waffle cookies, that would be wonderful," she said. "And come as early as you can." She paused for a moment. "I almost can't remember what it was like to have a big Christmas dinner here."

But Isabella knew that there was something else on Anetta's mind. "What else do you wish to talk about, Anetta?" she said.

The old lady smiled, surprised that the young woman sensed her mood. "Well…lately I've learned so much about the terrible effects of poverty, because now it has a face: Piccina. It's heartbreaking to think that those children are all like our girl—never having had cake or ice cream or any kind of present. They've never been loved. So I've decided—and I'll need your help, Mr. Connolly—I've decided to build an orphans' home. Maybe on the North Side."

Hugh looked at Isabella and then back to Anetta. "It will cost a great deal of money, Anetta. Maybe we can see if there is a place available that can be fixed up."

"I'll leave that to you, Hugh. I'm not worried about the money. I just want it done so that those children have a Christmas at least faintly resembling the one that we will have.

"This year they will have new clothes and presents to open, and a nice dinner. Father Quinn will say Mass for them on Christmas morning, and some of the nuns from the convent will be there to warm up the day."

"It's a first step toward changing their lives, Anetta," said Hugh. "You know now that those little girls will not become prostitutes, and the boys will not become gang members."

She was thoughtful for a few seconds. "Isn't it hard to imagine? Piccina as a prostitute in four years? How awful!"

"What will you call the home?" Isabella asked.

"I don't know," said Anetta; "I've never thought of that."

"Well, I think it should be named after an Irish saint," Hugh said.

"Which one were you thinking of?" Anetta said. "Patrick?"

"No," he said, "Brendan."

She was quiet for a few moments. "St. Brendan's Home for Orphans…I like it."

Chapter 15

THE NEWLYWEDS BECAME FRIENDS, bonding as strongly as a group as they did with each other. Once, early on before the weddings, Abramo called Hugh "Signor Connolly." Hugh waved the title off. "Listen, boyo, at the mill, just so they don't think I'm always favoring you, you can call me that. But as Molly's husband, I'm 'Uncle Hugh' to you. Okay?"

One night, Hugh and Isabella invited Molly and Abramo to dinner, and to meet Isabella's sister, who had moved to Youngstown at her sister's urging. When they arrived, they were met by Hugh and the children at the door. Abramo hugged and kissed each of them, even the boys. Molly, not really used to the open affection and expressions of love of the Italians, did the same. It was fast becoming second nature to her.

"Where's Piccina?" said Isabella's youngest son.

"Here," said Abramo, pulling the little girl forward as she nervously held her new father's hand.

Gianina hugged Piccina and brought her forward into the midst of the children to help her take off her coat. "Come with us. We want to show you our new rooms," the youngest boy said.

"Mommy?" Piccina said, turning to Molly to see if it was okay to leave them. Piccina was living the opposite of a normal life. She had learned to live as an adult, alone without parents or family, fending for herself in a hostile world. Now she was learning to live as a child, learning to trust the love, the gentle touches, and the tender mercies of people other than her new parents.

"Yes, my dear, we'll call all of you later," said Molly.

With the children gone, the room was quiet, with Molly and Abramo and Hugh left alone to catch their breaths. Then the door opened, and a lovely woman with mahogany brown hair walked in.

"Madonna," Abramo whispered when he saw her. Molly pinched his side and made him laugh softly.

"Molly and Abramo, this is my sister-in-law," said Hugh, "Signora Marina di Capua. Marina, my niece and nephew, Molly and Abramo Cardone." Marina curtsied gently. Isabella entered just at that moment with some wine and biscotti on a tray.

Molly and Abramo, upon seeing the two sisters standing together, a dark brown and black version of Italian loveliness, turned to Hugh in amazement. "I told you she was beautiful," Hugh said in response to their looks of astonishment.

"Are you twins?" Molly asked.

"No. I am the older," said Marina, "by one year."

The meeting between them was easy and warm. Marina was so much like Isabella that everyone felt that they had known her for ages. The dinner with four children and five adults was noisy and bright, with conversations and stories going all ways back and forth across the table.

Molly loved Italian food, especially the new dish they called "pasta." She had tasted noodles, but they were a blander form of what they had tonight, a tomato sauce with spicy, wonderful flavor. The dessert was the usual fruit and coffee and a cake made by Marina. It was all delicious.

Later, as all three women cleared the table, Molly begged her new aunt and her sister to teach her how to cook some of the exotic dishes for her new husband—pasta and that delicious bread pie called pizza.

Hugh was standing near the fireplace that crackled with the large logs that blazed all through dinner. His drink was on the mantle, and he was alone and quiet, watching the women. Abramo had been commandeered by the children to visit one of their rooms and comment on a display they had set up. Piccina was delighted with her new cousins, even though she had not known what cousins were. She didn't realize that cousins often come in packages, grouped by three in this case, and as talking, laughing, teasing, touching, and feuding siblings. To Piccina, feuding without the love that each of Hugh and Isabella's children felt for their parents and in their secret hearts for each other, meant malice and retribution. She had always lived like that. Now, feuds and animosities just moments old could be forgotten in the wake of new discoveries or interesting stories or surprise events. She learned that animosities and even anger, in the right house, among people who loved each other, are ephemeral and nonlethal.

Abramo had giving his blessing to the many constructions of blankets and pillows that created tents and secret passages, all decorated with signs and drawings on school paper. His work was soon done because new construction was about to begin. Piccina was one of the central figures in the undercover work, under chairs and beds and tables. She was busy.

Downstairs, Abramo came upon more noise: three women talking and laughing and cleaning. Hugh, standing aloof, studied them as they interacted. Abramo noticed that he was watching Marina as she came in and out of the kitchen. Hugh took a sip of whiskey, unaware of his nephew watching him.

"He'll like her," he said to Hugh. "He'll be as captivated by her as you are of Isabella."

"The hell you say, Cardone," Hugh growled. "I don't know what you're talking about."

"I'm talking about my father-in-law, as you well know," Abramo said in Italian.

"You dagos have a lot of witch in you, you know that?"

Abramo laughed. "Uncle Hugh, do you remember that night you first came to see me when I was making Brendan's frame? When Isabella answered the door, what did you do?" Hugh shook his head. "What did you do, *Zio*?" Abramo persisted.

Hugh took a deep breath and turned to face Abramo. "I fell in love," he said.

"Is the man who has been your best friend all your life so very different from you?" Abramo asked and gestured with his drink slightly toward Marina, who had just entered the room alone.

"But will she be captivated by him?" Hugh said.

"Look at her. What do you see?"

Hugh snorted softly. "Jesus. I see Isabella."

"You see one side of her happiness. The other side is in the AOH."

"What makes you so sure of all of this?" Hugh said.

"You and I both know what it is to be lonely, to long for someone wonderful. My beloved father-in-law is also like that. Is he not?"

Hugh nodded and was about to speak when the children came down into the room and the noise level inside shook the walls. Molly, Isabella, and Marina came into the room carrying cookies for them.

Before they began to share the goodies, Isabella called to the little girl. Hugh was standing near his wife, and Abramo was standing next to Molly.

"Piccina, come here, my dear. Tell Uncle Hugh your new name." The little girl came toward Hugh shyly. "Tell him, angel," Isabella said.

Piccina turned back to Molly, who nodded to her, smiling encouragement. "Cara," she said.

There was silence in the room. Hugh at first was motionless. Then he raised his hand to his eye to wipe a tear. Isabella urged the little girl closer to the front of him. The other children, and even Marina, did not know what had struck him so acutely, so they watched intently in silence.

When he took his hand away, he saw the little girl standing in front of him. He knelt down and hugged her, kissing her on the forehead silently, then on both cheeks. Then he stood up and looked at Molly and Abramo.

"He thought of it, Uncle Hugh," Molly said.

"It's both Irish and Italian," Abramo said, shrugging. Hugh walked over to his nephew and hugged him. "Thank you both. This means the world to me. And hearing that dear name will bring me joy for all my life. Does your father know?" he said to Molly.

"No," she said. "We'll tell him next. We just decided today when the judge told us we could have her for our own. We were afraid to name her until we knew for sure she was ours."

"Cara was the name of Hugh's beloved sister and Molly's mother, God rest her soul," Isabella whispered to Marina in Italian.

Abramo's aunt came to the door to let him in. "He's in his chair," she said, pointing to the parlor where Michele usually sat.

They spoke in Italian. "How is he doing?" said Abramo.

"He has most trouble at night usually…but it's getting worse."

Abramo walked quietly into the parlor. "Zi'Michele," he said, grasping his hand and bending over to kiss the old man's cheek.

"Abramo, it's good to see you, my boy."

"How are you getting along, Uncle?" he said as he sat down opposite Michele.

"I'm doing okay," Michele said. "What's the good of complaining? And how are Molly and that little girl?"

"Ah, they're fine. Molly tells me she's afraid that if she doesn't learn to cook like Isabella, I might run away."

Both men chuckled. "Dear Molly," he said. "Why would any man run away from such happiness?"

"That is what I tell her every day. But, you know, these Irish often look upon the dark side of life. They have to be reminded not to worry so much."

"I'm so happy I've lived to see your marriage," he said.

"You will live to see other marriages and births and baptisms, Zi'Michele."

Michele shook his head and was thoughtful for a few moments. "Only yours, Abramo."

"Zi'Michele…"

"No, my boy, you must know it's true. I will be gone before summer."

"Is it that bad, *Zio*?"

"I am getting worse, Abramo. My day is coming. But I will leave this world a happy man. You have been the blessing of my life, the son I've never had."

"Did you ever think when you saw me not even three years ago, that I'd have two wonderful girls like Molly and Piccina?"

"I always hoped for good things to happen to you, because of the pain you endured in Italy. I never imagined that they would come in the shape of two such fine women."

"They've been a blessing, *Zio*."

"You bless each other, Abramo. Your happiness becomes my happiness and Aunt Renata's happiness and Kieran's happiness and Hugh and Isabella's happiness and the Donna Reid's happiness. Remember that as you grow older. You are never so potent that you do not need all these good people in your life. There will never be a day when they don't enrich your life and bring you grace."

"I will remember, *Zio*," Abramo said softly.

"I know you will, my boy." He paused for a moment. "Abramo, I am not rich, but I have some money. I will leave most of it to you and Aunt Renata, and a few distant relatives I brought to this country. And Marco…I have given him the warehouse and the wine franchise. He has been my best friend for twenty years and has helped me grow prosperous in America. You are many things, son, but you are not a warehouseman. He deserves the business."

"I'm glad you did that. Marco is a good man. But I'll be all right, Zi'Michele. I do not need it. Give it to Aunt Renata and my cousins."

"No. I will give Aunt Renata the money she will need to buy food and shelter, to live. But you must give her the other sustenance she needs—yourself and your family. Please keep her in your life, Abramo. Please never let her be lonely."

He shook his head. "I will take care of her, Uncle. She will never be lonely."

"I have had a full life, Abramo. I have done some foolish things…I let the one woman I loved get away and marry someone else, all because I was too busy making money and too blind to realize what she meant to me. And for thirty years she was the blessing of another man's life, the mother of his children. When she died, I knew the pain I felt was deserved, and of my own doing. But in other ways it made me wiser, because ever after I always remembered how foolish I was at the most important moment of my life.

"But you, son, are the last great blessing I will have. That Irish girl will show you that some of us can have heaven here on earth. And Piccina will reveal to you the story of the little girl you once lost. For what you lost, you have found in her."

They lay next to each other, exhausted after their lovemaking. Molly smiled and kissed Abramo. "Are you truly happy?"

He looked at her and nodded. "I have you and a lovely daughter. I am part of two wonderful families. Every day I get more outside work as a carpenter and cabinetmaker. We will soon own this house. Piccina is finally ours. Except for Uncle Michele's sickness, my life is glorious."

Just then a sharp clap of thunder rolled above the house. Abramo got out of bed and put on a pair of underpants. Then he got back into bed. Molly was curious about what he did, because they usually lay together naked through the night after they made love. He lay back and took a deep breath, running his hand gently over her groin, instinctively enjoying the pleasure of her softness. They were quiet for a few moments.

Then there was a gentle knock at the door. "Yes, Cara?" Molly called.

Piccina opened the door, dressed in a simple child's nightgown. "Mommy, can I stay with you and Daddy tonight?"

Abramo motioned to her to come into bed. She ran to his bedside, and he picked her up with one arm and rolled her onto the bed between Molly and him. When she was situated, she raised herself up slightly and smiled, her right hand braced against Molly's naked breast. She bent over to kiss her new mother on the lips. Then she turned to Abramo. Molly had seen it before: the innocent, childlike look between them, the way she gazed deep into his eyes, searching for his soul, the look that they had dreamed the same dream, come true now that they were together, the look of love with that mysterious and irresistible connection.

Piccina touched his face, laying one hand on his cheek, brushing his hair back off his forehead. Then she bent down, placing her left hand on his chest and reached over to kiss him on the lips. Then she sat cross-legged on the bed between them, putting her hands together in a single silent clap, smiling as she faced them both. She seemed amazed by her happiness, finally knowing that all the evil that had come before in her life was small tribute for the joy and wonder at being loved by this man and this woman. God did care about her.

Joseph Greenhill rang Anetta Reid's doorbell one day in late February. When he was ushered in to the library, Anetta was waiting. "Hello, Anetta, how are you?"

"Fine, Joseph. Thank you for coming so promptly."

"My pleasure…but what can I do for you?"

"Well, I'm going to make some changes in my will."

"You are? Didn't we make it final and definitive just last year?"

"I was going to die soon, then. My circumstances have changed a great deal in the past year."

"Everything had changed," he said. "Do you know how much money you're worth now? You're one of the richest women in the country."

"How much?"

He opened the folder that he had taken out of his briefcase and read from it. "Your personal worth is almost fourteen million dollars...not to mention what your stock in the mill will be worth when U.S. Steel buys the Carnegie portion of your estate out. Remember, he agreed to give your heirs market value, and U.S. Steel agreed to it."

"Well, that's good. It will enable me to do some of the things I want to do."

"What do you want to do?"

"Well, to begin with, I want to leave two million dollars to Hugh and Isabella Connolly," she said.

"Hugh Connolly? Isn't he the executive at Reid-Carnegie that's also a politician in the Second Ward?"

"That's the one. Also, I'd like to leave the same amount to Abramo and Molly Cardone."

"Two million?"

"Yes."

He seemed troubled. "Are you sure you want to do this, Anetta? I mean...this is a great deal of money, far more than they would ever make in their lifetimes."

"I'm certain of it. Also, I would like you to arrange a trust for Saint Brendan's Home for Orphaned Children—six million dollars. That will sustain the home after I'm gone."

"What about your niece in St. Louis?"

"I've decided to lower her legacy to two million dollars."

"So you're cutting the current legacy in half?"

"Yes."

"But why are you doing all this? How long have you known these other people?"

"Most I have only known well about a year," she said.

He took a deep breath. "Look, Anetta, I've been advising you on your money for more than twenty years. Please don't take this wrong…but I'd like you to be sure of these changes. Has anyone tried to talk you into this? Against your better judgment?"

"Joseph, do you know what I did this last Christmas?"

"No," he said, curiously.

"Well, I had dinner here…but with fourteen other people, a bunch of Irish and Italians. And there was more laughter and joy and noise in this place than there ever has been, all because of those people.

"Do you know what I'm going to do at Easter? I'm going to spend it at Molly and Abramo's house. And Thanksgiving? At Kieran Harty's house. And Christmas next? At Hugh and Isabella Connolly's house.

"Do you know where I have spent the last eighteen Christmases? And Easters? And Thanksgivings? Right here in this house…alone. These people have changed my life, Joseph. Now I have four children who call me 'Grandma,' and now I receive visitors daily. Not a day goes by that at least one of several men doesn't visit. And I talk to or see Isabella and Molly every day. They ask for nothing and bring things always, things they cook or bake for me.

"Do you know when I last saw my niece? Four years ago… for two days. Since Anthony died, she has been here two times in eighteen years. When Brendan died, I received a letter of condolence from her with regrets because she was too busy to come. I receive no telephone calls from her, but I do receive a perfunctory letter about three times a year…short notes, really. So you see, she'll be well provided when I'm gone…for all I've meant to her in her life." She paused for a few seconds. "If she were not Anthony's only niece, his late sister's daughter, I would have left her a mere token for all the closer we have been. I'm afraid she's going to have to struggle along on the two million.

"No, Joseph, I've been lucky. These people have asked for nothing but my presence in their lives. None of them has the faintest idea that anything will change in their lives because of their kindness to me."

"Are you sure, Anetta?"

"I know what I'm about, Joseph."

"Anything else?"

"Yes. Molly and Abramo Cardone have a daughter named Cara Cardone. I want the child to have a quarter million dollar endowment upon her twenty-fifth birthday—no matter what her parents' circumstances are."

"All right. And your servants? You want to leave them more than we had provisioned in the last will?"

"Yes. John and Mary are to receive a quarter million dollars apiece. And each of the other staff members are to receive one hundred twenty-five thousand."

"Is that all?" he said.

"No. Kieran Harty is also to receive a quarter million."

"All right," he sighed. "All right. But if your money continues to grow as it has been? How will you disburse it?"

"I would like to see it pro-rated among the current beneficiaries with a third going to St. Brendan's and a third to the church and a third to the others."

"Again, Anetta, I'll do whatever you wish…but are you sure of this?"

"I've never been more sure in my life, Joseph."

Hugh was reading in bed while Isabella was checking on the children. In a few minutes she came back into their bedroom and began to take off her robe. Beneath it she wore a short, thin cotton nightgown that covered her torso only to mid-thigh, barely enough to cover her buttocks. Hugh loved to watch her when she was unaware of his gaze. She had perfect legs, he thought as he watched her. In fact, everything about her body was wonderful. She draped the robe over a chair and walked toward the bed, turning out the large overhead light and letting the nightstand lights be their only illumination. She still did not notice his intense gaze as she moved about, seeming preoccupied with something.

Finally, she came to the bed and got in it as she always did, with one knee first, then pivoting on her hip, then rolling on her back. He had never seen anyone get into bed with that uniquely smooth and fluid movement. For a moment he pretended to be ignoring her. Then he moved near her and began to stroke her back and her buttocks as he nuzzled her breasts. "Hugh?" she said softly, thrilling as always to his touch.

"Don't bother me. I'm busy," he said, kissing one of her nipples.

"Hugh…stop for a minute. I want to ask you something."

"So ask," he said flippantly, still nuzzling her breasts and ignoring her entreaty.

"I want you to do me a favor," she said as she moved toward him.

"My God," said Hugh. "You want to ask me for something when you're half-naked in our bed, right? The same thing you could have asked me when we were fully clothed downstairs? Must be one hell of a favor," he said, chortling.

She put her hand over his mouth and stretched herself on top of him, looking down into his eyes. His hands continued playing over her back and buttocks. "I want you to ask Kieran over to dinner this Saturday night…alone," she whispered. He let out a loud yelp. "Shh! Hugh! You'll scare the children—not to mention my sister." She was laughing softly as she chided him.

"I can't do that! You want me to bring my best friend over here, innocent an unsuspecting, to be bewitched by you two dago women? Not to mention Gianina, who can charm the dogs off a meat wagon?"

"I would do such a thing for you if you asked me," she said, faking a pout.

"You would, huh? And what do I get out of all this—leading an innocent lamb to the slaughter?"

"My everlasting love and affection," she said.

"You told the bishop I already had that when we got married."

She wiggled her hips against him and giggled. "Hugh Connolly, you are a devil," she said, "but I like devils sometimes."

Hugh became serious. "Abramo told me he thought Kieran would fall for her the same way I did for you," he said.

"You talked to Abramo about this?"

"Only after he came up to me and began speaking in tongues like you dagos often do."

She enjoyed his teasing. But then she grew thoughtful. "She has had a terrible life, losing her husband so young."

"But you did too. So did I."

"Yes, but neither you nor I have ever lost a child as she has."

"She lost a child? I didn't know," he said.

"Diphtheria," she said. "He was five years old…two years after Pierino died." She began to get tears in her eyes. "She has had a life of misfortune. I would just like her to meet a man who will make her as happy as I am."

"Are you happy?" he said softly.

"I have never been happier in my whole life," she said. "And it is all because of you."

"It's all because I love you so," he responded. She kissed him as he took off her nightgown.

It was ten o'clock, and the February winds were howling through the darkness. Kieran was alone in the AOH, sweeping the floor around all the tables that had chairs stacked upside down on top of them. He was moving tables and still stacking when Hugh entered. "You open for business?" he said, startling Kieran.

"Hugh? I didn't even hear you come in."

"So, how's it going now that there's one less AOH in the Valley? That was a hell of a fire on Walnut Way, huh?" Hugh said.

"Business has picked up…"

"So, you're going to rent out that little red front on the corner?"

"Yeah, someday maybe." He continued to sweep, glancing at Hugh out of the corner of his eye. "And you came all the way down here at ten o'clock on the coldest night of the year to talk about my business plans, did you?"

"Well…no. Can't a man come out and get a beer once in a while?"

"Last I recall, you had cold beer at your place. I sent Conor over with two cases last Friday."

"I guess I thought I'd just come out and talk a little," Hugh said cautiously.

"Jesus Christ," said Kieran, "now I'm really scared. What's on your mind, Hugh Connolly?"

"Not much. Where are the boys?"

"Ross is upstairs studying, Conor's at his new girlfriend's house, and Paul is asleep. And Molly doesn't live here anymore. Now out with it, Connolly."

"We want you to have dinner with us this Saturday night."

"Dinner, huh? Whose idea was this?"

"Actually, it was Isabella's. For reasons I will never understand, she's taken a liking to you and resists my efforts to convince her otherwise."

"And she suggested that I come to dinner?"

"Yeah, as a matter of fact. But I'm in on it, too. I want you to come."

"Yeah? Who's going to be there?"

"Just Isabella, the kids, me, you…and her sister."

"Forget it, Connolly."

"Damn you, Kieran, it won't hurt you a bit. It's only dinner."

"It's only matchmaking."

"You wound me, boyo. Do you think I would stoop to such underhand tactics?"

Kieran chuckled cynically. "Jesus Christ," he said again. "Get you own beer if you want it." After a pause he said, "Where'd this sister come from?"

"Philadelphia. Like Isabella, she been a widow for several years. She's moved back now that Isabella isn't running the boarding house anymore."

"Where does she live?"

"With me, for a while…that is, until she gets settled here. Or unless some guy decides he wants to be as happy as I am and takes her for his own."

Kieran stared at his friend for several seconds. "And you think that could really happen?"

"When people get a look at her, I sure as hell think it will happen."

"What's she look like?"

Hugh began to get excited now that Kieran was curious about how she looked. "She looks like Isabella…only one year older."

"But ten years uglier, right?"

"Wrong again, boyo. She's as beautiful as Isabella."

"There's no chance that'll be true," Kieran muttered.

"I tell you she is, man. And she lives and breathes at my house. Come see for yourself."

Kieran stopped doing any work and leaned his arms on his broom, staring at Hugh. "I don't know what's going on in my life, Hugh…except God's playing with me. My daughter falls in love and marries an Italian. My best friend falls in love and marries an Italian. Here we are, Irish as whiskey and shamrocks, and we start getting hooked up with all these dagos. What's the world coming to?"

Hugh snorted. "It's coming to some happy people, kid."

"But my dad would be turning over in his grave, and so would yours."

"Your dad never had the years of loneliness that you and I have had, Kieran, and neither did mine. They both died surrounded by wives and family, as old men. And truth be told, we might end up being happier than those guys ever were. You know, Kier, my dad never once had what I have with Isabella. I wonder if yours did."

"You're pretty damned sure of yourself since you married that lady."

"So are you coming or not?"

"What's she like?"

"I told you, like Isabella. Oh, I forgot, she has brown hair, and Isabella's is black."

"I don't mean what's she look like. What's she like?"

"Isabella says that the whole family always called her the sweet-tempered one."

"You are an honest-to-God bullshitter, Hugh Connolly. With a wife like yours, you're telling me that her sister's the one the whole family favors? What's her name?"

"Marina."

Kieran was silent for a moment, staring at his old friend. He liked the name, and Hugh knew it. "Is she really like you say? You're not conning me with these stories?"

"Yeah, kid," Hugh said seriously. "She's a stroke of good luck just waiting to happen. Remember, I gave you my sister and was glad of it. I know you'll be crazy about her, and I swear she doesn't know I'm here."

"If she's anything close to Isabella, she'd be special, Hugh," Kieran said softly.

"Thank you, boyo…Look, you know damn well we're both too young to spend the rest of our lives alone. Molly's already gone, and soon the boys are all going to be married and leaving. Who are you going to talk to in that big house? Your cat? Come on, son. There's nothing wrong with choosing happiness. God's sending someone your way who's a lovely girl, in all ways. All you have to do is decide to come to my place."

Kieran turned around and wiped a liquor shelf, thinking quietly for several seconds and ignoring Hugh. Then he turned back toward his friend. "What time is dinner?"